"Hold ~~still,~~ grumbled, ~~his~~ ~~fingers~~ ~~brushing~~ her pant leg.

"I told you not to touch me," she said, her body shaking uncontrollably.

It had to be her magic that was driving him crazy.

"Don't worry, it won't happen again," he said, voicing a direct order to himself. For his inner beast wanted Nina Rainwater in the worst way.

And she had no idea how much danger she was in at the moment.

Books by Connie Hall

Harlequin Nocturne

*The Guardian #108
*The Beholder #112

*The Nightwalkers

CONNIE HALL

Award-winning author Connie Hall is a full-time writer. Her writing credits include six historical novels and two novellas written under the pen name Constance Hall. She is thrilled to now be writing for Nocturne.

An avid hiker, conservationist, bird watcher, painter of watercolors and oil portraits, she dreams of one day trying her hand at skydiving.

She lives in Richmond, Virginia, with her husband, two sons and Keeper, a lovable Lab-mix who rules the house with her big brown eyes. For more information, visit her website or email her at conniehall_author@comcast.net.

THE BEHOLDER

CONNIE HALL

 Harlequin®

TORONTO NEW YORK LONDON
AMSTERDAM PARIS SYDNEY HAMBURG
STOCKHOLM ATHENS TOKYO MILAN MADRID
PRAGUE WARSAW BUDAPEST AUCKLAND

Recycling programs
for this product may
not exist in your area.

ISBN-13: 978-0-373-61859-0

THE BEHOLDER

Dear Reader,

Whatever you do, don't ask Nina Rainwater if she likes being the baby in her family. You see, she lives in the shadows of her older and more bodacious sisters, Fala and Takala, who have extraordinary powers. All Rainwater women are connected through white magic. Their unique abilities are passed down through the female line.

If you asked Nina about her gift, she'd probably tell you it's nothing. But don't be fooled. She possesses the gift of tongues. She can communicate with any creature, alive or dead, and she has sacrificed her whole life in using her gift to help others.

So when she discovers Kane Van Cleave, a beast of a man, with a sinister past and even bleaker future, she finally meets a creature she's unable to help....

Connie Hall

Foreword

It is said that the Creator formed the earth and all life. He left the Maiden Bear to rule over his creation. The newborn mother earth still spewed furnaces of molten rock. Earthquakes trembled and churned and gouged the hills and valleys of her skin. Consequently, all living creatures were thrown together helter-skelter, forced to establish hunting grounds in this tumultuous world. Maiden Bear hoped they would live in peace, but the animals and humans were neophytes, driven strictly by instinct alone, and many fought over sparse hunting grounds. There was much dissent, for the animals could not communicate among themselves or with any other creatures.

Maiden Bear knew she would have to do something so the animals could understand each other or death would reign supreme and the earth would become barren. So she sought out the Patomani tribe, her followers, and bestowed one female brave with the Gift of Tongues. This new emissary could translate the language of life and death and could communicate with any type of being. Consequently, the creatures communicated through her, and they learned not to fear each other as well as those different from themselves. Thus, order and peace were established, and every creature found its mark on the web of life.

Maiden Bear was so greatly pleased with the progress of her mediator, she decided to pass the extraordinary gift down through the Patomani female line to a deserving and sensitive soul.

"Take hope from the heart of man and you make him a beast of prey."

—Quida

Prologue

Blue Ridge Mountains

A feeling of doom woke Emma Baldoon. She glanced at the clock. Midnight. The witching hour.

She sat up in bed. In the silence her breaths sounded like the beat of huge wings. For two days now a strange quiet had saturated the air, squeezed every sound from it: the kind of stillness that swept over a graveyard at night.

Emma shivered, rubbed her arms and heard her four parakeets rustling in their cage. She left her bed. Her gaze swept the dark shadows in the cabin as she found the cage and opened the cover. Her babies thrashed around in the bottom, banging their bodies against the bars.

"Shh, quiet, little ones." She opened the door. In a

flurry of feathers they flew out and landed on the rafters, huddling together. It calmed them for the moment.

She glanced up at them and shook her head. Yesterday morning they had stopped eating. She thought they might be getting sick. Now she feared it was something much worse.

Suddenly the sheep bleated and baaed, their bodies ramming the paddock fence. If they didn't stop soon, they'd knock the fence down. Bessie, Emma's milking cow, caught the fever and lowed in distress. Even the chickens squawked in the coop. She firmly believed animals had a sixth sense when it came to danger, and they were definitely warning her. What was upsetting them?

Over the past twenty years, she had lived alone, ever since her husband, Harvey, had died. She had never felt insecure or afraid...until tonight.

She hurried back to the gun case. With trembling fingers, she groped for the loaded 20 gauge Mossberg. A long time ago she had learned the hard way that an unloaded shotgun was useless.

A growl pierced the night air, close enough to rattle the windowpanes.

Her breath froze in her lungs.

She recognized the cry of bobcats, bears and coyotes. Had lived with them all her life. This unnatural sound came straight out of hell.

The hairs at the back of her neck stood on end. Her heart raced and her skin prickled as she aimed the gun at the door. Her arthritic hands shook so badly she had a hard time keeping the weapon still.

Footsteps thumped up onto the front porch.

The knob shook.

Her finger tightened on the trigger, but before she could pull it, an invisible force knocked her down.

The gun clattered to the floor beside her. She reached for it, but an invisible claw tore through her chest, bored down into her very core. Molten lava spread to her organs.

Pain seared her, arching her back, slamming her down onto the floor again. She felt her life force being drawn out, burned out of her, blood boiling in her veins.

The door rattled angrily on its hinges, then something kicked it open.

Plop! Plop! Plop!

Emma felt something hit the floor next to her. Dear heavens! Her babies. Flames engulfed their wings.

She drew her last breath as her own body erupted into an inferno.

Chapter 1

Oh, no! Make it stop! Nina Rainwater grabbed the steering wheel with both hands but still weaved over the white line. The guardrail and sheer drop below filled her headlights.

She gasped and jerked on the wheel.

Tires swerved right and hit the opposite shoulder. Gravel crackled against the undercarriage.

She braked the car to a crawl and straightened out, heart thumping, keeping time with her pounding head. Close call, that one.

Sunlight gnawed at the edges of ominous clouds but refused to break through. Their angry billows engulfed and eddied and animated the rounded peaks of the Blue Ridge Mountains. A northern wind screamed downward and swept another huge, angry fist against her Taurus. The whole car shook.

It wasn't the impending storm that concerned her at the moment, but the terror and desperation that throbbed in her head and prickled her skin.

If she could only concentrate fully on driving. The shivers wouldn't let up. At the age of two, when she had first realized her own clairvoyant powers, she had innocently called her perceptions *shivers* because they made her feel as if she were trapped in a freezer.

If the entities involved were few, she could usually manage the shivers. But the more energies tangled up in the intricate web of thoughts, the stronger the connection and her reaction to them. The awareness she experienced now was legion, the massed fear a throbbing jackhammer in her brain, a siren song with no end.

The maddening thing was that her empathic abilities had limits. She couldn't tell if the shivers were coming from living or deceased souls. She had to actually locate the harmed being or animal, or its place of death, to detect that information. And if they didn't want to be found and stopped sending her messages, she couldn't find them at all. In those instances, she assumed they were souls and had moved on to heaven. Sometimes being a lightning rod for spiritual emotions was like playing hide-and-seek in a foggy labyrinth. But once she cornered and tagged the shivers, any physical distress she had experienced seemed insignificant when compared to the benefits of helping others.

A chill went through her, and she glanced at the outside temperature display in her Taurus: twenty-four degrees and dropping. She had already jacked up the heater as high as it would go, but she knew the closer she drew to the source, the lower her body temperature would drop. Until she found the source of the perceptions and helped the beings, the sensations of cold and her headache were hers to bear. As was this crazy northern clipper that threatened to toss her car over the side of the mountain.

Bits of sleet began to chime against the windshield. She turned on the wipers and slowly accelerated, fighting the wind to stay in her lane. Dark squiggles formed in her vision. Great! If she didn't do something soon, she knew the shivers would escalate into a full-blown migraine and she might end up running over the side of the mountain. She needed help and fast.

A relentless wind pounded the rooftops of Brayville, shaking shingles, testing wall supports, cracking icicles. Bits of sleet pinged the roof of Kane Van Cleave's Jeep as he drove down Main Street. The snarl of the wind drowned out the purr of the engine.

He coasted into a parking spot in front of the Wayside Café, then hopped out.

A frigid breeze hit him, raw against his face, piercing through his jeans and flannel shirt. He braced himself against the cold and easily fought his way inside the café. The cold didn't bother him. His inner-body temperature was five degrees warmer than a human's. But the wind was brutal this morning.

The bell on the door banged as he slammed it shut. His face and hands met the café's cozy heat. He felt them warming instantly as he scanned the seats.

Empty.

Figured. No one in their right mind would venture out in this weather without good reason. His reason hadn't arrived yet.

His long legs quickly covered the length of booths. The Wayside hadn't changed in forty years, and the sameness of it pleased him. He liked the comfortable '50s feel, the red and stainless-steel counter, the black-and-white asbestos floor tiles. Retro at its finest.

He inhaled the familiar smell of coffee, cigarettes and fresh meat and felt his mood lifting a little. As he strode past the oversized Felix the Cat clock, tail swishing with a steady click, he felt the plastic eyes following him. A Bubbler jukebox hugged the back wall, its bubble tubes glowing yellow and orange. The jukebox hadn't seen a modern hit in half a century. It only played scratchy 45s. The denizens of Brayville liked it that way; so did Kane.

He dropped a quarter in the box and picked E6, "There Goes My Baby." He chose a booth opposite the door and slid into the seat, his jeans catching on the duct-taped plastic. The scent from the layers of chewing gum stuck under the table wafted up to his hypersensitive nose. He frowned. It was almost as bad as the smell of a public restroom. Both were hard to take at five o'clock in the morning.

He picked up the ketchup bottle and opened it, hoping the scent would run interference. He plopped it down near the salt and pepper shakers and noticed the many sets of initials carved into the table. He'd left his own graffiti on the counter when he was sixteen. Teens of Brayville were compelled to leave their mark in the café, a right of passage. Kane could hardly remember being sixteen. Too much had happened. It felt like he'd lived a hundred lifetimes in those twelve years.

The sound of the Drifters finally sent Carrie bouncing through the kitchen's swinging door. She hurriedly tied a white apron around her pink uniform while walking toward him. For a female of forty, she appeared in good shape. She was petite, a small waist flaring to wide hips, lean arm muscles rippling below her short sleeves. A China Doll haircut shaped her red curly hair and just touched the bottom of her collar. Wrinkles creased the corners of her slightly upturned eyes and lent her face a catlike appearance. Carrie was a pride female who in human form revealed more feline physical characteristics than most. Like him, she was a seniph.

When she saw him, she froze midstride. Her usual jovial expression melted and her hands dropped like lead weights near her hips. Burnt-umber eyes narrowed and her Adam's apple bobbed as she swallowed hard. Immediately she dropped her gaze as befitted his alpha-male status within the pride.

Kane could smell the fear on her. The perverse side of him enjoyed it. "Hello, Carrie." He deliberately kept his voice brusque.

She jumped, seemed to realize she stood there dumbstruck and forced her feet into motion. "Hey, Kane." The cusps of her white fangs flashed in an uneasy smile.

Kane caught the slight shift, but humans never noticed it. They just didn't pay attention to subtleties. Every seniph had the ability to hide behind a human guise, but they couldn't entirely erase their true sphinx—half-man and half-lion—persona from the truly observant.

She paused well away from his table and drew out a pad and pencil. "How about that wind? Almost knocked me over this morning opening up. Never seen it so bad. Hope it doesn't bring us a foot of snow." Her voice hit on a nervous friendly note, but it sounded forced.

He enjoyed watching the pencil in her hand trembling as he said, "It might."

"Haven't seen you around for a while."

"The vineyard and the pride keep me busy."

"Right. Right. I guess you're wondering about the business." Nervous words tumbled out of her mouth. "It's doing just fine. I actually doubled the profits from last month. I think it was putting in that new warm cream machine that did it. And we got that new meat supplier. They know how to freeze raw meat—"

Kane interrupted her. "That's good."

He, like his father and all the Van Cleaves before him, had used his wealth to keep the pride together, and that meant concealing their identities from humans. He owned all the real estate in Brayville and the surrounding mountains. The pride kept the few businesses in town running, along with the Van Cleave vineyard. It was perfect cover for the pride.

She shifted nervously from one foot to the other at his silence, then said, "Sorry, I guess I rattled on. What can I get you?"

"Scalded cream with a shot of coffee, a steak, bloody, tuna, hold the mayo, and lots of hash browns. That's it." Fried potatoes and coffee were one of the few conventional human foods he craved.

"Not very hungry? Sure you don't want some trout? Came in yesterday." She feigned an eager-to-please demeanor. "It's fresh."

"That's all." He shot her a look that sent her scurrying.

She shoved the pad in her pocket, saying, "Sure, sure. Coming right up." Then she ran around the counter and disappeared into the kitchen.

Movement through the glass door drew his attention, and he spotted the motivation for coming to town at this ungodly hour: Arwan. She muscled through the wind, heading for the café. The gale flattened her down parka and sheriff's blue uniform to her tall, lean body and thin curves. A .45 Glock rode one hip, the holster thumping against her thigh as she reached for the door. Her platinum hair usually hung down past her shoulders, but when in uniform she always wore it in a bun. Oddly, the rigid style seemed impervious to the wind and hardly any strands had strayed.

Most females would look manly in a sheriff's uniform, but not Arwan. She was the pride's alpha female; she could make army fatigues look sexy. Her feminine mystique would always shine through. Although Arwan never flaunted her sexuality. In fact, she deliberately tried to disguise her beauty behind a tomboy persona.

The wind shoved her through the door. She banged it closed and rolled her eyes, taking a moment to recover and take off her gloves. Bits of sleet salted the floor and her boots. She spotted him and said, "Whew, some morning." She knocked the snow off her boots, then walked toward him.

"Yeah, we should both be home." He was eager to find out what had been so important that she couldn't speak to him over the phone.

She took off her jacket, then bent and sniffed him, rubbing first one cheek against his, then the other one. It was a casual greeting ranking officers shared in the pride. His highly developed senses picked up on the odor of twenty hours of perspiration clinging to her clothes, and he wondered what she'd been doing.

He scented her alpha pheromone, an instant love potion for most of the pride's males. But Kane had trained himself to ignore it. The slight vibration of her throat was harder to disregard. It wasn't audible to humans, only to seniphs. And it wasn't something she could control. All female seniphs of child-bearing age purred when they neared another virile male. It broke the ice, so to speak, when finding a mate. Earlier in his life, he would have been driven to pursue her and mate with her, but that felt like eons ago. He had a tight rein on his baser instincts now.

He turned his face away and motioned to the seat opposite him and said, "Sit."

She didn't seem to notice or care about his indifference and her expression remained a closed book as she sat. They knew each other too well.

She gazed directly at Kane in that forthright way of hers. "I'm glad you could meet me so early."

He noticed the heavy exhaustion in her eyes and recalled her scent and said, "You been out all night?"

She nodded, rustling the few platinum wisps around her temples. "Tracking."

He knew the extent of Arwan's self-reliance. She had to be desperate before she asked for his help. His brows furrowed in worry as he asked, "That why I'm here?"

"Yes, but…" She hesitated, using caution in choosing her next words.

It wasn't like Arwan to tiptoe around a subject. He'd known her all his life. She was the only seniph in the pride who didn't fear him. After that one night that had changed his whole life, he'd made certain he kept his distance and was never alone with anyone, Arwan included. And there hadn't been an incident since the first one. He had hoped he'd convinced her of that, but it seemed he'd never be rid of his hellish mistake or the monster within him who had made it. He didn't blame anyone for being cautious, but he still thought Arwan had a good deal more mettle than most. Though here she was guarded and angst-ridden about telling him something.

"But…?" He encouraged her to finish her thought.

"I don't know how to tell you this…" Arwan leaned back and sighed. She opened her mouth to say something, but Carrie approached their booth and set Kane's steaming cream on the table, along with a tiny pitcher of coffee.

She shot Arwan a sympathetic look at having to share Kane's booth, then said, "Hey, Arwan. What would you like?"

"Got a way to mainline caffeine?" Arwan forced a grin.

"Hard night?"

"Haven't slept good for the past week. My oil furnace has bit the dust. The radiators knock all night. Crummy luck, huh, since it's the coldest week of the winter."

Kane heard the lie in Arwan's voice, but Carrie seemed oblivious.

"Better get that thing fixed. Can't have you falling asleep on the job." Carrie noticed Kane's eyes on her, and she quickly glanced down at the table and said, "I'll brew up some strong coffee."

"Thanks. And give me the breakfast special."

"Right—cream, eggs, bacon and herring." Carrie nodded, then disappeared behind the swinging kitchen door.

When Carrie was out of hearing range, Arwan lowered her voice to a soft whisper. "Look, I couldn't say anything. You know how Carrie gossips, but we've got a gleaner in our territory." Annoyance tightened her lips. "And the bastard is wily as hell. I lost his scent and went around in circles all night."

They lapsed into silence, both frowning at the same time. Each knew what the other was thinking. Their unspoken words swung like a scythe between them.

Arwan's eyes filled with worry, and she gave voice to their fear, "What if it's Ethan?"

Kane flinched at the name. He waved a hand to stop her. "Don't say any more."

"But…"

"If it is my brother, the less you know the better. If you're questioned by the council, then you can tell them you came to me for help in tracking the gleaner."

"But I'd like to help you."

"No. It's better you don't know what I find. I won't have you forfeit your life because you're involved." Kane shifted uneasily, growing aware of the scars on his back. With vivid clarity, he recalled the punishment he'd received for letting Ethan go the first time. Seniph prides had remained hidden from humanity by observing the Book of Laws. He'd broken law number one: never suffer a gleaner to live. And he bore the physical evidence to prove it.

The council had warned him that if his brother ever returned and Kane didn't kill Ethan, then not even Kane's status as alpha could save him from the ultimate punishment: death. And Kane knew Arwan would endure the same fate if she was involved. No, he couldn't let her become embroiled in this. Ethan had left miles of destruction in his path, but Arwan wasn't going to be one of his casualties.

Arwan stared at her hands and looked miserable. "I hate this. You know, I love Ethan as much as you do. He was like a brother to me. You both were."

"I know. But he's a gleaner." Kane's expression darkened with resignation as he said, "Where did the attack occur?"

"The Baldoon farm. Found the animals fried and her body nothing but ash." Arwan shook her head in sadness. "I liked that old lady. For a human, she wasn't bad."

"Yeah, she minded her own business and never wandered onto our land. She didn't deserve to be murdered by a gleaner." Ethan's face materialized in

Kane's mind, and he hoped Ethan hadn't returned home. But Kane wouldn't put it past him. He asked, "Anyone cleaning up the site?"

"Jake and Clive are out there." At the mention of the two inept deputies she'd been forced to hire, Arwan grimaced.

"Can you be assured of their silence?"

"I threatened to rip out their throats if they spoke to anyone."

Kane knew Arwan had the strength to easily carry out the threat. When pushed, an alpha female could hold her own against most male seniphs—especially one trained in self-defense as Arwan was.

"Just make sure this—" she hesitated, not using Ethan's name "—gleaner is taken care of quickly. We don't want the press getting word of the murder. They'll be screaming spontaneous combustion, and every tabloid reporter in the country will be here. I only have so many mind-easing drugs on hand before we'll be forced to bring in the mind eaters."

Kane grimaced at the mention of mind eaters, demons with the power to erase multitudes of thoughts. Their powers were rarely consistent. They sometimes erased too much memory, and humans ended up with mental disorders or, worse, strokes. And their fees were exorbitant. But if the memory drugs didn't work, they were regularly employed to keep humans in the dark about the supernatural world.

"I'll handle the gleaner," Kane said.

"What will you do if it is Ethan?"

"What I have to." Kane chugged the contents of his

cup. The scalded cream tasted metallic and thick like blood as a vision of his brother loomed in his mind.

The channeled emotions avalanched through Nina's temples. She struggled to hold the car on course and thought of the one person who could help her.

Okay, technically her spirit guide wasn't a person but a magical being. But he was all hers and the only salvation she had at the moment. To summon him, all she had to do was think about him. *Koda, are you there?*

No answer.

Koda! If she had spoken the name aloud, she would have been yelling it.

No reply.

She made a face. Koda usually came to her rescue when the shivers became unbearable. *Where are you?*

Empty silence.

Okay, be stubborn.

Spirit guides tended to have minds of their own and eccentricities, just like humans. They could be annoying like some humans, too. Right now was a prime example.

They also couldn't be relied upon with any frequency. That's why when Nina began to exhibit her powers, her grandmother, Meikoda, had taught her a method of gaining control over the shivers herself, the Patomani Indian way, through meditation. Meikoda had always warned, "Trusting animal spirit guides can have dire consequences." Now more than ever, Nina realized the wisdom of her grandmother's advice.

An opening in the forest drew her gaze, and she spotted a narrow country road where she could pull off the parkway and deal with her headache.

She turned, her tires finding every pothole. The forest thickened into an evergreen wall on both sides of the road, thick boughs whipping and thrashing in the wind. Low-lying limbs thumped against her hood and roof. Hail pinged her windshield and sounded like rattling teeth.

She switched the heater to defrost as she searched for a place to pull over, but the curvy road descended at a sharp angle. There were no pull-offs, just granite mountainside to her right and a sheer drop to her left.

Just as she doubted if she'd ever find a place to park, she reached an open valley filled with fields of grapevines. Their twisted frozen stalks looked like contorted arms grasping at whatever moved. Something about them caused the pain in her temples to settle in behind her eyes. Another ripple of emotions shook her. Her teeth chattered as her trembling grew uncontrollable.

Thankfully, she spotted lights. Humanity. A small village. Relief loosened her tensed muscles. If the Fates were on her side, she might even find a cup of hot chocolate to meditate over. All she needed was a little quiet time to mask those foreign emotions in her head.

She crept past a green sign that read: Brayville, population 102. She reached the sheriff's office, a white frame building. Beside the sheriff's office sat the courthouse, a Romanesque stone structure. The building belonged in a bygone English countryside rather than in a Virginia mountainside. Knob's Grocery rested next to it. A boldfaced sign in the display window read: Fresh Meat Cut Daily.

She cringed. Man innocently believed that animals were not sentient and thus were unaware of pain, but Nina knew better. She had never been able to eat meat, not without being haunted by the emotional insight of the sacrificed animal. Her powers had sealed her dietary habits as a strict vegan.

The sidewalk appeared deserted, only a few lights shining from the tiny homes surrounding the village. Something about the place looked untouched, forbidding, frozen in a winter mountain spell. Another surge of shivers rippled, and her trembling became uncontrollable.

That's when she noticed the glow from an open sign. The Wayside Café. A definite windfall. She drove half a block and parked behind a Jeep and a sheriff's car.

She donned the gloves Mrs. Winston, a client in her pet-psychic business, had knitted for her. Dog faces flopped on the end of each finger and looked very much like Max, Mrs. Winston's depressed Scotty. The gloves were pretty horrible. Fashion accessories a child would wear, but Nina could never refuse handmade gifts from clients, particularly if they were as nice as Jane Winston.

As soon as she put her hand on the latch to open the door, Koda's telepathic thoughts dove directly into her psyche. *Wait!*

Now you show up.

I was in a meeting.

Koda's habitual excuse when he didn't want to be found.

I could have used your help back there.

You know the rules. I can't interfere. I can only take you to the Quiet Place and offer advice.

Then you could have taken me to the Quiet Place. I'd have settled for that.

Can't. Sorry. You've been using it too often. I've been warned.

Warned? It's mine to use.

It is a gift, and you've abused it.

I don't see that I've done anything so terrible. I needed the breaks. Being bombarded by constant emotions drains me. You know that. Truth was that at times Nina felt a hundred years old. In the Quiet Place, she escaped her responsibilities, avoided the shivers and cleared her head. What was so wrong with that?

I've been advised that you are using it as a crutch.

Well, excuse me. I thought I could use it at my discretion.

Not when it harms you.

I think I should know what is good for me and what is not—thank you very much.

You should, but you don't. Case in point—you could be in danger right now. Take my advice and don't go in the café.

But I'm freezing, and I've got a migraine coming on, and there's hot stuff in there to drink.

Don't go in.

Sorry, but there may not be another café within miles of here. I have to.

Suit yourself. This last was said in a snit, and his presence left her mind in a final whoosh.

"Go ahead, be that way," Nina said aloud. It hurt her head to speak, and Max's many faces blurred before her eyes.

She hesitated for one minute, staring at the inviting hot-coffee sign over the counter; then she held her throbbing temples and climbed out of the car.

Frosty air swirled through her jeans and up her coat. Pellets of hail stung her face. A gust tugged at the tight braid she had coiled into a bun at the back of her head. She felt some of the pins falling out, reached to grab them and missed. The thick black braid flopped down her spine, thumping against her. She ran to the door, snuggling her woolen coat closer around her neck.

Between fighting the weather and her headache, she wasn't paying attention as she opened the cafe door. A man startled her. She stumbled backward.

His hands shot out with superhuman reflexes and caught her.

The moment he touched her, a shiver speared her, a presence not totally human or animal, but both. A shifter, or two-skin as her people called them. She sensed the inhuman creature caged within his flesh, raging to be set free, tearing at her mind. She panicked and broke his hold on her arm. A pair of harsh jungle-green eyes and a hulking solid-muscled body swept past her peripheral vision as she wheeled and fled.

"Are you okay?" His resounding baritone rumbled

over the wind, the tones resonating from deep within his large chest.

"Yes—never mind." She yelled over her shoulder, running for the safety of her car. Koda had been right this time.

She jumped inside and locked the doors. She couldn't start the engine fast enough; then she sped away.

Abruptly it occurred to her that the temporary interruption with the shape-shifter had diverted her thoughts from the shivers, and her headache had subsided. Though she felt as tightly strung as a guitar string about to break. She couldn't forget the contact with the two-skin. His brutality and hostility had struck her with such force, she hadn't been able to discover what type of shifter he was. Just the thought of him now made her quake.

He might be somehow involved with the horrible emotions that had led her to the area. She knew some two-skins lived in groups. Menacing creatures like him could fill this whole village. They might be harming innocents.

She prayed not. She never wanted to feel that beast in him again, much less a whole crowd of them. When she found the cause of the shivers, and if she discovered that he or anyone else in this village was responsible, she'd have to stop them. Unchecked shifters mustn't be allowed to harm innocents.

She sped along the narrow road, into the teeth of the wind and freezing rain, the force trying to push her back toward Brayville. She floored it, and the shivers returned full-force, in all their swarming glory, guiding her toward the unknown.

Chapter 2

Kane watched the Taurus pass him as he waved to Arwan through the window of the café. Arwan was still eating, but Kane had lost his appetite after learning about the gleaner. Ethan may have returned. His brother had been foremost in his mind, until he'd bumped into the stranger.

After only a few seconds of gripping her forearms, an awareness still strummed through his veins. The contact roused his darker side. He'd worked years at marshaling those instincts and up until colliding into the human, he'd kept them under strict control. But her scent lingered in his senses. She smelled extraordinarily enticing, otherworldly, more than mere mortal. He'd stake his life on that.

And what about her reaction when they had touched? He'd felt her stiffen, seen those bright blue eyes widen in fear. Her face had paled in comprehension. Somehow she had sensed his supernatural aura. So what was she? Sorceress? Seer? Another shifter, the likes of which he'd never encountered before? Whatever she was, she had been snooping around here just when a gleaner had returned. Even if she had nothing to do with the gleaner, he had to protect the pride's privacy. He couldn't risk humans ever finding out that shifters existed. He had a nose for trouble, and that woman was trouble with a capital *T*.

He bounded into his Jeep and stayed well behind the Taurus. He'd have to follow her and find out exactly what she knew. She was definitely a threat and took precedence over tracking the gleaner. The gleaner could wait. This new prey could not.

The shivers led Nina to a dark and dismal dirt road at the base of a mountain, not fifteen miles from Brayville. A plywood sign proclaimed Baldoon Farm, No Trespassing. The blue-painted letters had dripped and ran together in an eerie way. A Bates Motel sign, if she ever saw one.

This was the location, all right. Every fiber of her being quaked now. She felt her body temperature steadily dropping, and she'd kill for something hot to drink. She crept up the mountain drive, aware she wasn't only freezing but fighting a rising case of the heebie-jeebies. The feeling that someone was watching gnawed at her. For the umpteenth time, she glanced at the rearview mirror.

Not a glimmer of a headlight. Nothing but sleet

hitting the rear windshield, forming long rivulets of icy water that glowed blood red from her taillights.

She thought she'd seen someone following her when she'd left Brayville, but the headlights had disappeared about five miles back. Must be a case of nerves, she assured herself.

If she could only leave this place… But she couldn't abandon the chorus of voices still crying out for help. Her conscience wouldn't allow her to leave creatures in distress. Her path was set, and she had to follow it to the end.

Her headlights revealed only a heavily wooded forest. Trees swayed and bowed to the storm, the weaker ones looking ready to snap and topple. The higher the Taurus climbed, the stronger the shivers shook her. Emotions scraped etchings inside her mind now. She could even translate the fear into words.

"Help me. I'm afraid. No, no, no! Don't hurt me, please!" And the monologue went on and on, mingling with terrified screams. It was a recording inside her head that wouldn't stop. Their pain and fear became a part of her.

Nina gripped the wheel and began humming to drown out the noise marching through her head. Sometimes it helped. Her voice drew to a fevered pitch; then she gave up humming and switched to singing "Coming Out of the Dark" at the top of her lungs. Thank goodness for Gloria Estefan.

The chrome bumper of a black-and-white police car flashed in the headlights not fifty yards in front of her. Brayville Sheriff's Department was emblazoned across the trunk. Why were they here? Were they covering up what that beast inside that shifter had done? Her skull still tingled where his massive hands had gripped her arms. The pull of those empty green eyes and the beast's anger was something she'd never forget. At the memory, icy fingers trailed down her spine and she stopped singing.

Hoping no one saw her lights, she flicked them off and reversed back down the drive, using only her brake lights to see. She found an abandoned logging road and backed into it, driving over waist-high weeds and bushes until her car was properly hidden. She parked and cut the engine.

She eased out the door, insides churning, head hurting as if a swarm of bees were building a nest there. She gulped back the bile of rising fear in her throat. *The Sixth Sense* was pretty on target when it came to seeing the dead. The moments before death were the images that surrounded a spirit while they were trapped on earth. It was never pleasant, always graphic and sometimes hard to endure. She preferred discovering living creatures, ones she could help, ones that gave purpose to her life and the gift she'd been given.

The incline hadn't felt this steep in the car, but now having to battle the elements and walk straight up made her pant to catch her breath.

Sleet stung her face, and she pulled her coat collar up around her neck. Despite the two pairs of long johns and thick jeans she was wearing, frigid air sliced right through her. She wished she'd worn two sweaters instead of one.

Fatigue gnawed at her. The shivers depleted her energy stores, particularly when she was awakened at 2:00 a.m. by them. She had been on an assignment in Monterey, Virginia, sound asleep at Sally's B and B, a nice, quiet Victorian home she frequented when she visited Comet, a perpetually depressed bloodhound. Old and arthritic, he felt useless. Nina's sessions with him always perked him up and made his owners happy. She wished she were helping Comet now, or nestled in that feather-down mattress she had left, anywhere but tramping through this cold and ice.

The realization hit her that she'd left her cell phone charging in the cradle. She couldn't contact her sister, Takala, or her grandmother. They had always been overprotective of Nina. Sometimes it made her feel loved. At other times, smothered. But she didn't want to worry them, so she periodically called them when she was on an assignment. They would be concerned when she didn't check in. She made a mental note to call them later—if she ever got out of this mess.

She kept to the shadows. The forest gave way to split-rail fencing and open farmland. The dark outline of a little cabin rested on the very top of the mountain. Its weathered and bowed roof and faded clapboards seemed to stand like an eternal testament against the many winter mountainous storms. The little cabin had kept its inhabitants safe for many a freezing January—just not through this one, she thought ruefully. She hoped they were still alive.

She scanned the four outbuildings behind the cabin. Most were hardly more than run-down shacks. One had a crooked stovepipe chimney. Maybe a smokehouse. The barn was bigger than the cabin itself. Huge rolls of hay were stacked five deep along one side. Tarps covered them, their edges flapping sporadically in the wind.

She moved closer to the barn, keeping low. Luckily the wind was at her back now and she didn't have to struggle to skulk along the fence.

No sign of the officers. Where were they?

When she reached the barn, she pressed her shaking back against the faded clapboards. Her whole body was a saltshaker in motion. Her lips were numb, and she knew they must have turned blue. She could hardly feel her legs and arms. She silently jogged in place to raise her body temperature; then she peeked around a corner. A pasture stretched out before her, frozen and gray. The land here was craggy with deep hollows. Dim lantern light glowed in one of the hollows. She sneaked toward it, keeping in the shadows of the fence.

When she drew close to the light, the wind carried the sounds of male voices and two shovels hitting the ground in tandem. She froze and listened.

"Go deeper, Clive. You heard what Arwan said. We don't want anything digging up the bodies."

"Don't tell me how to do my job, Jake," Clive yelled back over the wind. "Anyway, critters don't come back to a gleaner's kill."

Gleaner? That explained a lot. The high-priestess shamans of her people had been hunting gleaners for eons. The Patomani Indian name for gleaner was *dahacheewha*, or lion man. Gleaners were male seniph mutants, genetic anomalies caused by sphinxes and humans procreating. When a mutant gleaner reached adulthood, their DNA began to disintegrate. They consumed human souls in order to regenerate and sustain life. When gleaners killed humans, they emitted a force that spontaneously combusted every living creature within a hundred feet. She tried to find the good in all life, but there was nothing redeemable in a gleaner. They were killing parasites who sucked the souls from the living to survive. Shifter vermin at their worst.

She now knew that the shifter she had happened upon in Brayville was a seniph. Usually when she touched a shifter, she could pinpoint their animal nature right away. Their other half couldn't hide from her paranormal connection to them, and she might have figured out the guy was a seniph if the creature trapped beneath his skin had been a run-of-the-mill lion. But this beast was fierce, filled with anger and frustration and rage, barely contained within human skin. She'd only met two other shifters who frightened her more. One was a Kodiak bear, the other a Bengal tiger. Both were scary as hell, but neither frightened her as much as the Brayville seniph. She'd never look upon seniphs in quite the same way ever again.

Some two-skins could only shift at night when the moon was visible, some only when it was full. Most shifters were bound by the monthly cycle of the moon. Only the more powerful ones could change at will. And that seniph's beast was powerful enough to not be governed by the heavens. No, it had no boundaries. Thoughts of him sent an eerie tremor through her.

"I don't see why we're hiding the fact a gleaner's

come to the area," Jake said. "It's pretty obvious Ethan's come home. The council should know about it, too. They'll find out anyway, and then it will be our asses on a platter."

"You worry like a female. If we keep quiet, no one will find out. So shut your trap and remember—we don't report to the council. We report to Arwan."

Was Arwan the sheriff of that creepy village?

"I don't like it one bit, her hiding the fact that Ethan's home. And it's gonna lead to trouble, mark my words. Pretty obvious why she's doing it." Jake snorted with disgust. "To everyone but Kane, that is."

"You're just pissed 'cause she won't give you the time o' day."

"Oho, there you're wrong. I don't go following tail that's out of my league. You're the one with the hots for her."

"Admit it, you wouldn't toss her out of your bed," Clive said, his voice growing wistful.

"Alphas are too high maintenance and just plain snotty and high-strung. I'll keep my Mattie, thank you very much."

"She's about your speed. That's what's wrong with you, Jake, you settle too easy. You're always settling."

"Ain't a thing wrong with my Mattie," Jake said, growing indignant. "She's given me four little cubs."

"Okay, she's fertile, I'll give you that. And she's kinda cute. But I'm aiming higher."

"Tell you what I heard if you keep it to yourself." Jake seemed mollified by Clive's concessions concerning Mattie, and some of the anger had left his voice.

"Sure, what'd you hear?"

"The council's going to call a contention in a month if Arwan doesn't choose a mate."

"Aw, that ain't nothing. Every one knows that. And I won't be out o' the running then, now will I?" Clive said.

Nina couldn't see Clive from her vantage point, but she had a feeling he was sticking out his chest like a male peacock.

"You think you got a chance against Kane?" Jake's voice wavered as if he'd just spoken the name of the devil himself. "If I were you, I wouldn't even embarrass myself like that."

Nina wondered if this Kane was the alpha male.

"Just shut up, will you? You're getting on my nerves."

"'Cause you got no chance, and you know it."

"I mean it, shut up and dig. I don't want to be out here all night."

A loud chuckle; then Jake said, "Sore loser."

"Shut up, 'fore I shut you up."

Another dismissive chuckle under Jake's breath. Nina was already liking Jake over his companion.

She waited for the shovels to begin again, then got down on all fours and crawled forward. Frozen wet grass poked her gloved hands and knees as she crept to the edge of the ravine and peeked down. She gasped silently.

The two deputies were digging a mass grave. Light from a gas lantern shrouded their forms. They worked at superhuman speed, seniph speed, their shovels in fast-forward. One was tall, tow-headed with a buzz cut and a handlebar mustache. The other was shorter, stockier, with a gnomelike face. Both had the wide necks and meaty, solid musculature of two-skins. Even in human form they couldn't hide the fact that a muscular animal resided beneath their flesh. She would bet the gnome-faced one was Clive, because short, unattractive men overcompensated by flaunting their masculinity. And poor Clive had a lot of flaunting to do.

She glanced past them, toward the pasture. Her jaw fell open as she blinked away the sleet from her eyelashes. Carcasses, dozens of them. She counted a hundred sheep, ten cows and a flock of chickens all charred from being burned alive. All had been thrown into a crematorium, and the fire had gone out before they'd turned to ash. Their combined horror and misery crawled along her skin and crashed in her mind. It was too much, and her world began rocking.

She squeezed her eyes closed and let images of the Quiet Place, the serenity there, the tranquil peace, take the place of the mind storm.

When she achieved some semblance of control, she looked up again. The animals' spirits hovered above their bodies, advancing and ebbing in a palette of white mist. They resembled snowy figures on a television with bad reception, but their graven images at the moment of death were clearly discernible. Flames consumed the animals, their flesh melting away from bone. But it was the frightened look in their eyes that caused Nina to blink back tears. She glanced down at her gloved hands long enough to gather herself; then her sympathy turned to anger at the senseless and violent death the creatures had suffered.

Gleaners usually weren't this sloppy and destroyed the physical bodies they left behind by turning them to cinder and ash. This one must have been interrupted.

Nina forced herself to look up again. Where were the owners of the farm? Their spirits wouldn't be present, because the gleaner had consumed them. But since the gleaner hadn't finished tidying up, some evidence of their physical remains should be there.

She glanced back at the area around Jake and Clive. No evidence of human bodies near them. Had they already disposed of them?

Her attention shifted back to the animals' spirits hovering above their bodies, circling the air in chaotic flaming patterns. They were caught on a frightening merry-go-round and didn't know how to get off. She had seen this behavior among animals that hadn't resigned themselves to death and died suddenly or in turmoil. Sometimes it happened in slaughterhouses or dog pounds where animals where frightened and disoriented when they were put down. She detested the shivers that called her to these places.

Hear me, all of you. Her magic instantly translated the command to the language of the dead creatures.

The animal spirits turned in unison, all eyes gazing at her. A sudden stillness entered her mind, and the rapt quiet brought tears to her eyes. *You will be fine now. You can leave the earth in peace. I'm sorry you had to die this way, and I'll punish the gleaner who did this. Now rise and embrace your new destiny.*

The air suddenly thinned as if the earth's reality took a deep breath. The wind and sleet stopped. The earth's reality caught in a sudden suspended animation. The sky above her sucked the gravity from the air, and her body grew weightless. She grabbed a fence post and braced herself for what would happen next.

A fissure tore through the dark ominous clouds and into another dimension. The air smelled heavily of ions, like after a lightning strike, cleansed and pure. The sound of heaven's heartbeat rumbled from the opening. Then bright rays unfurled like a rolled-up tongue and fell to the earth. Grace and happiness flowed from this corridor, and the animals' spirits were drawn toward it. One by one they stepped onto the Path of Light. When all the souls were grasped, the corridor rolled back up in all its magnificence and disappeared in a flash and a twinkle. The wind and sleet returned in gale force and hit Nina. The sudden reality knocked her out of the trance that always caught her when spirits left the earth.

She held tight to the post, knowing Clive and Jake were oblivious to the ascension. She was one of the few chosen ones who could witness the transfer of spirits to the other side. Her people called it the Crossover. Koda said it was Nina's consolation prize for having suffered the shivers, one of his feeble attempts at making her feel better. Sometimes it worked, though, for it gratified her to know she was helping other souls.

Nina felt her body temperature rising again and her shaking slowing down. She crept away from the edge and turned to leave when voices broke the calm in her mind.

Help, help.

Oh, no.

Our mistress.

Nina cringed as the words and anxiety drifted through her thoughts. By the faint weakness of the signal, she could tell there weren't that many souls. But where were they?

She crept back along the fence and let the voices guide her past another open pasture, toward a trail that led straight into the woods. She hurried down the rocky path, careful not to turn an ankle. Traces of the rising sun tried to break through the dark storm clouds but had little success. She had to pick her way through the murky shadows.

The forest thickened into twisted brambles, cedars, hollies and pines. The wind failed to penetrate its denseness. The unnatural silence that teemed in the air raised the fine hairs along the back of her neck. She glanced behind her and saw no one.

She picked up her pace and reached a brook. It snaked along the path, its water gleaming dark blood-red in the shadows. Ground mist swelled along its sides, and gray vaporous fingers grasped at her feet and legs.

The path curved away from the stream, and she spotted two apparitions. Birds. Parakeets, maybe. Their tiny spiritual bodies blazed with misty flames as they flew around and around in circles.

Bring back our Emma, the birds chorused, their

voices shrill with apprehension. *Gone. Gone. Followed her here. Lion monster took her.*

Nina drew closer. Even though it was sleeting, the moisture did little to mask the unmistakable smell of burned human flesh. Something about the odor made her deathly ill, and she stopped to vomit. When she felt better, she knelt beside a small pile of ashes and touched them. They were cold. All that was left of Emma.

Hear me. Nina caught the attention of the parakeets, and they stopped flying in frantic circles and hovered, looking at her. *Was anyone else hurt?* Nina asked, hoping that the gleaner hadn't disposed of another human.

Only our mistress, Emma Baldoon. She loves us. We sing to her and we love her.

Nina felt their heartache and loss. Whoever believed animals didn't feel emotion or attachment knew nothing of their spirits. How could she explain to them that they'd never see Emma Baldoon alive again because she was nothing more than fodder for a gleaner?

Nina always thought of herself as the most levelheaded of her sisters. She hated confrontation, easily forgave and wasn't quick to anger. But when innocent creatures and people suffered needlessly, all her restraint snapped. Righteous indignation for Emma Baldoon and all of her farm animals smoldered in her as she asked, *Which way did the gleaner go after he did this?*

You don't want to know. Stay away from him.

Nina would like nothing better. The thought of tracking a gleaner made her insides churn, but she wasn't about to let this two-skin mutant continue to kill innocents. *Thank you for the warning, but I have to know.*

Into the rising sun.

East. Now that she knew where to look for the gleaner, she took a deep breath and enlightened them about Emma's death. She assured them that Emma would not be coming back and they need not wait for her.

The birds calmed and accepted the loss; then she helped their spirits ascend.

She turned to head east. That's when she saw two bright eyes staring at her, the fires of hell burning in the bottomless pits. Gleaner eyes.

Chapter 3

Nina froze, transfixed by fear. She couldn't let the gleaner believe he had the upper hand or he'd certainly kill her. At the moment, he had no idea of the extent of her power. Keep them guessing was an edge she'd discovered at an early age in dealing with the shifter and animal kingdom. She forced herself to remain calm.

The fiery eyes slunk out of the mist, and the gleaner's huge sleekness emerged. He appeared in lion form, walking on all fours. She knew from the stories passed down from the Guardians that gleaners and seniphs could shift their arm and leg joints and walk upright on their hind legs like humans. She also knew grown lions weighed between four hundred and six hundred pounds. This gleaner looked every bit as large. It was one thing seeing a lion behind bars in a zoo, quite another being stalked by a supernatural lion-beast.

Nina felt a cold fist of fear contract in her gut as she watched the agile muscles pumping beneath the tawny fur. His mighty mane quivered with each step. He moved with the stealth and confidence of a predator high on the food chain. A reddish aura emanated from his body, evidence that he'd just fed off of Emma Baldoon's spirit. His scorching eyes never left her as he ran a huge pink tongue over his lips, exposing three-inch-long fangs.

"Well, well, what have we here?" His deep voice rumbled loud enough that she felt the vibration in her own chest. He prowled closer on massive paws. "A little do-gooder."

Nina gulped past the sudden dryness in her throat. Remain calm, assertive, show him you're not afraid. She forced a smile right back at him, though her cheeks felt disembodied and plastic, and her lips must surely crack any second.

"Just cleaning up your handiwork." She tried to sound as cold-blooded as he had, though she was certain a drop of fear had slipped into her words.

The flames in his eyes narrowed the slightest bit, cunning burning bright in them. "I clean up my own plate." He ran his long tongue around his mouth.

Staring into his eyes was like looking into a bonfire. They both held the same hypnotic power. So this was how he lured victims to their death. She avoided his eyes as she said, "Not this time. You've been sloppy."

"I'll admit, I didn't expect the Brayville sheriff's department to be so prompt in arriving. But look what it brought me." He raised his flat black nose, and his nostrils quivered as he sniffed. "I smell human, but wait…" His nostrils flared, then he said, "You smell pagan. What are you, witch, conjurer, fairy, angel? They all work for me. Hmm! Your scent is different, inviting. But I think it's poisonous if you wish it to be."

"How perceptive of you." Nina didn't let her gaze waver from his nose. Here was where a poker face held the difference between life and death.

He slowly crept toward her, his eyes calculating, assessing. "Hmm! I'm guessing you're a siren of some sort."

"Wrong, sorry." She jammed her hands on her hips while scanning the area for an escape route. The path she had been on swerved to the right.

"Maybe it's time to find out." He bared his teeth in a wicked sneer; then he crouched to spring.

Before Nina could react, a roar thundered and shook the very ground beneath her feet. A seniph, in lion form, lunged out of the woods. An enormous furry body sailed past her.

The seniph landed on the gleaner with a loud thwack, solid walls of flesh hitting.

Nina staggered back, mind reeling, heart racing. She took cover behind some trees.

The creatures tore into each other. She kept her gaze on the seniph. He was even larger than the gleaner. He fought more aggressively, too. The gleaner had a hard time fending him off. She glimpsed familiar vivid green eyes. The seniph from Brayville?

Nina didn't know which was more frightening, the seniph or the gleaner.

In all her dealings with shifters and animals, she'd

never seen a more violent struggle for survival, all bared fangs, claws and tearing flesh. The two lions balanced on their hind legs, front paws locked in an unnatural human way, going for each other's throats. Their thick manes were the only protection they had, and in the gleaner's case it didn't seem to help.

The gleaner had taken more bites from the seniph, and deep gashes covered its fur. It struggled to hold its own. No blood poured from the wounds; gleaners didn't bleed. Their blood disintegrated as soon as it touched the air. And it took them only twenty-four hours to regenerate and heal, unlike regular seniphs, who healed faster than humans, but not half as quickly as a gleaner. In order to wipe out a gleaner, you had to stop its heart or cut off its head. A lot like vampires.

The seniph sensed his weakening opponent and used his weight to thrust the gleaner to the ground. In a second, he covered the gleaner, his massive weight pinning the gleaner's spine to the ground.

The seniph raised his mouth to rip out the gleaner's throat, saliva and blood dripping from his formidable fangs. But he paused, shaking his head in fury, as though his conscience warred with his animal instincts. His green eyes narrowed and looked expressly human and odd embedded in his lion features. He opened his jaws wider to bite, but instead of delivering the *coup de grâce,* he let out an enraged roar.

Nina felt the tremor of it inside her chest.

At the seniph's hesitation, the gleaner saw his chance and bit the seniph in the shoulder, gouging flesh.

The seniph growled out in pain.

The gleaner bit again and again as it rolled the seniph off with a twist of its body. Once free, it staggered into the woods. Then it broke into a limping gallop and disappeared into the forest.

Nina couldn't figure out why the gleaner hadn't fried the seniph, or why the seniph had hesitated in finishing off the gleaner. The seniph lay on the ground, unmoving, bleeding. His own hesitation might have cost him his life.

Since he'd saved her, Nina wanted to check on him, but the gleaner was getting away. She followed the fresh shiver trail of pain and anger the gleaner left in his wake and went after him. Now that he was wounded, he would be the hunted. How quickly the tide had turned, thanks to the seniph. She spared him one final glance over her shoulder, then shoved her way past the thick branches of a pine tree.

Kane's shoulder and arm throbbed as he heard a branch crack. He smelled the woman before he spied her skulking off into the woods. The little idiot was pursuing Ethan.

She'd get herself killed. Maybe she believed that now Ethan was wounded she might get the upper hand. Did she really think she had a chance against a gleaner?

She might not be as fragile as he thought. Maybe she could kill Ethan. Kane didn't want his brother destroyed. It wasn't Ethan doing the killing, but the gleaner. No, the brother he knew, the one he cared for, was in there somewhere. And if he needed proof of that, he'd witnessed it moments ago. Ethan could have killed

Kane easily with his power, but he hadn't. Ethan cared for him, Kane was certain of it. He would never believe Ethan was all monster.

Kane would give anything to have traded places with his brother. He'd been only twenty when Ethan showed signs of gleanerism. They had seventeen great years together; they were closer than two brothers had ever been. But when Ethan showed signs of the sickness, it all had soured. And in saving Ethan's life, Kane had betrayed his father's trust. When Nelson Byron Van Cleave lay on his deathbed, he whispered in Kane's ear, "This family was cursed the day you were born." How those words had tortured Kane. His father's prediction had come to pass, for everyone Kane had ever cared about, he'd destroyed or disappointed. The guilt of not being able to do something to help Ethan would always be Kane's burden to carry. But it was in his power to save Ethan again, and he had to try.

What possessed Ethan to return home and stir up so much trouble? It was sheer folly. Once the council learned of a gleaner being in the area, they'd assume Ethan was back. He'd be hunted down and slaughtered, if Kane didn't find him first.

What irritated Kane more was that the human had watched as he spared Ethan's life. She was an eyewitness to his one Achilles' heel, and if the council found out, not only would Ethan lose his life, but Kane, too. And Arwan might be dragged into it. Not to mention the meddling human.

Something had brought her to the Baldoon farm, but what? What kind of powers did she possess? He'd seen her stand up near the animal corpses, facing them, her expression one of fixed concentration, then she'd gazed up at the night sky as if seeing a vision meant for her eyes only. He had no idea what she was doing. Then he'd tracked her down the path where she'd walked right to Emma Baldoon's ashes, as if she knew where Ethan had killed her. The human had worn the same absorbed rictus on her face as before, as if she had been experiencing something preternatural. Whatever her power, he promised himself she would rue the day she came to Brayville or anywhere near it.

Despite the flesh wounds, Kane rolled over and up onto his feet. He licked the blood from his shoulder and front leg, then slunk off into the forest. He'd have to find the woman and Ethan. Damn them both!

Nina paused to catch her breath. She sat on one of many rocks that jutted into a secluded ravine and branched out over a waterfall. Solid icicles clung to the rocks and hung in long, sparkling rivulets below her and above her. Oaks and hickories crowded the rocks, their naked boughs bent and twisted and grasping at the promise of spring. She might have enjoyed the serene beauty, if she hadn't felt totally disoriented, lost and freezing.

The sleet had turned to a fine snow. Her breath formed white clouds around her head. She brought a hand up to shield her eyes from the flakes that the wind whipped at her face. The cold went right through her wool gloves, and she had to keep her hands in her pocket. Even so, she couldn't feel the tips of her fingers…or, for that matter, her toes. The hood on her coat did little to keep her face and cheeks and neck warm, and she felt the ice chaffing them raw.

Not to mention she had lost the gleaner's trail. Nothing stirred her thought processes. She couldn't pick up one sensation, one feeling, one vibration. It was as if the gleaner had vanished off the face of the earth. He must be using his gleaner cloaking powers. A sort of gleaner camouflage, a chameleon's trick, only more deadly, for it made finding them almost impossible. Flitter demons were capable of the same wiles. When her grandmother had been the Guardian, Nina had helped Meikoda track them. They were crafty killers, even worse than gleaners, because they could hide inside a human body. Flitter demons possessed a person, forced them to commit suicide, then took the soul and moved on to their next victim. It was hit or miss with flitter demons. If they were already entrenched in a human, they hid their emotions within the human's mind, and Nina had been no help to Meikoda at all. Sometimes Nina could discover them if they were moving from one body to another by concentrating really hard. Maybe she could do the same thing to track the gleaner.

She closed her eyes and concentrated. Something didn't feel quite right. Something heavy stirred the air where it shouldn't be moving. A breath maybe. A pair of eyes. The feeling of being hunted.

Her skin crawled as she opened her eyes and locked gazes with the seniph.

She gulped in air, every nerve in her body prickling. He was still in lion form, perched on a rock above her head, a commanding leonine predatory figure in the driving snow. He stood across the waterfall, about twenty-five feet away, jungle-green eyes narrowed on her, teeth bared. Even though he was yards away, he looked massive. His chest and body were so thick with muscle, his skin quivered with every breath.

She spotted caked bloodstains from the wound on his shoulder and front leg. The lesions appeared deep and open. By all rights, he shouldn't have been able to stand, much less track her. The main question was whether he could jump far enough to attack her. Those vivid green eyes paralyzed her. The black pupils narrowed like blade edges, daring her to stir. She was afraid to even blink. So this was how his prey felt.

Suddenly he leaped over the waterfall, sailing gracefully through the air as if he had wings.

She wheeled and jumped up and ran, slipping on the ice-covered rocky mountainside. Branches snatched at her pants, coat and face. A deer path led to the right, and she sprinted that way, heart hammering, adrenaline coursing through her body.

Thump! The seniph landed on the rock where she'd just been sitting.

The violent images of the fight between the seniph and the gleaner flooded her. She couldn't bring herself to stop running.

"If you make me come after you, you'll regret it." The deep bellow thundered through the woods, his closeness startling her.

She slipped on some icy leaves, lost her footing and slid straight down. A limb came out of nowhere. Before she could react, her head plowed into it. For a second, a vision of her flesh being torn to bits by huge fangs flashed before her eyes, then blessed darkness took her far away.

Kane saw the woman's head crack into a maple limb. Then she crumpled, her limp body rolling and bouncing down the mountain.

In three long strides, he chomped down on the back of her coat, dug his claws into the ground and instantly stopped her fall. The material ripped. A piece stuck inside his mouth. He spit out the wool, irritated at having to track her and chase her. Because of her, Ethan had cloaked himself and could only be found if he allowed it. Though the human had somehow followed Ethan until she lost his trail. What type of magic allowed her to track gleaners?

He gazed down at the hole he'd left in the coat. He'd severed it, lining and all. She was lying on her belly, half her back exposed. Her baggy blue sweater had ridden up her spine, exposing a ten-inch expanse of what looked like two pairs of white long johns. Was she wearing long johns under her pants, too? If so, her legs were too slender, even with the layers of material around them. Her low-top hiking boots were caked with snow. She was small for a woman and fragile looking, way too thin to suit his taste. He could snap her bones with one good swipe of his paw.

He tugged on the sleeve of her coat and rolled her over. Her long hair covered her face in jumbles of thick strands. He used an extended claw to gently swipe aside the thick jet-black hair, then stared down at her face. A large bruise was forming in the middle of her high forehead. He hadn't noticed from their first encounter, but she had a girlish face and soft rosebud lips. Impossibly long dark lashes, too. Her features were delicate, almost ethereal, and there was an air of purity about her that grated against him. There was nothing innocent about her intentions. Something had brought her to the area, and she had foolishly followed Ethan. Most humans would have run in the opposite direction. Not this female.

In animal form his senses were heightened, and he could hear her heart beating, every pulse point in her body drumming softly. Her mouth was open, and tiny clouds of her breath condensed in the air. He bent down, feeling the tips of his whiskers brushing her cheek. The sensation sent an awareness of her that made an eyebrow raise and his blood quicken.

He wanted to pull back, but he found himself moving in closer to suck in her breath, absorb her essence. Her scent was far different than that of most human females. Sweet and tempting, fey to be sure. She definitely gave off a supernatural impression, an enchanted vibe he couldn't figure out. Whatever it was, he found it fascinating and impossible to ignore. It was like being pulled by a leash, or feeling the hypnotizing tug of a full moon. It touched something primal in him, stirred a reckless yearning to fill himself with her. He hated being drawn to her, for he knew what might happen if he totally gave in to his urges.

He broke her spell by shaking his head. She'd

actually made him salivate, and droplets of saliva went flying from his lips. He licked his mouth and came to a decision.

He knew he was stronger in shifter form and could cover more ground. He stretched out his legs, morphing his hips and shoulder joints. Skin stretched, tendons popped and muscles writhed as he stood upright. He bent and scooped her up into his arms. It surprised him how little she weighed. She hardly put a strain on his wounded shoulder and arm. He ran back up the mountain with ease, trying to ignore the small and helpless way she rocked in his arms. He wished she hadn't come near him or Ethan.

In frustration, he threw back his head and let out a roar. The sound echoed through the mountains and carried for miles. He hoped Ethan got the message: contact him in some way. Why hadn't he trusted Kane enough to seek him out, rather than hide from him? Didn't he know all Kane wanted to do was help? Kane felt that familiar emptiness in his heart when he thought of Ethan, and before he could stop himself he was bending down to sniff the human's hair. Her scent was like a balm, and he let it wash over him.

Chapter 4

Charles Billingsly, Kane's butler, held ice on the woman's forehead while Kane searched through the belongings that he'd taken from her car. Charles, a seniph, was pencil thin. His balding pate glistened in the lights. Freckles dotted his nose, and his gray goatee and mustache were trimmed with mechanical precision. He managed Kane's home, Lionsgate, and its staff with the same meticulousness. Charles insured Kane's privacy was never infringed upon. Sometimes Kane wouldn't see a maid or gardener for weeks on end. Kane didn't know how Charles managed it, but he liked that the staff stayed well away from him and out of harm's way.

Ever since Kane could remember, Charles had worked at Lionsgate. Charles's family took pride in having served the Van Cleaves for over three hundred years in the capacity of butlers, maids, gardeners and chauffeurs.

Charles's wife did all the cooking on the estate, and his three sons supervised the vineyard and the making of the wine. Running a vineyard and an estate was truly a family affair, and Charles and his relatives were the closest thing Kane had to family, though he'd never allowed himself to get too close, for their own good.

Charles was the only person Kane permitted to cross that line. The butler had been there for Kane during the death of his parents, Ethan's disease and finally Kane's own reckless descent. He was loyal to a fault, would do anything asked of him and didn't seem afraid of Kane as others in the pride were. He'd always been a bulwark in Kane's life, the one person with whom Kane shared his true feelings.

Kane scowled over at Charles. An eager-to-please expression rarely left the servant's face, but at the moment he didn't look at all enthused about his task. He held the ice on the woman's forehead with two fingers while he kept a wary eye on her as if she were a sea hag about to rise out of the water.

Charles studied the woman's face. "There's something weird about her. Can you feel it?"

Kane paused from rummaging through the pockets of her torn coat. Nothing there but old tissues. He was glad that someone else experienced the odd attraction, and the allure he felt wasn't just his imagination. "Yes. What do you think it is?"

"Clearly magic of some sort. She appears human, but there's a definite enchantment about her." Charles bent and sniffed. "It's strong, too. I can feel the pull all the way to my insides."

"Me, too," Kane said, tossing aside the coat.

Charles bent lower, placing his nose above her face. Being that close to her caused the butler's stiff guards to come tumbling down, and a silly grin broke over his face. "What is it about her that makes you want to rub up against her and lick her? Kinda like taking a bath in warm crème. Good grief, she smells delectable…." Charles's tongue flicked out, his fangs flashing.

Kane felt a snap of possessiveness as he barked, "Get a grip, man. Don't fall under her spell."

Charles blinked and seemed to realize what'd he'd been about to do. For a moment, he looked flummoxed; then he regained his dignity. His cheeks turned red. He cleared his throat and straightened, backing as far away from her as he could and still hold the ice pack. "I'm so sorry, sir. She glamoured me. I just couldn't help it. She's—"

"I know," Kane finished for him. "Real trouble." Kane had asked Charles to tend her wounds because he feared making a fool of himself as the butler had just done. Now he regretted his hasty decision. He'd much rather have tasted her cheek than become aware of this envious feeling for her. He'd been so careful about keeping his distance from everyone. He wasn't about to let this tiny wisp of a human rattle his defenses. No, he was stronger than that.

"Imagine if a hunting party found her, the effect she would have on us all." Charles shifted the ice pack so it wouldn't fall. "Cleopatra herself didn't have the allure of this human."

"I know," Kane said flatly, recalling the history of

the seniphs. Cleopatra had been an enchanted alpha who had almost single-handedly destroyed her own pride because every male, including humans, fought wildly to have her. They weren't aware that when she tired of toying with them, they'd become quarry for one of her royal night hunts. This human might be as deadly. He trusted his instincts, and they were screaming at him that she was another Cleo, or worse.

Kane's brows snapped together. He purposely kept his gaze from her, not tempting trouble, as he picked up her purse. The leather-fringed bag was as large as a briefcase and made of patchwork neon colors. One of the ugliest handbags Kane had ever seen. No fashion-conscious woman in her right mind would carry something like this. But then this woman had to be out of her mind to go after a gleaner—unless she had hoped to use her temptress powers on Ethan, which might have worked if Kane hadn't intervened.

Kane noticed a slight tremor in his hands. He hoped it was from the wounds in his shoulder and arm and not that he was in close proximity to this human femme fatale. Opening the bag, he pulled out a rotting apple, some chunks of cheese in a baggy, a handful of hair clips of varying sizes and shapes, hand lotion, ChapStick, a pair of blue Ben Franklin sunglasses, several tampons— Charles pulled a face at the last bit of plunder. "Where the hell is her license?" Kane said.

Kane lost his patience and turned the bag upside down. A bright yellow wallet with a smiley face on it fell out. He glowered at it for a second, thinking he'd enjoy burning it when he was done with it.

Charles's mustache wiggled in distaste. "I'm not sure it's such a good idea to keep her here, sir."

"She stays until I decide what to do with her."

"But the Council, sir—"

Kane shot Charles a look that normally sent him into a hasty retreat. "Enough about the Council. I know the danger. That's why I'm sending all of you away."

Charles's bushy gray brows snapped together. "But the house, sir. Who will take care of you?"

"I'm quite capable of taking care of myself. And I won't put you in danger because of your loyalty to me. Go now, and leave with your family as soon as you can. And you haven't seen me or this human. That clear?"

Charles made a zipper motion over his lips. "Nothing, sir."

Kane thought a moment, then said, "And take your boys to the Rockies on me. They need a hunting vacation. So do you." A seniph's hunting vacation didn't include guns. It was all shifter and nature.

Charles still looked unsure, crushing the ice pack between his hands. "At least let me tend your wounds, sir."

"Nothing, remember?" Kane's expression said this conversation had ended.

Charles heaved a loud sigh and gave a final nod. He would have clicked his heels had he been wearing Army boots instead of a pair of galoshes. He set the ice pack on a side table, gave Nina a distrustful but longing glance, then said, "Call me, sir, if I can be of service."

"Thank you, you've helped enough."

Kane listened to Charles's footsteps clop through

the guest house; then the back door slammed. Charles's minivan revved up; then the heavy snow engulfed the engine noise. It had snowed six inches and was still coming down in thick gusts.

Kane had brought the human here for privacy. The guest house was almost a mile from the main house, and it was cleaned only once a month. The less the staff knew, the better. And now that he knew he wasn't imagining the enchanting allure of the human, he knew he had to keep her from everyone in the pride.

He pulled out a mound of credit cards from the smiley wallet. It seemed to be laughing at him, and he frowned as he found her license buried on the bottom. The mug shot made her look mousy and nervous, but she had a nice smile. He read on: Nina Rainwater. He paused over the name, couldn't place it, then continued. Twenty-one years old. She resided on the Patomani Indian Reservation. Well, that explained her tanned coloring—then it hit him.

He recalled why Rainwater had sounded so familiar. Fala Rainwater had just become the new Guardian. News of her reign had just reached the pride's council. They'd had a town meeting to announce it last week. So that's where he'd heard the name. He'd never met the Guardian, but he'd heard rumors, one being that the bloodline of the Guardian came from female Patomani Indians, more particularly Rainwater women. Meikoda Rainwater, Fala's grandmother, had been the prior Guardian. The Guardian was supposedly the most powerful shaman alive, defender of all goodness on earth. He cocked a skeptical brow at that myth. As far as he could tell, there was no goodness anywhere, and evil was winning hands down.

His thoughts strayed back to Nina Rainwater and her formidable relatives. If one of her relatives was the Guardian, what was Nina Rainwater? There were no myths or rumors regarding her powers, but he and Charles—and Kane suspected Ethan—had felt her influence. Had she been sent here to eradicate Ethan? That would surely complicate matters. And what about disposing of her? It might bring down the wrath of the Guardian as well as the Patomani council of shamans. Not if he steered them elsewhere and removed all evidence of her.

He wished he'd never seen Nina Rainwater. He couldn't let her go now, because she knew too much. And she'd had the ability to track Ethan quite a distance. Even Kane's heightened senses weren't able to trace *Ethan*. He gave off no physical scent; his body burned it off. And the snow had covered his tracks. But he noticed that when Ethan had cloaked himself, she had been stumped, too. Maybe there was a limit to her powers. Another mystery about her that he didn't like. Once he got the truth out of her, he'd have to take care that all evidence of her was cleaned out, and he'd have to dump her car far away from here. He'd driven it deeper into the woods, in a ravine, and covered it with leaves and branches. A temporary fix, but not for long.

Something bulged from the wallet's zipper compartment. He opened it and found her business cards: Happy Face Inc., Pet Psychic When You Need One, Day or Night. It had her name, email address and telephone number at the bottom. Perhaps her psychic powers had led her to Ethan. He hoped the Guardian hadn't sent her here. Just how powerful was she? He could still feel the hypnotic pull of her charmed body.

He turned and threw the hideous purse and wallet into the fireplace. He poked it, jabbing it deep into the logs, then looked at Nina Rainwater. She was still as death, but the color had come back to her skin, and her body had stopped trembling. She looked petite and lost in the king-size bed. Her hair fanned out around her head on the pillow. Firelight danced blue highlights along the thick dark strands. Charles had tucked her beneath the covers to warm her. With all those layers of clothes on, it must not have taken long.

Kane grimaced, remembering how he couldn't allow himself near her. Charles had put ice on the nasty knot that had formed above her brows, but it had still grown to the size of a quarter and turned purple. It looked like an all-seeing third eye, and he almost felt it staring at him.

He grew uncomfortable and poked the fire again, fighting the intoxicating force drawing him near her. He felt his beast growing aroused at her nearness, too. He quelled an overwhelming desire to crawl into bed and lay beside her, feel her skin against his, inhale her sweet breath again. He wanted to consume her and stop these insane cravings. He knew what a junkie must feel like, and he hated the vulnerability of it. He'd made a point of staying away from all women, human or seniph, since Daphne's death, and he couldn't allow Nina Rainwater to change that. No, her glamour had no power over him if he didn't allow it. All it took was self-discipline. And he had that in spades. And once she awakened and he questioned her, he'd be rid of her for good.

But what to do with her in the interim? He couldn't stay here and be this close to her. He jabbed at the fire again and scowled at the spitting flames that consumed her purse and blackened the smiley face on her wallet. Abruptly it occurred to him what he could do with her.

Nina awakened, her forehead pounding. Moldy dank air filled her senses and drew her brows together. A pain shot through her forehead. It all came back to her now: being chased by the seniph, bumping into the limb.

She reached up to rub her forehead but found her hands bound with duct tape. Her knees and ankles, too, mummy-style. Then she recalled the seniph chasing her. He must be holding her prisoner. Dread gripped her, and her eyes flew open.

Overhead a hazy dim bulb burned from a bare socket. It hung from a bare rafter in the center of the room, throwing dim golden shadows around her. She was in a dungeon—no, there were shelves and shelves of wine bottles packed around her. A wine cellar?

She raised her head and noticed she was lying on an old army cot. Someone had thrown a bunch of blankets over her—not very clean ones, either. They were moth-eaten and grease-stained and looked as if they had been down here longer than the wine. So her captor had tied her up in this horrible place, but worried about her comfort. How thoughtful.

She guessed she should be grateful she was still alive. That really didn't make her feel much better—especially now. So much for positive thinking.

Something rustled and chattered near her. The sensations of insatiable hunger and curiosity filtered into her thoughts. She shifted her gaze to the floor as two small creatures scurried beneath the cot, their long tails swishing, their feet making a delicate pitter-patter on the brick floor. Rats. The least of her worries.

The resourceful little rodents tested the legs on the cot to see if it would hold. Rats weren't so bad. She was always finding them and nursing them back to health. They were intelligent creatures and appreciative and always sad they wouldn't be able to talk to her anymore when she released them back out into the wild. She'd also helped rat owners when their pets were going through some emotional trauma. Most of the time they were just plain lonely and the installation of another rat into their cage did the trick.

It was the were-rats you had to watch. They marauded through urban areas at night. When they shifted, they turned into city rats as large as labs, but not as friendly. They'd grab humans in a minute and pull them down through a sewer drain and make a tasty meal of them. Lord help anyone who ventured down into their sewer territories uninvited. If she had to go down to discover the source of a shiver, she had to clear it with the local "king" first. And each city had its own monarch. It wasn't a pleasant experience dealing with were-rats. Regular rats received most of the blame for the damage were-rats left behind. Didn't seem fair. Maybe man would one day recognize his ignorance.

The industrious rats found a way to lever their bodies against the wall and the cot legs, then clambered up beside her. They reared up on their hind legs and sniffed the air for her fear. When they found none of the usual human dread that accompanied the sight of them, their eyes gleamed and their whiskers quivered. Their curiosity overcame the last of their reticence, and they crawled cautiously toward her.

"That's right, come on," Nina cooed, though she knew they couldn't understand her yet. If it had been their spirits she was communicating with, it wouldn't have been a problem, but in their present living state she had to touch them to give them an order they couldn't refuse.

One of the rats grew bold and edged along her legs and sniffed the blanket covering her legs and thighs. The other followed, its pink nose twitching. Brave One scampered up her leg and hopped onto her stomach.

She opened her fingers as wide as her bound wrists would allow and grabbed the rat by his neck. *Gotcha, my friend!*

He struggled in fear for a second; then her thoughts worked through him and he became pliant. She gave him a mental order. His free will balked for a nanosecond; then he relaxed and began gnawing on the duct tape between her wrists.

The second rat, a female, very pregnant, couldn't stay away. Mrs. Rat crawled up Nina's hip and perched in the hollow of her stomach. *Hello to you, too.* Nina stroked the rat with her index finger, and it looked content and a little dreamy-eyed. *Join your partner, thank you.* She felt the rodent's will become her own, then released it.

The female scrambled down her legs and paused near her ankles. She felt a light tugging as the rodent chewed on the duct tape.

You're good little soldiers.

They seemed content with the praise.

She decided to take advantage of them once more and asked, *Where am I?*

Van Cleave mansion, Brave One answered.

Good eating in the winery. Lots of grapes. Tasty, not like this nasty tape.

Sorry. Is the owner a seniph? She prayed the answer would be no, but she had a gut feeling her prayers were futile.

Yah-uh. Kane Van Cleave. We don't go near him. Seniphs aren't good. Make us afraid. We stay down here.

We don't want to die. Can't, can't, can't. Mrs. Rat's thoughts broke into the conversation.

Her captor's name was Kane Van Cleave. Her stomach clenched at the thought of him. She grew impatient waiting for her liberators to finish their job and asked, *Are there windows down here?*

No, no, no. Only one way in and out for humans—the stairs.

In a few minutes, the rats freed her. Nina jerked off the rest of the tape, stretched her wrists and her ankles, then rolled off the cot and pulled down her sweater.

She watched the rats scamper off into the shadows.

Now to escape without detection, hopefully. She found the staircase, eased up the stairs and reached the door. Gently, she tested the knob.

Locked.

She headed back down, hating that she was losing precious seconds. After a frantic search, she came up empty-handed. She had to elicit the rats' help again. They pointed her to a cabinet that held a bucket with old tools. She grabbed the flat-head screwdriver and sneaked back up the stairs.

After some careful twisting and jamming, she paused and listened at the door.

Nothing.

She eased the door open only wide enough to peer through.

Four gas sconces burned in a long hallway that seemed to stretch on forever. The ceilings had to be twenty feet in height. Dark mahogany wainscoting covered the walls. Beautifully carved rosettes and lions in different poses decorated the paneling. Gilded laurels and vines of flowers outlined the ceiling tiles. She could see a window at the end of the hall. Not just any window, but a massive arched thing at least fifteen feet high. It would have looked at home in a castle. Elaborate stained glass covered every inch. A huge letter *V* slashed across the middle, cleaving the glass into thirds. Ivy crept along the *V* and formed weird hieroglyphic-looking symbols. The darkness behind the window didn't do the work of art justice. She wondered how late it was and how long she'd been down in the basement.

The opulence and size of the mansion lent it a hollow,

uninviting feel that consumed everything, that seemed to say, "Enter at your own risk." Nina much preferred her grandmother's tiny rancher, where she had grown up. This place was too formal and austere, and, what was even worse, Kane Van Cleave could be lurking somewhere in this place.

She gulped, then made sure the coast was clear and quickly opened the door, hoping the hinges wouldn't creak. They moaned, but softly. Her shoes hissed on the Persian hall runner. Gritting her teeth, she tiptoed down the hall.

She could only turn left into another hall. This mansion felt like a giant labyrinth with no escape. A kingdom for a window she could open or a door leading outside, she thought ruefully.

She reached the sleeping quarters. All done just as lavishly as the rest of the house and in varying colors. She passed a blue, green, lilac and pink room.

She paused at the end of the hall and ducked in a yellow and gold room. She didn't dare turn on a light, but from the hall sconce she could see it was a beautiful room, with brocade gold and yellow curtains and a four-poster mahogany bed with a canopy that matched the drapes. The posters were as large as her waist: hand-carved and museum-quality.

She hurried past an armoire and matching writing desk; they looked as if Marie Antoinette herself had used them. She paused before the windows, miniature versions of the hulking stained-glass window she'd just seen. She gazed outside. At least two stories up. It had started to snow, too. She could see the flakes within the globes of lights that stretched along a vista of manicured lawn and an English garden. Was this the front of the mansion? She tried the latch.

Locked or frozen from age and lack of use.

With a heavy sigh, she gave up and returned to the corridor. In minutes she reached the end and another set of stairs, much grander, wider and spiraling downward. She peered over the carved railing. The staircase swept into a huge entrance hall, the likes which could make Donald Trump jealous.

Cautiously, she made her way down, her footsteps loud in the immense silence. The space was something to behold. She'd only seen one other to rival it, and that was in the Biltmore Estate. She had visited the North Carolina tourist attraction one summer with her grandmother and sisters. The Vanderbilts had nothing on the Van Cleaves.

The floor was solid white marble. In the center three steps led down to a monumental fountain. It gurgled and spewed water from the mouths of four full-size lions. A small rain forest of potted ferns and palm trees and flowers was nestled strategically around the base. Embedded lights shined up through the fronds and cast eerie shadows around the fountain. Over it all stood a black wrought-iron gazebo.

She counted four huge cathedral-type doors, spaced equally apart on the points of a compass, each leading off from the grand entrance. They were all closed. Kane Van Cleave could be behind any one of them, in beast mode, those predatory eyes waiting for her.

The hairs at the back of her neck prickled, every

nerve in her body screaming at her to choose correctly if she wanted to get out of here. She took a chance on the nearest door.

She tugged on the massive thing. The hinges creaked like dry, brittle bones. The sound drowned out the steady gurgle of the fountain and sounded like gun blasts. She cringed and slipped inside.

Humidity and warmth hit her right away and felt wonderful to her chapped skin. She was in a conservatory. There had to be a door for the gardener to get inside. Maybe she'd chosen the right way after all.

The scent of lush earth, moss and growing things filled the air. All she could see were green leaves and orchids of every variety. A waterfall babbled and trickled somewhere within the tropical forest of leaves, but she couldn't see it. It was too dark, and there were only dim solar lights along the pathway. The beauty had to be stunning in daylight—if you weren't being held prisoner in it, she thought dolefully.

She passed a sphinx statue covered in moss, then spied the glass door that led to the outside. Finally, salvation. Freedom. She could taste it and feel it. She headed down the narrow brick walk, carefully picking her way through the shadows.

A low, rumbling growl sounded behind her. It prickled the skin on the back of her neck.

Then something grabbed her from behind, and she screamed.

Chapter 5

Nina's back plowed into a muscle-bound brick wall. A massive arm clamped around her rib cage. The other hand gripped her neck in such way that if she moved her attacker could snap her neck. Long, powerful fingers pressed into her windpipe, while scalding breath singed the side of her neck and cheek. But the thing that made her dizzy and ripped through her mind like a machete was the sensation of Kane Van Cleave's inner beast.

"I can smell your fear." His deep voice was a husky growl in her ear; then he bent closer and sniffed her.

"Guess you like the scent. That why you take innocent victims?" she managed to ask, though a maelstrom of sensations bombarded her, sending her mind reeling in all directions. His face was a hair's breadth away from her, and she felt his thick beard stubble prickling her cheek. Each of his hot breaths sent warning goose bumps down her spine.

"My *victims,* as you call them, never live long enough for me to enjoy their panic."

Her breath quickened, partly from her growing terror and partly from his emotions darting into her thoughts, the onslaught too intense even for her seasoned mind. Loneliness, sorrow, self-condemnation, rage inundated her. She absorbed the depth of his physical pain, the wound in his shoulder and arm he tried to ignore when he moved. But worst of all was the aggressive and unpredictable stirrings of his predatory side, screaming at her from within his body, a force stronger and more visceral than his human emotions. She recalled the bloodshed and carnage she'd witnessed between his beast and the gleaner, and she knew Kane Van Cleave was capable of much more brutality than she could ever imagine. A shiver shook her even as the tidal wave of impressions banged against her mind, sucking her under. She felt disoriented, and her knees buckled.

He shook her a little and said, "Don't faint on me."

It wouldn't hurt to let him think she was a simpering Cindy that had passed out from fear. The weak damsel-in-distress routine could give her an edge. She let her head fall forward and go limp. He used the hand around her neck to grab her beneath the arms.

She summoned the last of her will and strength to twist and grab his arm with both hands.

"I demand you sleep," she ordered.

He continued to hold her.

Why didn't he drop? "Sleep!" she shrieked, summoning all her mental powers.

"I'm not in the least tired."

Why did he sound so smug? Why wasn't her magic working on him? Something wasn't right here.

"Any more tricks and demands?" He easily pinned her wrists at her sides. His burly arms were hot iron bands, one above her solar plexus, one across the top of her chest. If he exerted a little more pressure, he could break every one of her ribs.

She found it hard to breathe. She'd never felt so frantic, or trapped, or afraid of any creature in her life as she did of this shifter. She had devoted her whole life to her calling, communicating with any and all creatures, priding herself on being able to control shifters and their inner beings long enough to help them. But she'd never had her powers flunk out on her. And why now, when she was up against an alpha seniph and the discontented and angry beast inside of him? And if she lived through this, which she doubted at the moment, she hoped to never meet another one. She'd never felt so defenseless. Some situations in life could be humbling. She considered herself thoroughly humbled and at this seniph's mercy—if he had any. *Hear that, Koda! Okay, you were right. I shouldn't have gone in that café.* She hoped admitting he was right might go a long way in soothing his ego. Yes, spirit guides had egos, big ones.

"Your power in those little hands of yours, Miss Rainwater? It won't help you." Something in his voice sounded like he enjoyed her struggles, took pleasure in toying with her as a cat did with its victims before the kill. "What else can you do with those hands, hmm?"

"Evidently nothing at the moment," she said, still feeling her mind connection to him, ripping through her thoughts.

He grunted in agreement at that observation, and it seemed to pander to his male ego. "I'm glad you see it my way." He forced her arms behind her and bound them with a rope. "Maybe you'll stay tied this time."

She felt the rough hemp biting into her wrists and managed to gasp, "Okay, tie me up. I don't care. Just keep your hands off of me."

"Don't worry."

His disdainful tone cut her to the quick. Not that she was experiencing Stockholm Syndrome or attracted to this guy in any way, shape or form, but she'd always felt unattractive to men. And his rebuff just confirmed her innermost perceptions.

He quickly shoved her away.

She stumbled a step as immediate quiet settled in her mind. Her heart slowed. The normal rhythm of her own thoughts fell back in place. She locked stares with him.

He was a towering shadow above her, long hair flowing wildly about his shoulders, his breath heaving, fists gripped tightly at his sides. He looked ready to attack, as if the beast would emerge any second. He raised one long finger and shook it at her nose. "A warning. If you try to leave again, I won't be as accommodating next time."

"Why are you keeping me here? What have I done to you?" She stepped back from him.

His arm snaked out and grabbed her shoulder, bringing her up short. "Don't move, unless I tell you."

"Okay." She couldn't see his expression clearly in the darkness, but his resignation and detachment and iciness railroaded through her mind.

"Please, let go." She shrugged off his touch.

He dropped his hand and stepped back from her. "Do what I tell you, and you needn't worry about me getting close to you again."

"Fine."

"Turn around, and get moving." He pointed at the doors she had come through only moments ago.

She walked that way, feeling tropical leaves brushing her face and body. She scanned the conservatory for an escape route and felt him so close behind her the tips of his boots almost touched her heels. He'd definitely carry through with his threat, and this time he could lose the tenuous rein he had on his beast. She'd have to bide her time, if she had any to bide. "Where are you taking me?" she asked.

"To a more secluded spot. I'd hoped to keep you here for a while until I'd had time to decide what to do with you, but you've proven that's impossible."

"Please, I won't try to escape again."

"Right, and if you're selling bridges, I'll buy one."

"Okay, so I lied. Please let me go."

"No."

So much for reasoning with him. He'd kill her for sure. Fear edged a line down each one of her vertebrae.

But it didn't stop her from asking, "Why didn't you kill the gleaner when you had the chance?" Now that she thought about it, he had shown a surprising control over his beast in that moment that she had to admire. Still, she wished he had ended the gleaner problem.

"That's none of your business," he grumbled.

"I'm sure your pride wanted the gleaner destroyed. You guys risk exposure otherwise."

"Be quiet. You talk too much."

Nina clamped her mouth shut. She was certain Kane Van Cleave was harboring a gleaner. But why? This gleaner had to be stopped. If she got away, she'd find it and destroy it herself. But first she had to escape a more immediate threat: Kane Van Cleave.

Kane forced Nina to go out the servants' entrance and into the garage. He flicked on the garage light and herded her down an aisle past antique Porsches and Bentleys and Rolls-Royces.

He couldn't help but watch the sway of her coal-black hair that cascaded down her back. Blue highlights danced along the straight strands that almost touched her bottom, which was hidden by a bulky sweater and baggy corduroy pants. He decided he liked it down better than the tight bun she'd worn the first time he'd seen her. She was way too petite for his taste, her head hardly reaching his chest. Her hair was by far her most attractive feature.

"Jeez, these all your cars?" She gazed at the 1932 Rolls.

"My father's."

"Does your father know you kidnap women?"

"He's dead."

"Oh, sorry. What happened?"

"You're asking too many questions again."

"Is it a crime to be curious?"

"No, but it might get you in a hell of a lot of trouble."

His dark warning must have worked, because she clammed up.

When they reached his Jeep, Kane opened the door for her. "Get in, Nina."

"Wait a minute," she blurted, pausing to look up at him. "How do you know my name?"

"I know a lot about you."

"Like what?"

"That you ask too many questions."

"Hah, what else do you know about me?" Her brows narrowed, and her lips hardened with suspicion.

"I know you're a pet psychic."

"That's just my line of work—wait a minute. How do you know all this?" Her brow furrowed, her blue eyes sharpening.

"I searched your purse."

"Where is it?" She looked anxiously up at him.

He took pleasure in nodding and saying, "I burned it."

"That was a gift!"

"A gag, right?"

"It wasn't. A client gave it to me," she retorted. "And I happened to like it." Her full lips puckered in thought, then her jaw dropped a little. "Good grief! My business cards were in there—those things are expensive—and my wallet. Tell me you took that out?"

He shook his head and recalled watching the smiley face turn to ash. He hadn't felt that much pleasure in a long time.

"There goes my Social Security card and driver's license. Do you know how hard it is getting a driver's license now that they've cracked down with Homeland Security? You have to stand in line at DMV for hours. You burned them both? How could you?" She was so irritated now, words tumbled from her mouth like bullets from a loaded Glock.

He was getting a taste of Nina Rainwater's fighting spirit, and he was enjoying it. He sensed she was not the type easily riled, but once there the rhetorical questions alone could fill a man full of holes. He found himself wondering what it took to vex her in bed as he bodily picked her up and set her down in the seat.

"Wait! Stop! You can't do this!"

He slammed the door on her tirade and locked it. He had few pleasurable moments in his life, but this ranked right up at the top of the list. He walked around the Jeep and sat in the driver's seat. He saw her eyes widen and shoot blue stardust at him, and his mood plummeted about three flights.

She fought the ropes as if she wanted to strike him and said, "I bet you stood there, enjoying every minute of it. You did, I can tell. You're a sadist, a—" she searched for a derogatory moniker "—brute. That's what you are. Pure and simple. You're terrible—as if you didn't know that already. What made you burn them?" Her forehead wrinkled in realization; then she said, "Oh, I get it. You hoped to dispose of *them* like you're going to do with *me*. That it?"

"Pretty much," he said, starting the Jeep.

"You could have given them to charity. And what about my car?"

"I did you a favor and burned that, too." He'd hidden the Taurus in the woods to escape detection, but he hadn't done away with it completely yet. He didn't know why, since he could never release her now.

"You could have given it to someone in need."

He saw her force back the tears, but one escaped down her cheek. A sudden pang of guilt stabbed him, and he hated it. This pureness and innocence had to be an act, surely. It seemed genuine, and he was responding to it.

At his close scrutiny, she grew suddenly self-conscious. She flopped on her right shoulder, laid her head against the window and stared out the glass, making a show of ignoring him.

Good. At least they understood each other now, and she knew what to expect. He opened the garage door with the remote and the Jeep lurched out into the snow. He felt her silence alive and stabbing him. Or was that his wounds? He frowned, his mood quickly darkening.

The Jeep slid in the snow, and not for the first time. Kane struggled to keep it from slipping off the road. The pain in his shoulder and arm was throbbing now. He could feel the gauze bandages he'd dressed the wounds with soaked with blood that leaked through his shirt. He had wanted more time to take care of the injuries, but he had sensed Nina prowling through his house. Damn her, anyway.

He glanced over at her. She sat huddled on the right side of the seat, lying on one shoulder with her bound hands behind her, her back to him, pretending to sleep. Her thick coal-black hair covered her back. Was it as soft as it looked? He caught his hand as he reached to touch it. He forced his fingers back on the steering wheel and his attention back on driving. What was wrong with him?

He knew exactly what the problem was: her fey scent was sheer torment inside the closed spaces of the Jeep. The more he tried to get away from it, the more it overwhelmed his senses. It was a heady female mixture of salt, perspiration and a hint of soap all bound up within her unique, incredible pulsing aroma. He wanted to be wrapped in the smell, bathed in it, engulfed by it.

And there was no escaping her womanliness. It unmanned him more than any female he'd ever come in contact with. After the tragic death of his wife, Daphne, he'd made a point of avoiding the opposite sex, even prided himself on his state of celibacy. But that was before Nina Rainwater became his number-one nuisance.

What was it about her that made him feel so outside of himself, like he was struggling for control? And there wasn't anything physically special about Nina Rainwater. She wasn't like the human women whom he'd been attracted to in the past. She wore clothes too big for her, layers of them, wasn't tall and seemed all too fragile—except when she tried to use her mojo on him. Well, that had been a bust, or a ploy to throw him off. She might not be as helpless as she seemed. After all, she had untied herself somehow. No, he was certain the all-consuming attraction he felt around her had something to do with the spell she cast. How she did it, he hadn't yet figured out. But he would.

It irritated him that she had ignored him since they'd left the house and he'd had to put up with her silence hammering him. For some reason, he wanted her attention—no, *needed* it. It must be the magic that leaked from her. He glanced over at her again and noticed her shivering.

He remembered destroying her coat and said, "You always this cold natured? You have on two layers of winter underwear and your clothes." He was just the opposite, overheated. Cold didn't bother him, but she did.

"I'm always freezing—wait a minute. How'd you know how many layers of underwear I have on?" She sounded as incensed and prim as an old maid. She wouldn't turn to face him, either.

"Don't worry, I draw the line at raping unconscious women."

"But burning their personal items, tying them up and keeping them against their will is okay?" She huffed dubiously under her breath and continued to stare out the window and shiver.

"Believe me, I'd let you go in a heartbeat if I could."

"Then do it."

"I can't."

"Who are you protecting? That gleaner you let live?"

"Why did you come here?" His voice dropped to a growl. He felt the motor vibration as his fingers tightened around the wheel.

"I don't have to tell you anything." A razor stubbornness edged her voice.

"Who knows you're here?"

She hesitated, appeared uncertain, then reached a decision and said, "Okay, if you must know, my grandmother and sister. I'm sure they've sent out the troops to find me."

Could he believe her? Either way the clock was ticking. He needed to find Ethan and get rid of her. "Do they know about the gleaner?"

"They know, and you'll be sorry you took me and let him live."

He jammed on the brake pedal. The Jeep skidded on the ice, then slid to a stop. He gripped the steering wheel, waiting for his temper to settle down. As a child he'd learned to control his emotions. It was the first thing shifters were taught, if they wanted to live among humans. But this woman… Something about her incited his passions. All the wrong ones.

He looked over at her, cringing against the door, still determined not to look at him. He found himself contemplating what her body actually looked like under all those layers of fabric. Too puny and probably not worth the trouble of undressing her. He reached in the backseat and grabbed his spare coat, the one he kept for dirty jobs at the vineyard. There was also a pair of thermal gloves in the pocket.

He tossed them over to her and enjoyed watching her jump. "Put those on," he said.

"If you're ordering hostages around, you should at least use a civil tone. But I guess that's asking too much. I should have known," she said, her words prim with annoyance. She straightened in the seat, the coat slipping off onto the floorboard and pooling near her feet.

"Forgive me for not making your journey a pleasure, ma'am." His words dripped with the sarcasm of an overworked flight attendant.

She turned and gave him her full attention. "I didn't ask to come along, as you recall. And you may have forgotten this, but there's not much I *can* do with these on." She pulled at the ropes on her wrists and glowered at him.

Her face glowed with a blue spectral radiance from the dash lights. She had the brightest blue eyes he'd ever seen, the pure blue of a wind-tossed sea, and when they held him as they were doing now, he saw the center of a star blazing within them. Their frank clarity could strip a man down to his bare soul. The only thing that softened their stark veracity was her long lashes, as black as her hair and just as thick. Even when she was angry, they hooded her eyes in a sexy, modest way that seemed artlessly coy, as if she had no inkling of the impression they made. Nina Rainwater was an enigma. Either she was a great actress and knew of her bewitchery, or she had no idea her eyes could be used as feminine weapons. He had to admit, they were her best feature.

"I can't untie you." He leaned over and snatched up the fallen coat.

She gasped and stiffened and tried to scramble away.

She didn't get far before he held her legs down with his chest. She continued to squirm and he began to enjoy her struggles. He wasn't certain if she was afraid of him or repulsed by his touch. Either way, it caused a burning desire in him to toy with her, to dominate her. Where their bodies touched, a strange congealing sensation radiated through him, spreading warm honey over all his nerve endings.

"Hold still, I won't hurt you," he grumbled, his lips brushing her pant leg. He realized his face was between her knees, a truly dangerous place to be.

"I told you not to touch me," she said, panting like she was running a race, her body shaking uncontrollably.

He grabbed the coat and sat up. He noticed she seemed calmer when he wasn't near her. She stopped shivering and looked relieved. She scooted over until she squashed her hip against the door, getting as far away from him as possible. This dread of hers brought out his perverse side, and he wanted to rub his hands all over her. No, he wouldn't give in to that urge. Had to be her magic driving him crazy.

"Don't worry, it won't happen again," he said, voicing a direct order to himself. He felt the beast warring to take control. It wanted Nina Rainwater in the worst way.

It was all he could do to fight the desire to shimmer. It took all of his willpower as he leaned back in the seat, eyes closed, teeth clenched, his chest heaving.

She sensed something was wrong, then turned to look at him. "Are you okay?"

"Give me a minute." No, he wasn't okay with her in the seat beside him. She had no idea how much danger she was in at the moment.

"You're not okay?" She looked at his shoulder and arm. She reached out to touch his forearm, but pulled back as if she were reaching for a rattler.

"I am," he snapped. Why did she keep pulling away? Was she that afraid? Perhaps it was a good thing. She shouldn't get too comfortable around him for her own good.

"I don't believe you. You're bleeding," she said. "It's coming through your shirt."

He wished it was only loss of blood, but it was much worse, everything he'd struggled with for years, denying himself a normal life, trying to control that part of himself that he hated. What was it about her that incited him in every way, made him feel powerless against his desires, evidence of it pressing against his jeans. He'd never ached with an arousal like he ached now, nor had he been forced to struggle not to shift.

"I'm fine." He heard the beast's deep rumble coming through his own voice.

She frowned over at him. "You're not. Untie me. I can help you."

"Of course you will." He shot her a sideways

annoyed glance. He wasn't falling for her compassionate routine.

"Why can't you believe someone might care enough to not want you to bleed to death?"

"Why should you give a tinker's damn about me?" he asked out of wry amusement.

"Beats me, other than you could have let the gleaner kill me. I guess I owe you."

"I didn't do it for you."

"Why didn't you just let the gleaner finish me off, then?" Her tone sharpened and stiffened again, and he knew she was in a high pique. She shifted in the seat, leaning on her right shoulder again, giving her back to him. "It would have saved us both a lot of aggravation," she said, speaking to the window.

"You're right about that."

She huffed under her breath and lapsed into blessed silence.

He realized the coat had fallen down to her waist again. He wasn't about to touch it this time, now that he had a handle on his lust. Instead, he turned the heater up and shifted into first gear. He was already burning up, and he was certain it wasn't from the added heat.

Chapter 6

After an hour's treacherous drive, during which Nina had to yell at him at least six times so he wouldn't lose consciousness and slip off the mountain road, they finally reached a cabin. Considering his injuries and the dangerous driving conditions, it was a miracle they'd made it here alive.

Beyond the headlights and the blowing snow, she could barely make out the image of a small log home. The surrounding forest encompassed it, and the snow all but made it disappear in places. She made out a small porch, a stone fireplace and could tell it was one-story. The place had a sinister, deserted atmosphere, and Nina wished she knew where she was. The snow had ruined the visibility, and she hadn't been able to see beyond the headlights. If Kane Van Cleave died of blood loss, she'd die with him because she'd never find her way back in this blizzard.

She glanced over at him. He was barely conscious. He didn't have control over his shifting, and his head shimmered in and out of lion form. His hands, too. But his body remained human. He was leaning on the steering wheel, a blur of man, then beast, then man again. It was like watching a broken horror flick.

"If you value your life, you'll stay away from me when I change and do exactly as I say," the man spoke, his voice tortured. He continued to rest his head on the steering wheel.

She didn't regret one bit the fib she'd told about Fala and her grandmother coming to rescue her. At least he'd think twice about killing her right away—though at the moment he didn't look at all up to it. "Untie me so I can help you," she said. When he didn't respond, she added more firmly, "We'll both die if you don't."

He raised his head, his shoulder-length wavy hair transforming into a heavy mane right before her eyes. Then a feline untrusting face appeared. "You'll run away," his deep voice rumbled.

"If it's any consolation, I don't trust you, either. But I'm all you've got at the moment."

The human face appeared. "Come closer," he said, his voice low, almost seductive.

It made her breath catch in her throat. Shadows hid his expression, and an air of danger pulsed around him. She couldn't tell if he'd shift again. One misplaced word or quick movement could have disastrous consequences while he was in beast form.

Every nerve in her body humming, she inched closer. She squeezed her eyes shut, preparing herself for whatever he might dish out. She turned and raised her bound arms as high as she could. When she felt him tugging on the ropes, carefully so as not to touch her, she let out the breath she'd been holding.

As soon as she was free, she stretched through the sharp pains in each shoulder socket and her wrists. It felt wonderful to be able to move again. Then she saw him slump back into the headrest, struggling to keep his eyes open and focused on the interior light.

Now was the time to escape, but how far would she get before she got lost or, worse, froze to death? She had a hunch that if he hadn't discovered her identity and that her sister was the Guardian, he might have made a meal of her a long time ago. She was convinced that the perfect lie she'd told him about her family coming for her had been the only reason she was still breathing. If only that were true.

And, too, she couldn't leave until she discovered why Kane Van Cleave was protecting a gleaner. She could try mentally prying the information out of him, but his free will was a prevailing factor. If he didn't want to fully communicate with her, she couldn't access his memories. She'd only be able to feel his emotions, and that wouldn't be much help.

And there was that whole thing of leaving him to bleed to death in the middle of nowhere. No matter how rotten he'd been to her, she couldn't in good conscience leave him here alone.

A chill went through her, and she looked longingly

at the jacket crumpled around her feet. She didn't want to wear anything that belonged to Kane Van Cleave, including his old coat, but in this case comfort went before pride.

Reluctantly, she slid her arms into the sleeves. The wool was still warm from the heater, and it smelled like the outdoors, earthy, musky, braided with his spicy aftershave. She inhaled the scent and decided the combination wasn't half bad. The coat hung on her and fell down to her knees. She was forced to roll up the sleeves. She found the gloves and donned them, too. They were so large they felt like oven mitts on her hands. She wondered ruefully if he'd burned her Max gloves as well as her pocketbook and wallet. Nothing was safe around him—including her life.

Her face scrunched up in a glower as she got out of the Jeep. Snowflakes pelted her. Snow immediately drowned her ankle-length hiking boots. She shivered and slogged through the shin-high snow to the diver's side. She opened the door. The interior light glared on, and she grabbed the keys and pocketed them, then reached down and cupped a handful of snow.

He reclined in the seat, revolving between human and lion. She waited for the man to appear and stuck the snow on the back of his neck with an angry plop, making sure a thick layer of ice kept her palm from touching his skin. The part of her that resented being held against her will enjoyed this way too much.

It brought him around with a jerk. He raised his head and shook it, all man for a moment. His wavy golden hair was in ringlets around his face and shoulders, and

for a second she couldn't look away from his beautiful
jade-green eyes. His five o'clock shadow darkened his
square chin and the dimple there. He was gorgeous and
tempting, and she was certain he was no stranger to lust.
Most alpha shifter males attracted the opposite sex—
unfortunately, human and supernatural females were
not immune. Alpha males were formed by nature for
the express purposes of breeding. Just look at Brad Pitt
and George Clooney. Prime examples of alpha shifters.
Kane Van Cleave was right up there with them. Sperm
banks magnifique.

"Okay, look, I can't carry you," Nina said, annoyed.
"You're going to have to help yourself."

"Help myself," he repeated, his words slurred and
barely audible.

"Yes, I can't help you." She raised her voice as if she
were speaking to an elderly invalid. Her kindness did
have its limits, and one of those was touching Kane Van
Cleave. She stood back a safe distance.

"I'll do it." He pulled his long legs out of the Jeep,
knocking his knees against the steering wheel. When
he stood, he fell forward but caught himself by hanging
on to the door.

Nina saw him teetering, struggling to stand, and knew
if she didn't intervene he'd stay out here and not only
bleed to death but freeze. With distressing clarity, she
recalled the last time he'd touched her in the Jeep. She'd
been overcome by the beast struggling to emerge, its
anger and insatiable desires more than frightening. She'd
also been hit by Kane Van Cleave's own desire. It wasn't
a warm and fuzzy feeling, but a brutal yearning, much

like the beast's. She knew that animals and supernatural beings were drawn to her because they felt the mental connection she had to them, but it was a warm and fuzzy kind of attraction, bordering on mutual respect, trust and goodwill. It wasn't suppose to be sexual at all, nothing like what she'd just felt.

She'd also stewed over it for an hour—in between wondering if her life might end at any moment when the Jeep ran off the road. She didn't know how to categorize his attentions. Stick them in the flattered column or the out-of-his-mind-from-blood-loss category. She tended toward the latter. Handsome guys always zipped past their initial attraction to her and went straight for her bodacious beautiful sisters. Long ago Nina had decided she didn't need a man to be happy. She had her destiny of helping others, Koda and her Quiet Place. All of that had filled her life completely. The awareness hit her that her chosen lifestyle must have been part of what Koda had meant, that she had used the Quiet Place to escape living. But she was happy, wasn't she?

Totally, she told herself—until she'd crossed paths with this gorgeous brute. Now she couldn't stop the nagging miffed feeling that he wasn't the least bit attracted to her. It was her gift that drew him, and his own alpha libido. Anyway, she didn't want his advances. He was the enemy, for goodness' sake!

"Here, lean on me." She heard the sharpness in her own voice. She prepared herself to feel the deluge of emotions, but his weakness made his thoughts snarly, and thankfully all she comprehended was his light-headedness and a few animal impulses stirring.

She kicked the door closed with her foot, then slid her arm around his waist. She hadn't realized the extent of his size until she had to reach across his lumberjack back. It was sculpted steel beneath his coat. His heavy arm plopped over her shoulders. The contact awakened strange sensations in the pit of her stomach and a churning fear of the unknown. He was so male, so virile, so in her face.

He stepped in front of her, and she saw his lips coming at her.

"No, no, no!" She panicked and dodged his mouth. She let go of him.

He rocked back on his heels.

She caught his elbow to steady him and said, "Breathe deeply. Your brain needs oxygen." She was fairly certain he would have kissed a fence post if it had been near him.

He seemed to sober and cocked a shocked brow at her as if his ego had just taken a major hit. His long arm shot out, and he stroked the back of his knuckles along her jaw. "Never been clearer."

"No, I'm certain you don't have a clue about what you're doing." Warmth stirred in the darker regions of her body.

He leaned close again, their lips almost touching. He cupped her chin, gently, his fingers feathering along her skin, sending tingles down her throat. "Don't bet on it. And if you run from me, Nina Rainwater, you won't get far." His leonine features emerged, and his voice growled the last few syllables.

Nina felt the reverberations of the deep baritone inside

her own body. The very air between them vibrated. Every muscle inside her tensed. She felt his claws pressing into her chin. Panic caused her heart to hammer against her ribs, even as his hot animal breath scorched her face. It felt wonderful against her freezing skin. His jungle-green eyes had a spellbinding quality that thrilled and frightened her. She didn't know which terrified her more, the man or the beast. She couldn't forget that attempt at a kiss. No, she wouldn't go there.

She frowned and struggled to keep a sensible, even tone as she said, "I've no intention of running away. But let's not forget who needs the help here." She pursed her lips and eyed his bleeding shoulder and arm. His shirt was covered in blood. "If you want my help, I'm setting some ground rules. Keep all body parts, including your lips and hands, to yourself. Got it?"

"Stop bewitching me."

"I'm not."

"Witch."

"I'm not a witch, and I resent your name-calling."

"Resent all you like." His face turned human again, and his rough fingertips slowly traced a line down either side of her throat until his index finger rested at the base of her jugular vein.

She'd heard many stories that the jugular wasn't only an erogenous zone for seniphs but was the attack point for killing—just like with vampires. He stroked the delicate skin, intrigued by her pulse there. His nostrils flared as he sniffed her. "You're afraid. Good. Should be." A wolfish gleam burned in his eyes, even as snowflakes collected on his eyelashes.

If she didn't get things under control, he'd change again and either have her for dinner or his curiosity could escalate into something much worse, something that she refused to explore with a kidnapper.

She gathered all her bravado and knocked his hand from her neck. "I'm not afraid, and you're going to be a gentleman from now on," she said.

"Not very likely."

Okay, he asked for it. She forced her will into him.

Resistance met her, and her magic bounced back at her. Her powers were still off. He grimaced as if he had felt her prying into his thoughts; then he swayed and narrowed his eyes suspiciously at her.

She scowled at him and said, "Either you keep your end of the bargain, or I leave you right here. I'll just go inside and get warm and comfy. What's it gonna be?"

A sardonic grin twisted up a corner of his mouth. "Admit you're a witch, a hex weaver."

Nina sighed and knew his stubbornness was going to be a problem. Since she was freezing and didn't want to stand out in the snow any longer, she said, "Okay, I'm a witch full of tricks. Anything else you want me to be?"

"Afraid."

"Okay, I'm a witchy fraidy-cat." She didn't give him time to answer and said, "Good. Now that we've established my finer points, let me help you."

"You can't. It's too late." He looked devilishly handsome and sexy and hardly able to focus on her face without his heavy lids closing.

"I like a challenge. Let me try."

He waffled for a moment on trusting her, then reached over and leaned on her shoulder.

Nina slid her arm around his waist and guided him toward the cabin. He weighed much more than she, and it was difficult keeping him in a straight line.

"Nina Rainwater… A witch who refuses to be kissed."

It was the first time she'd heard her name on his lips when he wasn't angry, and she liked the deep resonance of it bounding from inside his chest. What she didn't like was the bullying tone he'd used after it and the fact he'd spoken as if he were giving a press conference about her.

"Don't make generalizations about my character. You don't know me at all. And I've kissed thousands of men." Thousand was stretching it. Three, max. She could count her dates on one hand. Pretty pitiful love life. It was disconcerting that he could read her so well, even when he was light-headed. But she was not a witch. He was way out of the ballpark with that one. "Now if you'd hurry it up, we won't turn to ice cubes out here."

"I'm hot."

"Yeah, that's an understatement," she said ruefully.

He nodded in agreement, sending his long golden hair down into his face; then his brow furrowed as he concentrated on walking.

She felt the steady loss of blood mellowing him considerably. In fact, she detected his strength slipping away. No matter how maddening he was, she didn't want him to die. "Okay, a little more and we'll reach the steps," she said, hurrying him along.

"Steps," he parroted.

"Yes, you have to climb them."

He acted like he hadn't heard her and walked like a drunken man, zigzagging through the snow toward the porch. She felt his hand shifting where he touched her shoulder, his claws pressing into her skin, then his finger tips as he shifted.

"Where are we?" she asked.

"Our place."

What had he meant by our? Had he referred to a current lover? Was this a cabin he kept for other more sordid activities like forcing hostages here to party with their jugular then dispose of them? She quelled a panicky feeling and turned her mind back to helping him stay upright. "How much land do you own?"

"Two thousand acres."

"A small country. How far from civilization are we?"

"Boonies."

She thought of the journey back to Monterey she'd have when she left. The roads were almost impassible even with the Jeep. Soon there'd be no leaving unless on foot.

She pulled him up the two porch steps and paused before the door. "Is it locked?"

"Open."

"You're pretty confident no one will break in."

"No one would dare." Even weakened as he was, the warning in his voice caused chills of fear to ripple through her. "I defend what's mine."

Her memory swung back to the fight he'd had with

the gleaner, a stark visual aid depicting just what he meant by defending. Though he appeared vulnerable and at her mercy, her skin still grew clammy from the tension of being this close to him.

With a wary eye on him, she propped him against the cabin and tried the door. The hinges and lock looked ancient and rusted. With a big shove, she flung the door open. Darkness and a musty, unkempt smell met her. She took an instant dislike to the dark, closed-in place. A coldness lingered in it that didn't seem penetrable by any kind of warmth.

She felt around for a light switch by the door. When she found it, she flipped it and nothing happened.

"Wasting time. Electricity rarely works. Use generator."

"Great. Stuck out here in blizzard, in the middle of nowhere, with iffy electricity, no cell phone. Could things get any better?" She shook her head. "Of course not. Come on, then."

"Nag, nag, nag," he mumbled.

"And I guess you're Mr. Perfect Kidnapper." She grabbed his arm, none too gently, and helped him cross the threshold. She slammed the door with her foot, then stared into the dark room. "We need candles."

"Mantel."

"Where's a chair?" She wanted to speed things along and stow him somewhere.

"I'll find it." He let go, and she heard his wet feet plodding unevenly on the floor.

"Which way to the mantel?"

"Left...no, right."

She made a face in the darkness, then heard him plop down on something. She went in search of the candles, arms outstretched, feeling totally at the mercy of the dark room.

Without a disaster, she crossed the floor and found the wall. The hewed and sanded logs were smooth to the touch as she felt her way down them.

"A little farther."

She'd forgotten that he could see in the dark with his heightened senses. "I should've made you find the candles," she said.

A loud snort came from the other side of the room. It was the beast's voice, low and grumbly and cranky. "No one makes me do anything."

"I bet," she said.

"Believe it." His voice sounded weaker, human again.

"Oh, I do," she said, patronizing him. Her finger connected with the mantel. She felt across the top and found the candles and a lighter. "Aha, found them." She grinned, delighted with the discovery. Quickly enough she had the candles lit. There were five large ones, each in its own canning jar.

She surveyed the cabin. It was one large room, divided into a kitchen and a sitting area. The waist-high hearth stood before her. It was made of smooth river stones, the prettiest part of the cabin. The living-room area was furnished with two huge leather sofas and a rugged pine coffee table. The braided rug that covered the whole room added a little homey warmth. It didn't seem as bad as her first impression.

The galley kitchen was small but appeared well-stocked. Pans hung from a rack over a stove. Open shelves held a set of dishes. Someone had added a feminine touch by lining the shelves with little muslin skirts. A door stood off from the kitchen. She raised the candle higher and peered through the doorway at the iron railings of a bed. The only bedroom?

Van Cleave had flopped down lengthwise on one of the sofas. He looked pale, and he'd stopped shifting. Blood darkened the whole front of his shirt. She noticed her borrowed coat had his blood on it, too. His eyes were closed, and he looked still as death.

Nina ran to his side and checked the pulse in his neck.

He was still alive, but his clammy skin felt ice-cold.

She hurried back to the fireplace and used the logs and kindling there to start a fire. Then she grabbed a quilt off the bed in the bedroom and threw it over him.

She had to stop the bleeding. She found a bathroom off the bedroom and in it an extensive first-aid kit. She pulled out butterfly strips and gauze and bandages.

She noticed a modern sink and faucet in the kitchen and an old hand pump, which meant the cabin probably had running water when the electricity was on and the electric pump was working. Yeah, but that didn't help right now. She went to the hand pump and primed it. It groaned in protest; then icy water flowed into the sink. Nina knew how to operate a hand pump. Her grandmother kept a manual pump in the backyard for when they lost power—and it seemed to go out a lot on the reservation. The value of running water was one of the first things you learned growing up in the country.

She filled an iron pot with water and warmed it by the fireplace. She found a towel and set up the first-aid kit near him and the pan of warm water.

She threw more logs on the fire. The room began to heat up as she undressed him, not an easy feat with someone so much larger than she. The jeans were impossible to get off, and touching the zipper just didn't feel right. She left them alone, but it was impossible to miss the worn places in all the right places, accentuating his lean hips, muscular thighs and the masculine bulge between his legs. No, the pants were definitely staying on.

She forced her attention back on undressing him. She rolled him from side to side and pulled off his flannel shirt. That's when she spotted the raised scars that crossed his back. Whip marks of some kind. No one should be beaten that badly. An unbidden surge of sympathy for him overwhelmed her.

She blinked it away and forced her gaze back to his bare chest. She took in his torso, all sculpted abs and muscles. Candlelight did strange things to his skin, and it glimmered gold with an exotic iridescence that only shifters possessed. He was beautiful, even with the blood smeared over the golden hair on his chest.

She tried not to look at the line of hair that went down his belly and below his jeans while she extracted the blood-soaked bandages. She cleaned the wounds on his chest, shoulder and arm, then moved down his belly to the caked blood that had pooled around the waist of his jeans.

She stopped there and assessed the wounds on his chest. Two were very deep and jagged on his upper shoulder. Three were on his forearms and biceps. An open gash slashed very near the base of his neck, but it wasn't as bad as his shoulder injuries.

She tried to use the butterfly strips, but he was bleeding too profusely and they wouldn't stick. If she didn't do something soon, he'd die for sure.

She glanced around, then walked over to the fireplace and pulled out the poker. She'd never attempted this before, but she'd seen it done in the old Westerns her grandmother liked to watch. She prayed it worked. She thrust it into the fire and didn't take it out until the tip was burning red hot.

She gulped, summoned her courage and thrust the poker down into the deepest gashes, cauterizing them. He bucked and thrashed but didn't wake up. Thank goodness, because she could smell the scent of burning flesh, and it sickened her. It was the same scent the gleaner had left behind when he'd killed Emma Baldoon. Bile rose in her throat, and she ran to the bathroom to vomit. After she rinsed her mouth and splashed icy water on her face, she returned to his side.

Once cauterized, the wounds stopped bleeding. She smeared antibiotic ointment on them and bandaged them tightly, winding the gauze around his whole shoulder. She couldn't help it, but her fingers itched to touch his powerfully built body. It seemed safe enough. Her fingers trembled as she explored his muscular contours.

He really was an exquisite male specimen. Her heart began to pound as she felt her body becoming excited. She'd never explored a man's body at her leisure. She'd just never gotten that close to want to stroke a man intimately. She'd petted two-skins in animal form, but that was different. She was helping them. Touch was a powerful tool for healing. But touching Kane's bare skin didn't feel useful, it felt naughty and forbidden, something she could easily grow to enjoy. She pulled her hands back, afraid of her own response. He was her abductor, she reminded herself.

She meant to draw her hands down to her side, but her fingers paused over the swollen wounds. It was a shame, but now his chest would be as scarred as his back. Seeing such perfect male beauty damaged in such a way saddened her, and she wondered again who had put the wounds on his back.

He was shivering now, uncontrollably, his teeth chattering. It brought Nina back to her senses and she scolded herself for enjoying the wicked little pleasure of exploring his body. She went in search of blankets and found them in the bedroom cedar chest, along with a down comforter—a nice surprise.

On her way into the living room, she paused before the dresser. She held the candle close to three pictures sitting there. One was of a beautiful woman, standing outside. She had bright blond hair, laughing, upturned, catlike brown eyes and full, smiling lips. Her face exuded confidence, and Nina was willing to bet she was an alpha female seniph. She was stunningly gorgeous. No doubt one of Van Cleave's conquests. An unwelcome pang of jealousy nagged at her. Silly, she chided herself, but it wouldn't go away.

The other picture was of a couple. Gray streaked the man's golden hair. He wore the stern, harsh expression of an unforgiving taskmaster. The woman was smaller, auburn-haired, and her face held a frail smile. Her eyes looked trapped and needy and full of sadness. If the picture was any evidence, they weren't a happy couple. Were these Kane's parents? The man's handsome features resembled Kane's in many respects.

The last photo was of Kane, his arm around a younger man. They each held up two huge bass they had caught, grinning like proud fishermen. The younger man was almost as tall as Kane, but smaller in stature. He had the same deep green eyes, but there was something unsure and unknown behind them, and his smile was there for the camera. His tawny golden hair was cut short. He was definitely one of Kane's family members. The resemblance to Kane and the older man in the photo was unmistakable.

Her gaze strayed back to the pretty woman, and she frowned as she left the room. She spread the blankets over him and waited. He stopped shivering and looked peaceful and quiet.

Suddenly she felt very alone and weary, events of the past day and a half and all the stress that had accompanied them folding in on her like a landslide. She craved her quiet place, but knew that if she summoned Koda, he wouldn't take her there. He'd already made that plain. Abruptly she felt depressed and exhausted and trapped with a man who saw her only as a hostage.

She forced back her present depressing situation and felt hunger gnawing at her gut. When had she last eaten? She couldn't remember and dragged herself to the kitchen. After rummaging through the cabinets, she found a bag of pretzels and a stash of sodas. Then she strode to the living room. She sat on the floor and leaned against the sofa next to Kane. Not a very substantial meal, but the pretzels filled her empty belly and the sugar in the soda tasted like manna from heaven.

When she was full, she blew out the candles and pulled some of the down comforter over her. It took only a few moments of listening to the fire popping and Kane's deep, even breathing before her eyes grew heavy and closed.

She missed the face that peered in through the window and the two flaming eyes that stared at her.

Chapter 7

Kane woke, aware of the agonizing burning below his skin. Then he remembered driving here, but not much else. Had Nina Rainwater escaped? He thrust open his eyes, only to find her asleep on the floor near him, curled up at the base of the sofa, cocooned in a comforter. The pulse beating in her throat was the only sign that she was alive. A half-eaten bag of pretzels and an empty soda can turned over on its side lay beside her.

He peeled back the comforter and let his gaze roam over her. She was lying on her side in a fetal position. Her mouth was slightly open. He traced the line of her sultry and pouty lips, perfectly sculpted, her deep, even breaths gliding through them. Long, sooty lashes formed dark half moons on her cheeks. Her thick hair was voluptuously mussed around her face and shoulders. She looked small and childlike, but womanly and desirable, too. Something about her made him want to stare at her like this forever.

But he forced his gaze back to his own body. He remembered blood, lots of it. He lifted the ton of blankets on him and peered at the wounds. She'd changed his bandages and managed to stop the bleeding. She must have helped him walk inside, too. Most captives would have left him to die or gotten their revenge. Nina Rainwater had a kind heart. The notion disturbed him, made him feel beholden to her and responsible for her. He found himself reaching down to rub a strand of her hair between his fingers. It felt like tantalizing silk caught in his fingertips. Everything about her felt surreal, enchanted, bewitching.

He stared at her luscious full lips. Vaguely he recalled trying to kiss her and the way she had pulled back from him. Always keeping her distance. He had a fuzzy impression of the term "witch" coming up several times. He remembered being angry that he couldn't control his shifting and wanting to dominate her and feel her not pull away. That he remembered very clearly.

He tamped down the notion. He had to keep his distance. She was like this insatiable thing eating away at him, chipping away at his resolve.

Her eyes fluttered open, the blue in them reaching down deep inside him. She smiled, and two deep dimples formed in her cheeks. He'd never seen a more stunning face in his life. It almost hurt to look into those eyes, and he found himself staring at her lips. They were red and plump and glistening.

She must have felt the awkward moment between

them, too, because she sat up and said, "How are you?" She yawned and stretched, and he saw that she had small but nicely formed breasts under that bulky sweater and endless pairs of underwear.

"Better," he said. "Why did you do it?"

"I was hungry." She looked over at the pretzels.

"Not that. Why did you stay with me?"

"Because I couldn't leave you." She sounded matter-of-fact as if it were the most natural thing in the world for her to do. She began finger-combing her long hair.

"You should have," he said, intently watching her fingers sliding through the glossy mane. He wished it were his hand.

"Do you realize what you're saying? You could have bled to death."

"If our situations were reversed, I would have left you and escaped." He knew he sounded harsh and callous, more to convince himself that he didn't feel anything for her.

"Well, you're lucky then that I'm not you." She threw her hair over her shoulder, and it hit her back with a plop.

"Can't argue that point."

"Have we found some common ground?" she asked, her eyes searching his.

She seemed to peer straight into his innermost self, the dark place that had destroyed all he cared about. Someday he knew it would destroy him, too. "Doubt it," he said flatly.

She arched a brow. "I don't know. You might have been heartless yesterday, but today, after you've felt a random act of kindness from someone—" she pointed to her own chest, and he got another eyeful of her breasts "—could you honestly say you wouldn't have helped me?"

"I'm not letting you go, if that's what you're fishing for." He shot her his most dangerous look, the expression that warned others to be on guard.

"I'm being serious here. I'm not trying to manipulate you. Would you have helped me?"

He looked into her searching blue eyes and told her what she wanted to hear. "Maybe, if I could have gotten away."

"I'm glad you're not a total lost cause."

"I wouldn't bet on it. The world is full of darkness, and you can't change that."

She met his eyes squarely, unblinking. "Only if you seek it out."

"No need to go looking. It finds you."

"If you invite it in. You see, I have this theory." She raised her brows and had that forthright untainted expression that he was beginning to recognize and appreciate. "That if you do one good deed, then you receive that measure of kindness back tenfold. And it registers in our consciousness and changes us and allows more goodness to enter our lives. Same thing with evil. It comes in if we allow it."

It physically hurt to not reach down and grab her and show her his own form of happiness. It took all of his concentration as he said, "Then you don't believe in absolute evil."

"Of course I do." She cut her eyes at him. "Demons

are evil and unredeemable, but creatures such as yourself, who have two skins, and those like me—" she motioned to herself "—who are all human, we have a conscience and therefore free will and the capacity and receptiveness required for goodness to drop seeds. And we can control our destiny and not let negative energy in our lives."

Kane studied her a moment. She seemed so trusting and naïve and genuinely serious. He didn't think this was a Little Miss Sunshine act. He was seeing the real Nina Rainwater. He wished he wasn't so jaded by life and said, "You're young and easily taken in. What until you've lived awhile."

"You speak like you're ancient. You couldn't be that much older than me." She cocked her head to the side, and her hair fell over her shoulder. It was a flirtatious gesture, used by females over the ages, but he was certain she had no idea that she was doing it as she asked, "How old are you?"

"Twenty-eight. Old enough to know that if you believe what you just said, you're the most gullible human I've ever met."

"Or the most evolved." After a hard look, she grew quiet and looked offended. Her cheeks reddened from shyness or anger, he couldn't tell which.

Kane immediately regretted his words and said, "It's got to be frustrating keeping such a positive outlook."

"Really, it's not. But I guess for someone like you, who carries around so much gloom and doom, it might be."

"I don't look at the world with blinders on."

"I don't, either."

"I bet you've never experienced real emotional pain." He couldn't draw his gaze from the pout of her lips and those fathomless blue eyes crowned by the heavy black lashes that tied him up in knots. He hadn't felt like this since he was fifteen and had lost his virginity.

"Oh, my gosh! I'm a receiving tower for emotions." She threw her hands up in dismay.

"Really?"

"I communicate with all creatures, alive or—" She caught herself and looked suddenly annoyed at what she had just revealed.

"Dead?" he finished for her. She was a magnetic telepath, an ethereal diviner. So that's why he'd felt so compelled to be near her. He'd never met anyone like her. To keep her talking about herself, he asked, "How do you deal with it?"

"I've learned how to cope by finding the bright side. And don't think I haven't had disappointments in my life."

"Name one."

"I've never met my mother. There. How's that for disappointment?"

"You're not vested in the relationship, so you're really not feeling loss there."

"Okay, *quid pro quo*," she said, her blue eyes flashing.

"Who do you care about?"

"My brother. Back at you. How do you feel when you have to watch those creatures you try to help die?"

"I don't like it, and I question why I've been given

my powers, like I'm being tested or failing miserably."
She seemed to come to a realization, and bottomless
sorrow marred her face. "Honestly, I hate it sometimes."
Emotion stirred the blue glass in her eyes.

So Little Miss Sunshine wasn't all sunshine. Having
helped her realize that made him feel like a heel at the
moment. He wanted to give her back her little bubble
of optimism, no matter how fabricated it was, and take
away the sadness he'd caused. But there was nothing
wrong with her facing reality and learning that it bit
you on the ass every time you dropped your guard. He
didn't know how to console her, so he said nothing.

She cleared her throat, blinked back the tears and
said, "I've never admitted that to anyone. Not even my
sisters. Maybe not even to myself."

"I'm glad you told me. I thought anyone so optimistic
about life couldn't have lived it, but I was wrong." It
took a lot for him to admit that, but he felt she needed
to hear it and he needed to say it.

"It's okay." She smiled, but only a little. "I thought
the same about you." She pointed to him. "Anyone as
rich as you couldn't have any reason to be cynical or
gloomy or lonely, but I've felt it in you. So deep it hurts
me. So I guess we were both wrong about each other.
Because until you walk in someone else's shoes, you
really don't know what they've gone through."

So that's why she shied away from him; she channeled
his beastly emotions. He'd never felt so exposed. She was
able to look into the darkest corners of his soul. Was he
really so bitter about life or so miserable? It had been
such a gradual progression and acceptance that he'd

never really taken stock of his existence. And he didn't like her doing it for him, so he changed the subject. "It must be a burden, your power."

"You have no idea, but I have a place I can go—" She paused, seeming to grow uncomfortable at what she was about to say. She pointed to him. "Enough about me. Tell me about your pride. I never knew a group of seniphs lived here."

"We took great care that no one knew. We're a close-knit group and keep to ourselves. We had to be, living near humans."

"So you've been settled here a long time?"

"Hundreds of years."

"Tell me about your family."

"Not much to tell. My parents owned the winery. They're dead now."

"You mentioned a brother."

The conversation was shifting in the wrong direction, so he said, "We're done with Twenty Questions."

"Why?" She tilted her head and looked over at him in that sexy but innocent way of hers.

"It's better we don't know so much about each other." He refused to look into her eyes, and his gaze landed on the beating pulse at the base of her neck. He groaned inwardly.

"If that's the way you want it." Her back went broomstick straight. Her guard went up, and the warm, fascinating light died in her eyes. "I'd almost forgotten you'd tied me up and made me come here." She shot him an accusatory glance.

He realized he enjoyed sparring with her as much

as he enjoyed watching the blood pulse in her neck. He said, "Believe me, I didn't have a choice."

"We always have more than one option." She took his measure and grimaced at what she saw.

"Not in your case," he said. It was a harsh reality to admit, but he had to make it plain to her who had the upper hand.

"We'll see about that." The steadfast gleam in her eyes hardened, and the threat in the watery depths matched his own for intensity.

He fought an urge to grab her and show her who was dominant, but she stood out of his reach and rubbed her arms. "You mentioned a generator. Where is it?"

"I'll help you with it." He tried to sit. Pain stabbed his shoulder and arm, and he froze, panting hard.

"Stay." She held up a hand as if she were giving a command to a dog. "I don't want you bleeding again. Though..." She tapped the side of her cheek. "Come to think on it, I wouldn't mind another round with the poker."

"What?"

She grinned with a craftiness that surprised him. "Never mind. I'll find the generator on my own." There was a self-sufficient confidence about her that annoyed him.

"You can't start it."

"Don't tell me I can't do something. I may be small and—what did you call me? Oh, yeah—'gullible,' but I certainly don't need your help with a generator. My grandmother has one. I start it all the time when our power goes out on the reservation." She wheeled in a huff and gave him her back as she flounced out of the room and headed for the back door.

He heard her stop in the kitchen. She must have realized she'd gone off half-cocked as she shouted, "Where can I find the generator?"

He didn't know why, but he found himself grinning like a fool as he said, "The shed out back." He couldn't remember the last time he'd grinned like that.

"Fine."

The door slammed as she left.

For a second he wondered if she would return, and he found himself on edge, listening for her footsteps. If she was going to leave, she would have left last night. He relaxed back against the pillows and thought of her.

Nina Rainwater seemed all goodness and kindness and vulnerability, but she had a temper and a feisty determination, qualities he could even grow to admire. Still, he couldn't trust her not to harm Ethan.

And what about the magic that surrounded her? He now knew why she shied at physical contact. She could feel his darkest desires, and they disturbed her. He didn't like being laid open to anyone, especially her.

But that wasn't the only problem with her. Her powers of attraction worked on him constantly. Was she as pure and virginal as she seemed? He wanted to explore that possibility, but he couldn't. No—he *wouldn't*. He frowned until he heard the generator roar to life. Then a grin twisted his lips.

Nina left the shed, glad to be out in the fresh air. The shack had been small, freezing cold and smelled of gasoline fumes. And she had hardly had enough room to pull-start the generator.

She sighed with relief as she left behind the loud hum of the engine that still rang in her ears. The sleet had put a hard crust on the surface of the snow, and with every step she had to break ice.

Luckily, the snow and sleet were tapering off; so was the wind. The sky looked lighter, too. The gunmetal clouds had turned to whale gray. Tiny flakes, mixed with ice, fell on her face and head and thumped against the borrowed jacket. The smell of Kane still clung to it and surrounded her. She found herself taking large whiffs of the material. He really did smell great and made her drool when she looked at him, though she couldn't say there was anything inwardly likable about him.

She had to admit he could be charming and easy to talk to when he wanted to be. Hadn't he expertly steered her into talking about the pain involved with losing those she tried to help? But when she had inquired about his personal life, he clammed up.

She wished now she hadn't been so honest with him. But hadn't he made her realize why she sought out the Quiet Place so often? It was the loss that depressed her and made her feel in need of rejuvenating.

She might have helped him realize something about himself if he hadn't been so secretive about his life. She couldn't stop wondering what in his past had made him so unhappy, cynical and remote. Maybe it had to do with his parents or brother. She had noticed a sadness drift into Kane's expression when he had mentioned he cared about his brother. There must be a reason mentioning his brother had upset Kane and ended his few unguarded moments of candidness. He had said, "It's better we don't know too much about each other." Initially, that had hurt her because she'd told him something very personal about herself. It was only right he reciprocated.

But now that she wasn't near him and had time to think, she was glad he'd said it. She had let down her guard, but his words had made her aware of her present danger: that she was snowed in with a kidnapper, someone who was in league with a gleaner. No, now that she thought about it, it was better they stayed away from the personal stuff.

Her brow wrinkled in thought as she trudged through the white, crusty blanket. She felt her pants and long johns getting soaked. The cold went right through her shins and ankles and down into her hiking boots. When she bent over to knock away a piece of ice sticking to her corduroy pants, something caught her eye. She hadn't seen the large tracks on her way out to the shed. They were snow-covered, but the deep indentation of them was unmistakable. Their trail led from the woods to a cabin window, then back into the woods.

She stuck her hand down into the impression. The animal's foot was three inches wider. It wasn't a bear track. She knew from helping bears that they left a barefoot-human type of print. The image of the gleaner flashed in her mind, and a chill slid down her spine.

She straightened and looked off into the woods. The trail led toward the mountaintop. Every warning signal in her body went off as she sensed something lurking behind the trees, a waiting malevolence, taut and heavy. She sensed a pair of eyes watching her from the shadows. Was the gleaner out there, spying on her, waiting for the right moment to pounce? The hairs along her neck crawled, even as a feeling of doom settled over her.

If she wanted to survive, she had to be vigilant and one step ahead of him. Impossible with Kane around. She had to be rid of him so she could fight the gleaner.

And why was the gleaner stalking her and not making his move? Was he waiting to ambush her alone? She remembered how Kane had hesitated and the gleaner had savagely attacked, but he hadn't killed Kane. Maybe the gleaner just wanted her. A plan came to her, and she filed it away for later use.

Thankfully, she was only a few yards from the cabin, and she darted back inside. When she closed and locked the door, she let herself breathe again. She knew a locked door wouldn't stop a gleaner's killing powers, but it sure felt good to have four walls battened around her.

Her heart calmed while she stripped off the large coat and wet boots and peeked into the living room to check on Kane.

As if he felt her, he turned to look at her. His tawny hair fell down around his square jaw and shoulders. The stubble on his chin had thickened. He had pushed the blankets down to his waist, and she got an eyeful of brawny biceps and washboard abs above his jeans. She had wrapped the bandage over most of his pectorals, but she could see the swelled muscles there. She remembered every ridge and valley of his body beneath her fingertips when she had tended to his wounds. That strange heat he'd awakened in her began churning in her belly, and she blurted, "I'll find something for us to eat."

He gave her a noncommittal nod, looking aloof and brooding and wickedly handsome.

She ducked back into the kitchen and took cover there. She must stop getting all woozy around someone who had pushed her away and saw her as nothing but a captive. Stupid, stupid. She scolded herself as she heard the refrigerator turn on and an electric water heater popped in a closet. Modern conveniences, finally. She decided she'd wait for the water to heat up while she shed her wet socks and rolled up the hem of her damp pants.

Next she explored the refrigerator. Hardly anything there; only a few bars of cheese and two bottles of wine. Bags of French fries and frozen steaks filled up the freezer. Even though the electricity had been off, the two-inch layer of frost encompassing the freezer had kept the bags frozen solid. She guessed Kane hunted his own food in the nearby woods when he came here. In seniph form he would be the ultimate predator. The vegetarian in her frowned at the thought.

She gave up on the refrigerator and dug deeply into the cabinets. Her plunder consisted of coffee, granola, a box of Pop-Tarts, some instant powdered milk and beef jerky, along with cans of tuna fish, caviar, hash, beans, Vienna sausages and beef stew. On the side of a cabinet, she discovered a whole wine rack filled with Van Cleave wines. They had a pretty wheat-colored label with black lettering. She read the labels: Merlot, Rosé,

Zinfandel, Chardonnay, Blackberry, Blueberry and Pear. If she were a wine connoisseur, the offerings might have impressed her. The strongest thing she drank was herbal tea. Sad, her life was so boring.

She wished she had found a stash of chocolate milk or hot chocolate. Now, that would have excited her. Nothing really appetizing was here, but she could make something out of it.

She put the coffee on and searched for glasses and plates. That's when she felt a presence. She whipped around to find Kane standing right behind her.

She jumped and said, "Good golly, you scared the life out of me." She noticed he wasn't standing straight. His shoulders were hunched a little, his expression a tableau of repressed pain as he tried to look all macho and threatening. He hadn't put on his shirt, either. The fact she couldn't drag her eyes away from his tanned body scared her much more than the actual act of him sneaking up on her.

"Did I?" His mercurial green eyes sharpened on her as he leaned against the door jamb.

"You shouldn't be up."

"I wondered what you were doing in here." He watched her like a bored cat watched a mouse.

"I told you."

All pretense of polite interest slipped from his face, and his eyes narrowed with an aggressive, deadly glint. "Something happened to you outside. What?"

"Nothing happened."

"It did. I smell the fear on you. I smelled it when you walked into the cabin."

Boy, there was no concealing anything from that feline sniffer of his. It could be a problem. "I—I—" she floundered for a lie "—saw a bobcat."

He stepped over to her, blocking her way. "And it frightened you?"

"Yes." Nina noticed he had trapped her against the sink. Her head barely reached his chest, and all she could see was his burly upper torso, the golden hair there peeking out the top of the bandage.

"You said you can communicate with all creatures. Can't you just send the bobcat away?" He stepped closer, inches from her. Heat radiated from his body felt like a luscious wood stove that had just been stoked.

She found herself wanting to crawl into that heat and let it warm her all over. "If they are alive, I have to touch them to control them. It could get tricky with a bobcat." She heard the tremor in her own voice, even as adrenaline soared through her veins. It made her light-headed, and her breaths were hardly more than pants. The pull of his magnetism ran unhindered inside her.

"So, you can touch animals and control them?" His mouth lifted in a sneer of a grin.

"That's right." She nodded.

"But not me."

"No, not you for some reason." She flexed her fingers, wishing she could bend him to her will.

"Can you also kill an animal with your power?" His eyes took on a sadistic gleam as they sharpened on her face.

This was a touchy subject that she didn't want to explore with him, so she said, "Why do you ask?"

"I need to know where we stand."

"You needn't worry that I'll harm you."

"Unless, of course, I stand in your way of something. Now answer my question, does your power kill?"

"Okay, okay." She threw up her hands. "Yes, I have stopped animals' hearts before, but only if they are near death and in pain. If it's in my power to help, I can't let them suffer. I can feel their anguish," she said, feeling a dam of emotions break in her. Angry tears filled her eyes. "I just can't drive by an animal hit by a car and left on the side of the road to suffer. So, yes, I end their torment. Is that what you wanted to hear? I don't go around killing for the pleasure of it." She felt tears streaming down her cheeks and couldn't believe she'd grown so angry. She never yelled at anyone. But he had made her feel as if she had to justify her power to him. She'd never admit she remained depressed for days and stayed longer in the Quiet Place after a road stop.

"Thank you for being honest," he said, his voice almost contrite. He raised a hand to touch her arm.

She leaped back and watched an indifferent veil fall over his expression. "Don't touch me." She swiped at the tears with her sleeve and said, "I have to be honest, but you're not. Seems one-sided to me."

"What do you want to know?" he asked, his harsh mask in place.

"Why are you protecting the gleaner?" Nina pressed him with unflinching eye contact. She wasn't about to let him skirt the issue as he'd done last time.

His brows narrowed and he ran his hands through

his golden hair, shoving it back from his face. Finally he said, "He's my brother."

She digested the information and asked, "That's why you couldn't kill him?"

Kane's fists clenched in irritation. "Yes."

"It's nice you care for your brother, but surely you know he can't go on killing innocents. A gleaner is the worst creature imaginable. Evil personified."

"I know that, but we're family. We share the same blood," Kane said, his voice escalating. "I'll send him to a place where he can't hurt anyone."

"He kills humans to survive. He's a parasite."

"Not to me. And there are sick humans who wish to die. They come to him for help."

"Emma Baldoon didn't wish to die." Nina's voice became as impassioned as his own.

"You should have stayed out of it. I would have handled it."

"You had your chance, but you didn't."

"And I suppose *you* can. You don't have a chance against a gleaner...or me." He bent his head so their lips almost touched. His eyes narrowed and glistened with danger.

Nina held her breath. Her own pulse roared in her ears as she felt his hot exhalations on her face. His whole body was one large flame, burning her. Would he try to kiss her again? She didn't know how she'd feel about it if he did. Part of her wondered what it would be like.

She managed to say, "Don't bet on it."

He eyed her critically for a full minute, then said, "Perhaps I've underestimated you. You're as deadly as me, Nina Rainwater." Bitter triumph rasped in his deep voice; then his eyes turned cold and cryptic, and he stepped back from her. He crossed his arms over his burly chest as if putting up a barrier against her.

She felt instantly deflated. Too late, she realized he'd been baiting her to find out more about her powers, and he was enjoying it way too much. He hadn't wanted to kiss her at all. That was okay; she felt the same way, she told herself.

"That's right, and don't forget it." She shook a finger at him. "And stay out of my way when I find him."

"You will not harm my brother." His gaze narrowed ominously.

"I'm sorry, but it's inevitable. And if you had stopped him when you should have—"

"If you hadn't interfered, I could have reasoned with him." His words trailed off into silence, his eyes boring into her face.

"Looks like we're both at fault," Nina admitted.

Seconds of silence ticked by.

Her words seemed to calm his temper. After a moment, he said, "How did you know about the Baldoon killings, anyway?"

"Does it matter?"

"Yes."

"The animals' dead spirits led me there."

He watched her with that mercurial gaze of his. "What were you doing when I saw you near their bodies? You looked absorbed, as if you were doing something."

"I was helping them find their path. They were distraught and lost by the violent way the gleaner destroyed them." She bit her lower lip, and her frown deepened in an unpleasant memory.

"How did you track Ethan when he was cloaked? I need to know."

"He couldn't block out all the traces of his emotions from me in gleaner form. When he's human, that's a different story."

"So you can help me find him."

"I can locate him if he's frightened or has killed animals."

"He'll have to consume another soul again in a week. We'll wait out the storm. Then we'll see if you can pick up anything." His expression lightened, as if he had just discovered a solution to an impossible calculus problem.

She had no idea why, but she couldn't destroy the one glimmer of hope she'd seen in his face, so she said, "I'll help you find your brother. Now, please go rest while I fix something to eat."

He eyed her long and hard, then finally turned and left.

Nina welcomed the distance. At least her heart could settle down and she could think. She couldn't forget how he'd stroked her neck and made her shiver all over—no, she had to get it out of her head. She was not attracted to him.

Then it hit her. In a moment of sheer weakness, she had revealed the full extent of her powers to him. She had agreed to find his brother, succumbed to Kane's alpha powers of persuasion. She just made a deal with the devil—or, in this case, someone protecting a devil.

Well, she'd had no choice. Gleaners were evil, whether they had brothers who cared for them or not. And in the end, she'd find a way to destroy the monster.

Nina sat at the kitchen table with Kane. He refused to eat on a tray like an invalid, and he had hobbled to the kitchen table. He sat next to her sipping coffee and gnawing on beef jerky. It was a little stale and didn't look all that yummy, but it was protein.

Nina ate cereal with warm powdered milk. Not the tofu burger with onions and mustard as she wanted, but it contained calories. She was aware of Kane watching her with that fixed stare of his, and she felt her hands trembling from a sudden case of nerves.

She shifted uneasily in her chair and swallowed. The cereal seemed to stick in her throat, swell, and make it impossible to swallow. She gave up eating and sipped her coffee.

"You warm enough?" he asked, his deep voice a low purr in his throat.

"Not really." She didn't know if being near him made her shiver or if she was cold.

"There's some extra clothes in the bedroom closet you can wear."

"Thank you." He was actually being accommodating, which prompted her to say, "That's nice of you. I don't believe you're as mean as you'd have me believe. I think that's your way of pushing everyone away."

She'd hit a nerve. His eyes softened for the briefest of seconds, revealing a wealth of hidden emotion he kept hidden from the world. For a fleeting moment, he wore the expression of a wounded animal in a trap, crying out for help but willing to bite the hand that freed him. Something in her heart ached for him, even though she didn't want to feel anything. She almost touched him but stopped herself before she did something foolish.

"It's not a defense mechanism, I assure you. I've done things that would send you running in the opposite direction." His gaze followed the lines of her hair, down to her breasts, then slowly rose to meet her eyes.

"I don't frighten easily." She tried to sound offhand, but his assessing glance had caused a waver in her voice.

"I murdered my wife," he said, tossing out well-chosen words that were meant to shock her.

All of his words and actions seemed carefully executed to isolate him from others, so she pretended the disclosure hadn't surprised her and said, "You have no idea how world-weary I am when it comes to death. I've seen six lifetimes of it. What happened?"

His breathing increased, as if he were fighting a huge demon inside him. His expression turned distant. He leaned back in the chair. It creaked loudly in the silence. "I don't even remember doing it." His fingers tightened in fists as he rested his forearms on his knees and clasped his large hands.

"I don't understand. How could that happen?"

"I don't know. I fell asleep, and when I woke up she was dead, maimed, her blood all over me…." He paused, his expression full of torment. "I'd shimmered and killed her in my sleep…somehow."

"You recall nothing about that night?"

"Only the stark reality of waking up and finding Daphne dead. Bitten so many times her face was hardly recognizable."

"And you've been living with the guilt." So that's what was eating away at Kane Van Cleave. "Were you arrested for the murder?"

"The council ruled it an accident and said I couldn't be held accountable, since I'd shifted and couldn't remember. Sometimes tragedies happen like that among us. If we become too impassioned and our animal instincts take over."

"Do you usually remember what you do when you shift?" She leaned against the table and crossed her arms over her chest. "I know some lower forms of shifters don't, like were-dogs."

"We're nothing like them," he said, snarling in disgust. "Some things are vague when we hunt, sometimes. Depends upon how strong our animal instincts become and when the moon is closest to the earth."

"So that's when it happened?"

He nodded.

She knew that the phases of the moon affected the earth's tides and weather patterns, but also governed supernatural and natural beings as well—including humans. Homicide rates, suicides, major disasters, psychiatric admissions, stabbings, shootings, accidents, birthrates and fertility all went up during a full moon. Nothing new there. What wasn't known was that the same thing happened in the supernatural community. Man couldn't handle that bit of truth. Patomani lore stated that the moon and earth were sisters. One could not survive without the other, and the moon controlled the inhabitants of the earth's many dimensions. It gave the word *moonstruck* a whole new meaning.

"You're not alone, you know," she said, running a pointer finger over a deep notch in the wooden table and listening to the coffee pot dripping. "The moon does crazy things to everyone. Can't tell you how many times I've been called away on jobs during full moons because some animal turned vicious. Had a hamster once, Bacon. He turned into a little Tasmanian devil when the moon was full. Attacked his owner so much I had to make monthly visits."

"Did you help him?"

"Yes, and the owner, too."

"What happened to Bacon?"

"Oh, he had a fit one night and died from the stress of it. Vet said he probably had a stroke. Poor Bacon." She shook her head and remembered wishing she could have been there to help the hamster.

"You really hate losing a single creature under your watch, don't you?"

"I do. And the poor owners love their pets. They're the ones who suffer."

He snorted as soon as she mentioned love. "They knew the consequences when they decided to take in the animal. Pets die. Why should you feel sorry for them?"

"Probably the same reason you carry the guilt of your wife's death."

"Two different scenarios. I'm responsible for her death. You're not when it comes to your clients."

"Are you any more responsible than me?" she said reasonably. "If you think that, then you must believe you are above all this." She gestured to the natural world around them.

"I should be." He scowled down at his clasped hands.

"How can you say that? Every soul's destiny is in the Book of Life."

"That what you believe?" He looked at her as if she were an innocent child about to put her finger in a light socket.

"It's what my people believe," she said adamantly.

His brow crinkled in a frown. "Survival of the fittest is our religion."

Nina heard the emptiness in his words and couldn't help but feel touched by it. "What about love? Seniphs don't love?"

"Love is weakness. You care for someone, you get hurt." He spoke as if the word *love* left a bitter aftertaste in his mouth.

"My spirit guide says love is the glue that holds the universe and all its dimensions together."

He shot her a cynical glance. "Spirit guide?"

"Yes, Koda."

"Pulling my leg, right?"

"No," she said, rolling her eyes. "He's an honest-to-goodness angel—I think."

"You don't know?"

"If you want the truth, I think guardian angels are above spirit guides. But he's all I got."

"Male, huh?" His lips thinned.

"Yes."

"And how does this Koda guide you—when he's not filling your head full of drivel about love?"

Nina was sorry now she'd said anything about Koda. Come to think of it, he was the first person outside her family whom she'd ever told. She hadn't meant to tell him; it had just slipped out. She wasn't about to justify Koda's existence to anyone—even though he wasn't all that good of a spirit guide. "Just forget it. The point I was trying to make before I digressed was that you're extremely arrogant if you think you're so powerful that you're above all the dynamic forces of nature. What I'm trying to say is that you're a seniph, with feral instincts that can't be repressed at times. Your wife's death was a tragedy, to be sure, but you said yourself seniphs don't always remember when they shift, and it was ruled an accident by your pride's council. You're an alpha male—"

"All the more reason I should never have let myself shift unchecked. The council ruled it an accident, but my people fear me, go out of their way to avoid me."

She heard the emptiness and loneliness in his voice and said, "You have to forgive yourself before others can."

"I'm not one of your sick pets. I don't need your advice." He tensed, his expression darkening right before her eyes. He stood, and the chair scraped the floor. Even hurt, he moved with such agile speed and grace that she could hardly follow him with her naked eye.

She sucked in her breath, waiting for him to attack, but he only stalked past her on his way out of the kitchen.

He walked hunched over. She didn't have to touch him to know he was feeling pain, physically and mentally.

When she could breathe again, she told herself she was glad that he'd left. But she still wondered what would have happened if he'd shifted and lost control. Another icy tremor shook her.

She felt sorry for him. From the few moments she'd managed to get him to open up to her, she'd learned that his guilt was harming him in ways he didn't even realize. No wonder she had felt such penned-up hatred from his animal side. Kane's own self-loathing fueled the beast's inner discontent, a vicious cycle in which they were both caught. And pointing it out only angered him. It was too bad she couldn't use her magic on him, but her powers were limited. Emotions were not hers to command; she could only perceive them and sense a being's inner turmoil. She could try to communicate information that would help their present state of mind or take them out of harm's way, but she couldn't control how they felt. And Kane had plenty of history troubling him.

Her problem was the gleaner. He may have come to the cabin to see Kane, or to finish them both off. At the thought of facing the gleaner, her gut clenched and her stomach began to hurt. Last time, she had almost lost her life, but she wouldn't be as careless this time. Would her powers of suggestion work on Kane's brother, since they didn't work on Kane? She prayed so.

Kane flopped down on the couch in the living room. It occurred to him that he'd spoken his innermost thoughts to her. He hadn't been able to talk to anyone about Daphne's death, not even Charles, and he didn't like divulging his emotions like this. What had possessed him to spill his guts to her? It was that magical attraction of hers. She lured him in, and he heeled like an obedient puppy. Well, he was no one's faithful pet, and she'd find that out soon enough.

Chapter 8

Later that night, Nina sat at the kitchen table. She'd stayed well away from Kane most of the day and kept herself busy cleaning the cabin. He had steered clear of her, too, and feigned sleeping. She had just put his supper of steak and French fries on a tray and left it near the sofa so he could eat alone. He had grunted a thank-you as she had hurried out of the room. She really didn't want him near her while she ate. He'd make her nervous and give her indigestion—among other things.

She was enjoying eating without his brooding presence near her. In fact, it was a welcome change. She looked out the window at the drifts. Snow weighted down the younger evergreens' limbs, bowing them until they touched the ground. It really was beautiful, and she might have been able to relax and appreciate it… if Kane Van Cleave weren't in the other room. But at least she was by herself in the kitchen. She spent a lot of time alone in her job, driving from one assignment to another, and she was alone in the Quiet Place. Alone was comfortable for her.

The snow and sleet had stopped, but it was still overcast. Gray shadows covered the forest and gave it a deserted and threatening appearance. It was almost sunset, and the dying sun cast purplish blue shadows on the snow.

She didn't hear Kane's footsteps behind her—he prowled rather than walked—but she felt him enter the room. The kitchen suddenly shrunk about six feet on all sides.

He carried his plate and cup of coffee. He hadn't touched his food, and he was joining her. Just ducky. So much for peace of mind.

Thank goodness he'd put on a shirt, but the first few buttons were open in a *V*. His golden chest hair peeked through. She found it hard not to stare at his chest as he sat down.

She drew her plate closer to her and felt his left knee brush against her leg beneath the table. Nina felt a small vibe of emotion coming from him, but it was just a brief encounter and their clothes muddied the transmission. She slid her chair back a safe distance.

She stared out the window, unwilling to speak to him first. He'd been so indifferent and distant throughout the day that he'd have to initiate the conversation. She suddenly lost her appetite. He stared at the table and sipped his coffee. The pair of them made a gloomy tableau.

Finally he said, "Good coffee."

"Thanks." She kept the response offhand.

"Steak and French fries are good, too. Where'd you learn to cook?"

Okay, he was actually talking to her, complimenting her instead of threatening or ordering her around. He must be up to something. Had he come in here because her power drew him, or was he feeling gregarious? The last thought almost made her giggle out loud. She decided to roll with it and see what happened.

"My grandmother taught me and my sisters to cook—well, all except my oldest sister, Fala," she said.

"The Guardian?"

Nina nodded. "Takala teases Fala about that all the time. Guardians can do anything and everything except cook. But I'm certain Fala could cook, if she tried. She just hates it and never applied herself in the kitchen. Stephen will have to do all the cooking in that family, or they'll be eating out a lot." She grinned, thinking about the couple.

"Stephen?" He looked mildly curious.

"Her new husband. He's a warlock. I've never seen two people more in love. Stephen would do anything for Fala—including taking cooking lessons."

"The novelty hasn't worn off yet."

"And it won't," she said adamantly and added, "Stephen loves Fala. His love will never wear off. If I wanted a husband, then I'd find someone just like Stephen." Another handsome face materialized in her mind, one with tawny long hair and brutal jungle-green eyes. She forced it away.

"So, you're content without male companionship?"

"I have Koda."

"I'd like to meet this spirit."

He wouldn't. He was just being spiteful, sneering like all get-out. "If you do," she said, "you'll probably be dead."

That quieted him. Nina chugged the last of her lukewarm coffee and got up and put her plate in the sink. She began running water to do the dishes. She felt his eyes on her, making her squirm and play with her cup handle, and she said, "You should probably go lie down."

"Been doing that all day. I'd rather stay here."

"Annoying me?"

"Yes." A sliver of a grin slipped across his lips, but it didn't stay there. He stood, favoring his wounded side, and brought his plate to her. He grabbed a dish towel and waited patiently for her to pour dishwashing liquid in the water.

"What are you doing?" she asked.

"Helping you."

"You shouldn't be up."

"I can do this."

They stopped speaking and worked together, but it was in no way a companionable twenty minutes. She was too aware of him standing beside her, too cognizant of his eyes watching her like a cat watched a caged bird.

She was careful not to touch him when she handed him the dishes and pot, but he towered over her, and his nearness was like an unavoidable brick wall that filled her personal space. She sighed inwardly when they finished the job.

"Is it possible to take a shower?" she asked, filling in the silence.

"The heater should have hot water now. You'll find Daphne's clothes in the closet. She was taller than you, but you might find something to use."

And prettier, Nina finished his unspoken thought. He hadn't gotten rid of her clothes. He must have cared deeply for her, for all his ridiculing of love. Before she knew it, Nina found herself asking, "Is that a picture of your wife in the bedroom?"

"Yes."

"How did you meet?"

"Our marriage was arranged at our births."

"Is that something that happens in a lot in prides?"

"With alphas it does. Keeps the pure lines going."

Nina wondered if he could marry a human but kept that question to herself. "So she was an alpha female?" she asked.

"Yes."

"Did you have children?"

"Daphne miscarried three times. Then we stopped trying. It happens with purebred seniphs sometimes. It's gotten to the point that we're often forced to breed with humans to introduce new blood into our genome."

"What are the offspring?"

"They can be human or shifter."

"So you have humans in the pride?" This was all new to her. She'd never known any of this.

"They become outcasts. Some leave the pride to live with their own kind."

She heard herself asking, "Wasn't it hard marrying someone you didn't know? Did you care for Daphne?"

"Not at first. We were complete strangers. She came from a pride in Russia. Of course, after we married, we grew closer. Then she got depressed when she couldn't carry children. She begged me to take another mate, but I wouldn't...." His brows met in a pensive line, his words trailing off.

Nina saw that she had dredged up painful memories for him and regretted it. He'd stuck by Daphne; that was admirable. Emotional connections didn't drive the seniph world. It seemed acceptable to have arranged marriages and take a new mate if the first one didn't produce. But Kane seemed to have more human ideals.

The awkward silence that followed intimate disclosure hovered between them. Nina wanted to put her arms around him and hold him and help him forget his tragic past. Instead she quickly said, "Thank you for helping with the cleanup." She dried her hands, folded the towel, then hurried out.

She couldn't wait to get away from him and feel her body settle down again. He caused all sorts of butterflies and heart palpitations and unwanted yearnings. She needed distance between them. Lots of it.

Kane watched her leave, her hair almost touching her bottom. He didn't know which bothered him more: his wounds, the fact he couldn't stay away from her or the desire she fueled in him. He felt the evidence of it aching between his legs.

Thoughts of her naked in the shower would drive him nutty. He couldn't even stay out of the same room she occupied, and he'd found himself crawling into the kitchen to be near her like a lovesick human and regurgitating things in his past. If he stayed in the cabin, he'd end up doing something stupid like joining her in the shower. He would conquer this attraction to her, even if it killed him.

He decided to check the gasoline level of the generator so she'd have enough hot water to bathe with. And, too, he could see exactly what lies she'd been telling him earlier when she'd been frightened of something outside.

He ignored the pain in his chest and arm and put on his boots, then stepped out the back door. Cold air bit at his face and hands as he strode through the snow.

He smelled Ethan right away. The familiar musk of him lurked in the air. He'd been in gleaner form, and he hadn't cloaked himself. That's what had spooked her. Ethan could have harmed her, but he hadn't. A familiar possessiveness caused him to grit his teeth. He didn't want to feel anything for Nina Rainwater, but somehow he'd grown to care for her. A big mistake. Ethan was his first priority.

Why hadn't Ethan come in? They had hunted around the cabin as boys, cooked many a marshmallow in the fireplace together and tried to scare each other with ghost stories. He certainly had to have sensed Kane was inside, willing to help him.

Kane topped off the gasoline level in the generator, then followed the tracks. Hopefully Ethan was nearby, waiting for him. He thought of Nina. She wasn't going anywhere. And if he found Ethan without her help, all the better.

Nina rubbed her hair with the towel, still shivering even though she wore two pairs of leggings, knee socks and a pair of borrowed Liz Claiborne jeans from Daphne's closet. They were too long, and she'd had to roll them up a couple of times. Her own corduroy slacks she'd draped on the end of the bedpost to dry.

Daphne had very expensive taste in clothes, all designer stuff. And it had been a little eerie going through her things. But Nina needed clothes desperately, and warmth, and Kane had invited her to use them. Having seen Daphne's belongings, Nina had tried to visualize what life had been like as Kane's wife, wanting children and the pressure of not being able to give him a child. The expectations alone must have been hard on her. Nina knew what it was like to be flawed, overlooked and put aside. But Kane hadn't done that with Daphne. His wife's own self-abasement must have gone a long way in feeding her depression. Nina knew that in her own case her powers and the love for her family were the governing factors keeping her on an even keel. Everyone needed their Prozac in whatever form available.

While rummaging though Daphne's closet, she had found a black turtleneck and a wool sweater from Ann Taylor. The sweater was too big, just the way she liked it. Daphne must have been a size ten. Nina was a six.

She'd also found a pair of knee-high snow boots with a thick lining. They were too big, also. But nothing several pairs of socks couldn't cure. Growing up, Nina had always gotten her sister's hand-me-downs, and she'd learned creative ways to make shoes fit.

She finished towel-drying her hair, then found a brush among some makeup in a drawer. She brushed the tangles out of her hair, then decided to let it dry naturally near the fireplace. When she stepped out into the living room, the emptiness settled along her senses. All she heard was the distant roar of the generator. She had no idea when she had become so cognizant of Kane, but she knew without a doubt he wasn't here.

Alarmed now, she looked outside for him. The Jeep hadn't moved. She went to the back window and peered out. She spotted his deep footprints right away. They followed the gleaner's.

His brother might be setting a trap for Kane. She remembered seeing a jacket in Daphne's closet, and she grabbed it and hurried outside.

She followed Kane's tracks into the woods. They led straight up the mountain. Before long she was panting and out of breath and imagining all sorts of horrible scenarios involving Kane: like his brother killing him and his body being fried. Gleaners, she knew, could consume seniphs' spirits if they were in human form. What if she couldn't reach Kane in time? What if she failed to get her hands on the gleaner before he burned her to cinders and devoured her spirit?

She gulped at that thought, but it didn't slow her down. She waded through the snow. Each step a triumph.

She tried to stay in Kane's footpath, but his strides were much longer than her own. Her feet slipped, and several times she stubbed her toe on a log.

She saw movement ahead of her and was overjoyed when she saw Kane's large form. He faced her, leaning against a tree, holding his chest.

She ran to him and threw her arms around him. "I'm so happy to see you. Are you okay?"

She crushed herself against his hard body and buried her face in the warmth of his broad chest. His emotions filtered to her, and she sensed disappointment, frustration, confusion and pleasure. Was he actually happy to see her?

He wrapped his arms around her and held her tightly. "You came out here to find me?"

"I was worried."

"Were you?" He sounded incredulous and a little gratified. He lifted her chin and searched her eyes for she knew not what. Then he kissed her.

She let herself enjoy the moment, feeling the power of his lips electrify her, cause her breasts to tingle and a sweet ache to bloom in the pit of her belly.

His lips were warm and supple, unlike the man himself. The coarse stubble on his cheeks and chin chafed the soft skin on her face and sent a warm prickle down her throat.

He deepened the kiss, his mouth becoming hungry and ravishing. He tensed all over, his grip on her tightening, trapping her completely. Even if she wanted to, she knew she could not escape him now.

His damp curly hair touched her cheeks and forehead,

while he ran his tongue along her tight lips until she instinctively opened them.

He plundered her mouth; then his wide hands explored every curve of her body. She kept waiting to feel the seniph's ardor, mix with the man's, but Kane's passion was stronger, blocking out the beast's. It grew fearsome, an all-consuming yearning. If she cared to admit it, it thrilled her like nothing she'd ever experienced before. The part of her that wanted to feel desired and beautiful and as tempting as her sisters wanted to stay suspended in his arms forever.

She'd only dreamed about kisses like this. Sure, she'd let a few boys on the reservation kiss her, but it had never gone past the casual date and door smooch because inevitably one of her sisters would be home and her date would become instantly smitten with them, which had only added to Nina's shyness and insecurity.

She felt no such inhibitions now, and she dove her hands in his thick hair and pulled his head closer to her. Her body trembled uncontrollably with desire and longing.

He moaned as if in pain; then he moved his hands up under her coat, exploring. His palms found her breasts. She arched against him as he kneaded and teased her nipples through her bra until she thought she might scream.

She ran her hands over his large chest, learning the impenetrable hardness there.

His breathing grew rapid and shallow, his body trembling from holding back his desire. He growled in a wounded, out-of-control way. Then he cupped her bottom with his hands. Before she knew it, he lifted her up off the ground and set her against a tree trunk. He began moving his erection against the sensitive flesh between her thighs.

She felt the material of her leggings bunch up inside her thighs, rubbing her in all the right places. She moaned softly and gave herself over to him, unable to think of anything but the waves of yearning he forced inside her.

"You feel too good," he moaned, continuing to thrust his hips against her, driving her back against the tree trunk.

She wrapped her legs around his waist and clung to his neck, feeling the friction of his hardness, moving faster, making her sigh with her own need.

He cried out, a deep, guttural wail. She felt him pulse against her once, twice; then he was still as death, panting, his breath like a furnace on her face. In fact, he had warmed her all over.

The fury of his passion had simmered, and he rested his head against the tree trunk above her and still held her penned against the tree. She could feel his whole body trembling. Nina clung to him, aware they had just shared sex fully clothed.

"I'm sorry," he said. "I was rough. It's been too long." He set her down gently, and she saw a wet spot darkening the crotch of his jeans.

Her knees felt wobbly, and she had to lean against the tree to steady herself. "The rough part wasn't bad. Maybe a little hurried, though." She touched his cheek.

He pulled away from her. A coldness settled over his

features, and she knew she had lost him emotionally. Their intimacy was quickly being drained away by his wall of aloofness. In an attempt to reach him again, she tried to stand on her toes and kiss him.

"No, Nina." He stepped back, looking at her as if he couldn't decide whether to grab her again or get as far away as possible. "What just happened shouldn't have. You charmed me and made me do it."

Nina blinked up at him, his rejection stabbing her worse than a blade. "Oh, so now you're blaming it on my power." She heard the hurt bubbling up in her own voice.

"What else was it?"

"For your information, I've never had anyone or anything drawn to me sexually like that. Creatures want to be near me because they trust me. They don't want to mate with me." She jammed her arms over her chest and glared at him.

"Then it must be only carnal lust on my part. I've been celibate too long."

"Well, then you better go pull another prisoner from your harem." She wheeled around to leave.

He caught her shoulder and stopped her. "Why'd you lie to me? You knew he'd been here."

"I didn't tell you for this very reason." She waved an angry hand toward his wounds. She noticed his shoulder was bleeding again. Abruptly she felt embarrassed and guilt-ridden and hurt by his sudden coldness.

"You don't need to worry about me," he said. "You should be more worried about yourself."

"You're right, I should." She knocked his hand away

and ran back down the path. "And don't ever touch me again."

"Nina!" His bellow echoed through the woods like a shotgun blast.

But she kept wading through the snow. She got in a parting shot and yelled over her shoulder, "And don't speak to me again unless you shift. Your beast is so much more likable than you." She rarely lost her temper. It felt great to yell at him—to yell at anyone.

Pig-headed man that he was. He'd just denied wanting her, but she knew he desired her; she had felt his lust. In fact, she felt the intense untamed need within him to feel stroked and desired by her. She had wanted to make him admit as much. But she had her pride, and he'd stomped on it. She hadn't been prepared for the rejection or the sharp pain in her heart that it had caused.

When she reached the cabin, she ran to the bedroom and locked herself inside, berating herself for being so openly demonstrative and wearing her heart on her sleeve. He was a brute, a beast, not worth caring about. She buried her face in a pillow and sobbed in earnest.

Kane marched into the house, cursing his weakness around her. She had shut the bedroom door, and he paused there. With his acute hearing, he listened to muffled crying. He took a step toward the door, then froze, his fists clenching. Oh, God, he'd never wanted to hurt her. Never wanted to feel indebted to her for saving his life, to witness her caring side. He hadn't wanted to lose control and take her like an animal, but he had. He didn't want any of this. Yet not comforting her was the hardest thing he had ever done in his life. But if he went to her now, he'd soothe her, and that would lead to full-blown, in-the-raw sex. After that one little taste of her, he felt frustrated, unsatisfied and still throbbing for her. He had to admit he'd never get his fill of Nina Rainwater. He had to control this lust, or it would open up a Pandora's box.

And one thing he couldn't understand was why she had said she preferred his beast to him. Talk about a blow. She had no idea what he could unleash on her. She'd never find out, either. No, he'd vowed never to let himself get close enough to a woman to repeat the same mistake he'd made with Daphne. Nina was his prisoner, nothing more. And damn it, she was going to stay that way.

And part of his losing control was her fault. Why hadn't she pulled away from him like she was supposed to, like she'd done in the past? No, she'd gone running into his arms. He'd never forget her face as she'd done it, either. The concern he'd seen there was real. No way she could have faked the frantic look in her eyes, that look of concern.

He'd seen it in Daphne's eyes. No matter how bitter and disappointed she had become at not giving him children, her gaze had always softened when she had looked at him. And that's what still haunted him. That trusting gaze. Had she looked at him that way before he'd torn her to pieces? In his nightmares, Daphne's expression tortured him night after night. He'd wake up right before he bit her, sweating, gasping, the image of Daphne's trusting face burned into his psyche. And when he'd seen that same expression on Nina's face before he kissed her and lost all his self-control, it had driven him to the brink. That's when Nina had tried to respond to him again. Daphne's face had flashed in his mind, and he'd had the good sense to push Nina away. She had looked so open and hurt and betrayed, eyes glistening with tears. He thought he'd felt all the torment he could, but having seen her expression and hearing her cry now was ten thousand times worse. He couldn't let himself go down that path again. Not with someone as sensitive and vulnerable as Nina Rainwater. He couldn't. He had to make her loathe him. That shouldn't be too hard.

He walked into the kitchen, his shoulder and arm burning, along with a lower body part. He could smell Nina all over him, tormenting him. He went to the Jeep, found a pair of clean jeans and a shirt he'd packed, then took a cold sponge bath. He cleaned his wounds, applied pressure to his shoulder. When the bleeding stopped, he bandaged it himself. Then he dressed.

His thoughts strayed back to her as he yanked a bottle of wine out of the rack and broke it on the counter. Chunks of glass shot out all over the kitchen. He tipped it up and drank from the jagged edge. He needed to numb his mind to her. The merlot tasted bitter and sour, but he chugged it anyway.

Chapter 9

Nina woke, her mouth wet with drool. She had fallen asleep with her face in the pillow and Daphne's coat still on. Darkness covered the bedroom. What time was it? It felt like the middle of the night. And it was freezing, too, not an ounce of warmth in the room.

She pulled a quilt off the bed and wrapped it around her shoulders. Through the small window, she stared at the moon. The glowing globe shot an eerie shimmering gray over the snow. Shadows darkened the most recent trail of footprints she and Kane had left in the snow. The humiliation of finding him burned through her all over again. But she couldn't stay in this room. She was starving, thirsty and cold.

She grimaced and felt her way to the door. Complete silence made the cabin sound like a tomb. The generator had stopped running outside. She sensed Kane inside, but where was he?

Earlier she'd heard thumps or loud crashes, like glass breaking. But she refused to open her door and find out what Kane was doing and went right back to sleep. Not that a locked door would have kept him out if he had wanted to come into the bedroom. But it had established her territory, and being part feral creature that he was, he'd respected that. Thank goodness.

It had given her time to nurse her wounds and smother any delusions she might have harbored of caring about him. She also had a plan for ditching Kane and tracking his brother that she would implement in the morning—if he was asleep. She had only let him believe she was his prisoner to make sure he was okay. Well, he seemed fit enough if he could go tramping in the woods after his brother, and she was done worrying about him.

She straightened her spine, summoning her courage, then eased open the door and peeked out into the living room.

Empty, save for the hiss of the fire. He'd thrown logs on the grate some time ago, and they were slow-burning embers now, casting flickering shadows over the empty couch. She heard a chair creaking from his weight in the kitchen, the very room that held food.

She cursed her luck. She had hoped he'd be asleep. She heard the scratch of rough material sliding against material, then a thump, thump. What was he doing?

Candlelight flickered from the kitchen, so he wasn't in total darkness. It probably wouldn't matter if he was, with his acute sense of sight. She wished her powers had come with some kind of superhuman physical strengths.

She inhaled deeply and grabbed a candle from the fireplace mantel, lit it as quietly as she could, then padded into the kitchen. She knew he had heard her because the thumping had stopped. Gingerly she walked into the kitchen, the candle held high. When she saw him, she stopped.

Three broken wine bottles gleamed on the table near him. They lay on their sides, empty. He sat in a chair with two hiking backpacks at his feet, stuffing a sleeping bag in one of them. His eyes glistened in the light like sharp pieces of jade, his expression menacing, deep frown wrinkles creasing his brow. An air of wary aggressiveness hovered about him, as if she were his enemy and he was contemplating her every move. He had never looked more dangerous.

For a moment she only eyed him. He seemed wired; his body had grown rigid the instant she had walked into the room. His piercing gaze stayed on her.

"You're up." His deep bass voice broke the frigid silence.

"Yes."

"You're wearing her clothes." His eyes slowly traveled the length of her body, taking in the jeans and jacket beneath the blanket around her shoulders.

When his eyes settled on her breasts, she felt her face redden. Their last encounter became a vivid rewind, and she felt his hot mouth on hers and his large hands exploring her body. With agonizing slowness and clarity, every frame moved through her mind. She recalled what happened afterward, how he'd hurt her. Thankfully that wiped the explicit images from her mind. She pointed to the rolled-up cuffs of the jacket to distract his roving eyes and said, "A little long."

He merely grunted, his gaze still eating her alive.

It was so intense she felt her skin prickling and tingling. "Why are you still up?" she asked, forcing a bored tone into her words.

"Can't sleep."

Most people looked really bad when they didn't get any sleep, bags under the eyes, sunken cheeks, dazed sleepwalking look. Not him. His eyes were sharp green glass. His five o'clock shadow had darkened on his chin. His golden hair fell down to his shoulders in waves. And oh, boy, he looked good, even more handsome. She just wished he'd stop staring at her like she was a tasty morsel he was about to crunch down on. He had no right, after pulling away from her.

"What are you doing?" she asked tersely.

"Packing. We're finding Ethan."

She hadn't expected this turn of events, and her mouth dropped open. So much for her plan. She had hoped to find him asleep and tie him up, but that wasn't going to happen. When she could speak again, she said, "But your wounds."

"I have found a great painkiller." He motioned to the broken bottles.

"But the Jeep is snowed in."

"We're going on foot."

"There's fifteen inches of snow out there." She jabbed a finger toward the window.

"He won't expect us to be on foot, and we might have the element of surprise."

She set down the candle on the counter and said, "This is crazy. We'll both be sitting ducks. He could kill us at any time."

"He won't hurt you as long as you're with me."

"What if I'm not with you?" She jammed her arms on her hips.

"You will be."

"You're assuming an awful lot."

He leaped up, stepping over the backpack, his height and size dwarfing her. He wasn't favoring his wounded shoulder. The wine must have worked its magic. He didn't even look tired, or tipsy, only arrogant and smug and willfully capable of anything. "It's not an assumption," he said, his voice soft with threat.

A tremor shook her. She smelled wine on his breath, mixing with his own feral musk, and she had a hard time concentrating. She couldn't meet his eyes and not want to touch him, so she stared at his burly chest. At least he was wearing a shirt, a clean blue flannel. Golden chest hair peeked above the top two open buttons. She remembered running her hands over his chest—*get a grip, will you?*

She counted the buttons on his shirt, six, and cleared her mind enough to say, "Whatever it is, I don't appreciate being bullied. But I guess you can't help being like that, now can you? A leopard never loses his spots." She was surprised at the calm evenness in her voice. "And don't think for one minute that what happened between us gives you the right to make decisions concerning

my life. I'm going because I agreed to help you—"
and she needed to destroy his brother "—but it's not
because you're ordering me to go. And you were right,
our little interlude shouldn't have happened. It was a big
mistake." She thrust out her arms wide, showing him
just how large a blunder it was. She hoped that gave him
something to chew on. See how he liked getting some
of his own medicine back.

"Fine." His voice's sharp edge sent chills through
her. "Now we leave."

She turned, but he grabbed her shoulder, his fingers
digging into her skin. He bent until his lips almost
touched her neck. Then he said, "By the way, lions don't
have spots, and we have much bigger fangs." He gave
her a Cheshire smile, showing all his white gleaming
teeth, the points of his fangs evident.

His hot breath sent goose bumps down her neck. For
a minute she felt her heart stop as she wondered what he
would do next. Part of her, the part that melted around
him, hoped he'd kiss her.

Suddenly, he released her.

That was for the best, she told herself. At least she
could think. And she didn't think much of his harassing
tactics. Well, she wasn't about to let him know that he
affected her at all. If he could be cold and heartless,
so could she. Her stomach ached with hunger, and she
found the courage to ask, "Have you packed food?"

"Yes, but those are our provisions." He rummaged
through the cabinet and handed her a box of toaster
pastries. "That should hold you. Now, let's go. You might
need this." He picked up the quilt that had dropped on

the floor and draped it over her shoulders. He pulled a pair of Daphne's pink ski gloves from one backpack.

"Here, put them on."

Nina did his bidding, knowing she could wear twenty pairs of gloves and still be cold out there in the snow. In fact, she didn't think she'd ever warm up around him—unless they had sex again. That would be Hawaiian paradise in the middle of a Blue Ridge Mountains winter. She had to admit the heat in his body made her the warmest she'd ever felt in her life. And when she thought of their coupling in the woods, it still made her insides do strange things. But he'd pulled away from her emotionally, and she didn't know how to reach him, or even if she wanted to be hurt like that again.

She had no idea how this would play out when she met his brother again. It irked her that her powers wouldn't work on Kane and that she might have lost them for good. They might not work on the gleaner, either. When she was alone she'd call Koda and find out if he knew what was wrong.

Kane zipped up the backpacks and hefted them both over his good shoulder. They must have weighed fifty pounds apiece. They bulged with sleeping bags, a tent and cooking gear. He handled them like they weighed hardly more than a pencil.

"If you're so certain he won't hurt you, why didn't he just come in and speak to you?" she asked.

"I don't know. That's why I have to talk to him."

"Do you have any idea what brought him home?"

"Must be a good reason. I just have to find out what it is. Now, get moving."

He gave her a little nudge out the door. Cold air hit her, and she cringed. The moon beamed silver dust over the snow, glistening bluish gray. But the moonlight couldn't penetrate the darkness that engulfed the forest. At the edge of the cabin's backyard, the dried and dead limbs clawed out from the forest and grasped at anything that moved. The lethal appearance of the forest made her shiver. She wrapped the quilt tighter around her shoulders and trudged forward, her hiking boots slipping on her heels and Kane breathing down her neck.

"What's the matter?"

When Kane touched Nina's shoulder, she stumbled in the snow. He caught her elbow before she fell. She'd been absorbed in reading a distant emotion and hadn't been paying attention. He had her full awareness now.

"Are you all right?" he asked.

"I'm okay," she said, a little disoriented, because Kane's impressions and the other signal were coming at her in stereo. She blocked his out and zeroed in on the other perception. The cold dulled her reception somewhat, but the agony she sensed was excruciating. "Oh my gosh!" She gripped her waist with both arms as a shiver tore through her.

"What is it?"

"Something I've picked up." She shrank from his touch.

He regarded her with chagrined bewilderment, as if she had surprised him by her reaction.

She added, "Sorry, but you're breaking the connection."

"To what?"

"I don't know. A creature's in trouble. I hope your gleaner hasn't struck again." She shot Kane a reproachful look. She didn't like thinking of Ethan as a person, or calling him by name, so "gleaner" would have to do.

"Didn't you say you'd lost his trail on the deer path?"

"Yes." She'd been following his emotional trail for close to an hour. About a mile back she had lost any sense of him, and she was certain he'd shut down his thoughts on purpose. She believed he was leading them on a wild-goose chase and enjoying every minute of it, then this new feeling had struck her.

"It isn't Ethan. He wouldn't have attacked so close to us."

"You have a lot more confidence in him than I do. I think he's capable of anything, including setting a trap for us." Nina eyed the forest around them. She couldn't shake the feeling of being watched, or an impending feeling that something bad was about to happen.

"He could have killed you, but he didn't. You're safe as long as you are with me," Kane said, impatience sharpening his words.

She doubted that. The only way they were both safe was if her powers were working. She hadn't been able to contact Koda, so she had no idea if she was defenseless.

His voice broke into her thoughts. "Are the sensations strong enough to track?"

"Yes." Nina held her aching temples and stood very still. Like the dowser she was, her internal compass instantly found the point where the emotion was strongest. At least that part of her powers was still working. She pointed north. "It's coming from there. But it's off the trail we were following."

"Head that way."

She started toward the emotion's origin, but Kane's large hand gripped her shoulder. "Let me go first."

"Okay, I'll point the way." At his touch, she perceived his bravery and concern and need to dominate the situation.

He stepped in front of her, and she was glad to let him blaze the trail. He carried the backpacks on his left shoulder, so she fell in on his right side. Evidently, she wasn't close enough to suit him, so his gloved fingers slipped into hers.

Nina stared down at their joined hands. His fingers were so long they wrapped totally around her hand. They felt strong and warm, fitting so naturally around hers. She could easily get used to this attention. She should break the contact, but she couldn't, and she found herself squeezing his fingers tighter, which earned her a curious look from his piercing eyes. And she felt his emotional meter heat up again. His gaze softened for a brief second; then he was back on alert, scanning the woods for signs of his brother.

The trail drew her attention and she double-timed it to keep up with him as he shoved aside thick brambles, sidestepped oak trees and hollies. Snow capped the dense trees and brambles and hardwood seedlings. In places it was a maze of solid white.

A strange emptiness pervaded the forest. As thick as

the trees were here, there should have been animals and birds, but she hadn't seen one creature, heard anything other than the crunching tread of their footsteps in the snow. She felt like an explorer in one of those sci-fi B movies, moving through the tundra wasteland of a deserted planet. Any moment now an alien might pop out. Maybe it already had, and it was leading them into a trap.

"Veer left," Nina said while she shoved on his burly arm. She felt the shivers getting stronger, and she whispered, "Try to be quiet. We're close."

"You're the one making the noise." He frowned at her feet as if he were insulted.

He was right, Nina realized. His steps were hardly audible, the stealth of a hunter in his every movement. She sounded like a herd of stampeding cows. Well, he was forcing her to jog to keep up with him.

"Show off," she whispered back.

An amused and overconfident grin toyed with his lips. He resembled an evil forest god who had a reputation for taking advantage of innocent young damsels. And his libido waltzed into her thoughts, loud, clear and strong.

It was making her hyperventilate, and she pulled her hand free of his and pointed him ahead. "Go on. I'll bring up the rear."

"Don't get any ideas of taking off," he warned, his breath hot on her ear.

A tingle soared down her neck as she said, "Stop threatening me, and be careful."

His smile almost stretched the length of his mouth,

but it vanished before it had a chance. He crept ahead, a blurry moving shadow among the trees. She followed much more slowly, groping and picking her way through the dark ice.

When he'd gone a hundred feet, he dropped the backpacks. They made no sound as he stood behind a tree. He'd spotted something. He waved her forward.

As quietly as she could, she crept up and joined him. They stood on the fringes of an outcropping of rocks that jutted out from the mountain, a sheer drop below.

On one of the rocks, a female coyote stood with two pups. Near them, a steel trap held the paw of her mate, a large male. The female and pups whimpered, while the male licked and chewed at his ensnared front paw. He'd been at this a long time, and his flesh was bitten, torn and bloody. The male's anguish was what she was feeling, along with the fear and helplessness of the female and her pups. She was glad the gleaner hadn't killed again and that she could actually do something to help.

"Please stay here," she whispered. "You'll scare them."

He nodded, but he didn't look happy about it. "I'll find who set that trap on my land, and they'll be sorry they're alive."

By the menacing promise in his voice, Nina had no doubt he'd carry through with the threat.

"Here." Kane thrust a flashlight in her hand.

"Thanks," she whispered and edged forward slowly, not wanting to frighten them. The female leaped protectively in front of her pups.

It's all right. I'm here to help, she communicated telepathically to them. They could all hear and understand her, and it assuaged their fear. She could feel they were beginning to trust her.

Can you? the female asked, doubt in her eyes. *My mate's hurt. In pain. Nothing I can do.*

Let's see. Nina stepped onto the rocks and carefully approached the male. *Don't be afraid. I'm here to free you.*

She shined the light on him and saw he was trembling, his lips snarled over his gums from pain, fangs showing. Nina decided to try and see if her powers worked on the coyote, so she set down the flashlight and gently touched his head with both her hands.

Instantly, he reacted to her touch, relaxing, her magical connection to him breaking down his fear barriers. *You will not feel this. Sleep.*

The coyote's eyes closed, and his head flopped down on the rocks. Instantly, the pain Nina was sensing silenced and she felt a blessed wash of quiet in its place. Then it occurred to her: she still had her powers. They just didn't work on Kane. Why not? Would they work on the gleaner? That was the big question.

Nina fumbled with a lever, and the steel jaws popped open. This wasn't the first trap she'd come across, and it wouldn't be the last. The hinges rasped like rusty spikes being pulled from wood. She gently extracted the mangled paw from the steel teeth. Luckily it was a small trap and had only caught the paw below the joint. The wound looked better than at first sight. The male hadn't chewed much of the flesh off. Most of the tendons and muscle were still intact.

In a fit of rage, she wrenched the trap free from the pin holding it into the stone. Then she flung it off the rocks. It sailed out into the night and down the mountain. It took a while before she heard it hit the ground below.

"I need something to wrap his paw," Nina called out to Kane.

He came forward, and the female coyote must have sensed he was a seniph because she backed up several steps, fangs showing, and forced the pups behind her.

It's okay. He won't hurt you.

She didn't look convinced and growled.

Kane kept his distance so he wouldn't frighten her even more. He set one of the backpacks down and pulled out a roll of gauze and antibiotic cream.

"What else you got in there?" Nina asked.

"Whatever you need," he said, shooting her a sidelong glance. His wicked forest-god leer appeared as he produced a pair of scissors.

Careful not to look into his eyes, she crawled over and grabbed the supplies. She turned her attention back on the male. She slathered antibiotic cream over the wounded paw, then wrapped it.

She turned to the female. *He'll wake up soon. You should not stay here. The poacher who set this trap will come back.*

We'll leave.

Is there a place to warm up around here?

A cave with a hot spring about three yards toward the rising sun.

Thank you.

Nina and Kane left them, listening to the pups nipping and playing with each other as the female licked the male's face.

When they had gathered up their supplies, Kane said, "That was pretty amazing, watching you do that. You showed no fear, though the male looked ready to tear you to pieces."

"Kinda like how you look sometimes," she teased.

"You wouldn't get a warning from me. I just bite." His voice had that sensual edge that sent hot waves into her belly.

She found herself reliving that all-too-short passionate moment they'd shared. Then she scolded herself for it. She couldn't stand another rejection like that again, even if the melding had awakened desire she didn't know she was capable of.

The hard edge left his voice as he said, "You really do have a gift."

"Is that a compliment?"

"Take it however you like."

"A compliment, then."

Nina saw him rubbing his wounded shoulder and said, "Are you okay?"

"Yes."

"You're bleeding again, aren't you?" She couldn't keep the exasperation out of her voice. Was recognizing physical limitations only a problem with alpha shifters, or were all men stubborn like him?

"Not much."

"Why didn't you say something? I know of a cave we can go to." She had hoped to talk him into going to the cave to thaw out her toes, but now there was a twofold reason for going.

"How did you find it?" he asked casually.

"The coyote told me."

"And you believe a coyote?" His lips curled cynically.

"Actually, animals do not have the guile to lie, unlike shifters and humans." She saw his golden brows snap together in a scowl, and she enjoyed getting that little dig in. "The cave's just east of here."

He slid his large warm hand into her gloved one as naturally as if they held hands all the time. The ease with which he did it surprised her. Maybe she'd been too hasty in judging him. Maybe he could open up, a little. Then she felt him responding to her touch, that insatiable desire flowing through him and into her.

He tried to repress it, but it was a marching band parading through her mind. When she couldn't take it any longer without responding, she pretended to trip and broke the contact.

"Oops." She grabbed a tree trunk.

"Are you okay?" He reached for her.

"Yep, just dandy." She leaped back from the pure fire in his hands. If she touched him again, she'd be all over him.

He took her measure with his keen eyes. "Can't take the heat, huh?" A wicked look of triumph gleamed in his vivid green eyes.

"What?"

"You're reading me."

"Am not."

"Uh-huh." A calculating light blazed in his eyes.

It seemed like the more she drew back from him, the more he seemed drawn to her. Maybe it was the feline part of him that enjoyed the hunt. What would happen if she allowed him to catch her? Her last thought sent a shiver through her. She felt him eyeing her as she ignored him and plodded through the snow.

Chapter 10

Nina followed Kane along a narrow rocky path that went straight up. She panted heavily and lagged behind, unable to keep up with him.

Kane turned and shot her an impatient look. "If you take my hand, we can go faster."

"I'll make it." She was determined to keep her distance.

Annoyance forced his brows together as he paused long enough to pull up a limb protruding from the snow. He broke off a good-size straight piece of wood, then handed it to her. "Here, use this."

"Thanks." It fit her hand perfectly and would make a fair walking stick.

He turned and continued up the slope, both packs swaying on his shoulder. Even though he was wounded, he climbed like a goat through the snow.

She watched the confident sway of his wide back, the way his golden hair twined around his shoulders. She couldn't help but look at his tight butt and corded thigh muscles pumping as he climbed. Good golly, he had a nice body. She felt his hardness between her thighs again, his hands on her breasts, his tongue in her mouth. Her breasts tightened, and an unbidden ache settled in her lower belly. She just refused to let go of their woodland encounter. Look at something else. She did, his butt, dead center in her line of sight.

"Do you think we're close?" Nina huffed, more from her own desire than being out of breath.

"Yes."

"You sound really certain."

"I've been here before."

"Nice of you to tell me."

"Didn't think it mattered since you had the coyote giving you directions." He shot her a sidelong glance with an added flash of his white teeth. Mother Nature sure knew what she had been doing when she created alpha seniphs. A male shouldn't be that wicked and tempting.

Thankfully, he turned around, went a few steps, then dropped out of sight.

She hurried to catch up and found the cave's entrance, overgrown with snowcapped honeysuckle and blackberry bushes. A small path used by animals to frequent the cave veered off to the left. She took that path.

Warmth hit her as soon as she entered, and she breathed it in. Her frozen cheeks and lips began to thaw. Pitch blackness surrounded her, and she turned on the flashlight. The cave looked about thirty feet wide, but its height was half that. The rounded-smooth craters of the ceiling dropped drastically, then met a wall of rock with deep fissures. Farther in, the flashlight could not penetrate the darkness. Nina couldn't see Kane. A moment of panic seized her as she thought of his wounds.

"Kane," she called, worried.

"Here." His rumbling voice echoed from the cave's shadowy recesses.

She followed his voice to where the cave walls narrowed and spotted him squatting by the backpacks; the ceiling had dropped so low, he couldn't do much else. The light hit the commanding bone structure of his face, the square, even brow, the perfectly shaped noble nose. For a moment his skin glowed luminescent gold, and the sight of him caused the breath to catch in her throat.

"You're blinding me." He squinted at her, then rummaged through a backpack.

"Sorry," she said, not realizing she'd been staring at him and pointing the flashlight right in his face.

She forced her gaze from him and shined the light on spirals of steam drifting up from a hot spring. The pool was about ten feet wide, clear, rocks shimmering in the bottom. It looked shallow, but the depth of clear water could be deceiving.

She heard a pop, and saw that Kane had opened a bottle of wine. He dropped the opener back in the backpack and held it out to her. "Want a sip?"

"No thanks.

"You have a first-aid kit in your backpack. We really should check out your shoulder."

"We'll leave it for now." He turned up the bottle and took a long pull on it, watching her intently now.

Heat filled her traitorous body as she said, "So, you knew about this cave?"

"Yeah. Came here as a boy with Ethan." He pointed the tip of the bottle toward several crayon drawings on the wall. One was of a stick figure with a cape on it. The other was a better rendering, and she could make out a human form, wearing Batman's costume.

He motioned to the stick figure. "Ethan drew that. Must have been about six at the time." Sadness softened the hard gleam in his eyes.

"You colored the other one?" Nina crouched low and touched the sketch with her fingers. She imagined two happy brothers playing here, unaware that one of them would become a monster.

"Ethan used to call this the Bat Cave. I was Batman, he was Robin." A parody of a smile slid past his lips. "The spring was our Bat Pool. We killed many a villain down at the bottom."

"You must miss him," she said. She felt her heart go out to Kane. It couldn't have been easy for him, watching a brother he cared about slip away from him. For a brief moment she saw through the emotional wall that he'd erected, and she glimpsed a faraway sadness in his expression that wasn't guarded. She wanted to reach out to him and take his sadness away.

"After he left, I did. I wished I could have traded places with him."

"His sickness wasn't your fault."

"I know, but I felt helpless. All I did was run the winery and secretly mail a care package to him every now and then."

"You had to keep it hidden from the pride?"

"Yes, or there would have been hell to pay."

"Then you did everything you could."

"Not enough." He ran a finger absently around the top of the wine bottle.

It broke Nina's heart to see the utter bleakness in his expression.

"Do you really think you can save him?"

"I have to try." The cold aloofness settled back in as quickly as it had come.

It was miserable knowing Kane would be hurt by Ethan's death, but he would have to be destroyed. Thoughts of the pain his brother's death would cause Kane ate at her.

"I hoped he'd think of this place and make camp here, but no such luck." He shrugged his burly shoulders, then took a long draw on the Zinfandel, as if it might dull his disappointment.

Kane could have informed her that there was a chance they might find Ethan here. His lapse just drove home the fact he would sacrifice her or anyone that stood between him and his brother.

Sorrow settled in the pit of her belly. It shouldn't bother her, but it did. What did you expect? He's your kidnapper. And the man who'd made her feel real passion, whether she wanted to admit it or not.

She watched Kane's large Adam's apple working

in his throat; then he set the wine down and shed his jacket. It was hard to miss the inch-long dark spot of blood on his shirt, stark against the blue flannel. His shoulder wound had bled, but not as much as she had imagined.

He turned and eyed her, those spellbinding green eyes shining like emeralds in the light. His tawny beard had thickened along his strong jaw and sensual mouth. With his lumberjack flannel shirt and worn jeans, he looked like a rugged, virile gold miner. He gazed at her like she was the gold vein he wanted to mine. He was so handsome and irresistible her heart skipped in her chest.

"What's the matter?" The wary glint in his eyes softened for a second.

"Nothing. Where're the bandages? It's time to redress your wounds."

"Don't need them."

"Why?"

In seconds he unbuttoned his shirt and had it and the bandages off.

His body drew her attention, and she got an eyeful of his broad shoulders and muscle-bound chest and the golden hair spattering it. It tapered to a thin line and trailed along the ripples of his abdomen, then disappeared below the waist of his jeans. He faced her, hiding the scars on his back from her view, but he kept his eyes on the pool. Blood had soaked the bandage on his shoulder. The spot wasn't wide and looked as if it had stopped bleeding on its own. But the dressings needed changing.

She said, "Please, let me get the gauze."

"Don't. The spring water will do the trick." He made quick work of the laces on his hiking boots, then his shoes hit the ground with heavy thuds. He tore off his socks, exposing perfectly formed feet, thick, strong ankles and long toes. His agile fingers went for the button on his jeans.

Nina realized what he was about to do. She dragged her eyes away and turned around in a hurry. "This is a bad idea," she said.

"It's just a dip. You can join me." His voice was deep and husky and layered with all sorts of erotic promise.

"I don't think so."

"You afraid of me?"

"No." She was afraid of herself.

"Good, 'cause I won't seduce you again."

"Keep it that way." The sexual part of her he had awakened hoped he didn't mean that; still, his rebuff stung.

Something about hearing his jeans hitting the ground in a sensual whisper made her breath quicken. Her fists tightened at her sides as she conjured up an image of what he would look like totally naked, his body dripping with water. She licked her lips and recalled his hard shaft thrusting against the soft flesh between her thighs. She squeezed her eyes tightly closed as a wave of heat slid down her belly and into her groin. But then she recalled what happened after he'd spent his lust. How she'd tried to reach him emotionally and he'd almost bitten her hand and pulled away. No, she didn't need another rejection. Or a man, for that matter. She was happy—well, until

Kane Van Cleave had taken her prisoner and made her feel real passion.

"I'd say you have a choice to make," he said with wry amusement. "Join me, or not."

Nina disliked that languid challenging tone in his voice, as if he'd won and was just waiting for her to cross the finish line.

The air was warm, much better than outside; still, she was freezing. The steam coming off the water was sauna hot. She felt the damp heat from where she stood. Getting naked was a narrow path to disaster, but she was fed up with her well-ordered life. She wanted to do something impulsive for once, live in the moment.

A loud splash sounded behind her. A deep, contented moan issued from the pool. "You coming in or not? It's about a hundred and two degrees. The water feels like silk—"

She couldn't resist any longer and blurted, "Okay, since you promised to keep your distance." She flicked off the flashlight and thought she heard a derisive snort, but he could have been clearing his throat.

Pure blackness surrounded her; then she went to work disrobing. The cover of darkness gave her self-confidence, and she quickly began peeling off her layers of clothes.

When she shed the last of her long johns, she felt the cool air on her skin, sending goose bumps down her naked flesh, hardening her nipples against the inside of her bra. It occurred to her that this was the most impulsive thing she'd ever done in her life. In the past, her every move seemed driven or calculated by the feelings of others, or by her powers. This she was doing because she wanted to. It felt like she was soaring. She couldn't remember one day without the weight of her gift ruling her life, even as a small child. She'd never really felt the freedom and reckless abandon of childhood. Meikoda had said Nina was born with an old soul. She didn't feel old now. She felt young and vibrant and just a little daring to be skinny-dipping in a pool with an alpha shifter.

She unhooked her bra and kicked off her panties.

His breathing grew shallow and rapid. Did the water feel that good?

She groped her way to the pool's edge, the blackness dense and blinding. "Where are you?" she asked. "I don't want to jump on your head."

"Move a little to the right." His husky voice rasped through the cave's emptiness.

Nina froze and gasped. "Oh my god! You can see me." She put her hands over the isle of hair between her legs, using them as fig leaves. Luckily her long hair fell almost to her waist, covering her breasts. How could she have forgotten he could see in the dark?

"Don't cover up, Nina," he said, his voice caressing her name. "You're beautiful." His words were filled with deep sexual overtones that promised ravishment and sensual kisses and something much more intense than their interlude in the woods.

She could feel the alpha magnetism spilling from him like a fountain, filling the whole cave, bombarding her, somehow touching every inch of her body. Her heart began to thunder in her chest; then an ache of arousal poured into her breasts and belly. "You're despicable," she managed to say, her voice tremulous.

"Yes." He sounded proud of that fact.

In the next instant, he showed her how ruthless he could be.

Chapter 11

Kane's innate night vision utilized body heat, and Nina's petite frame glowed like a red beacon in the darkness. He drank in the sight of her, long hair spilling over her quivering breasts, flat waist, sensual bottom and shapely thighs, all exposed for his viewing pleasure. When he first met her, he had thought she was too small. But after seeing her naked, the high, pointed breasts and slight, flaring hips that tapered to shapely thighs, he knew she'd hidden a luscious body beneath the layers of clothes. He had wanted her for centuries it seemed, and seeing her naked and exposed ignited a need to protect her, to cover her, bond to her, drink his fill of her. He had wanted to keep his distance, but he could no more deny his desire for her than he could stop breathing.

He zeroed in on her position and stood up, the water

only waist-deep. In seconds he had his arms locked around her hips.

"Ohh!" she yelped as he pulled her off balance.

He caught her in his arms, then dunked her underwater.

She came up sputtering and spewing and swatting at his chest as she said, "Totally unfair."

"I know."

"I thought you said you wouldn't seduce me again," she said, her voice jagged and unsure.

"I lied. Don't you know better than to trust me?"

"You're despicable."

"I know. What else am I?" He shifted her so that the front of her body slid down his chest, the wet slickness singeing him. When her feet hit the bottom, he clasped his hands around her, pinning her arms at her sides.

"Brute," she said, not struggling now.

He kissed her, taking his time, running his tongue along her lips, nipping her lower lip. No need to rush things this time. This time he'd savor every inch of her, commit it to memory, for he knew this would never happen again. "Anything else you want to call me?" he asked.

"Give me a minute, I'll think of something," she said in a yielding bedroom gasp.

He felt her breathing grow rapid, even as her body become soft and pliant in his arms; his for the taking. He released her hands, and she touched his chest, splaying her fingers, pressing and discovering. Her fingers left a trail of fire on his skin, and he moaned, feeling his nerve endings going crazy, every part of his body demanding more of her attention.

She opened her mouth for him, and he explored the dark, sweet recesses, the taste of her stirring him like no female ever had.

He ran his tongue and the edge of his teeth along her jaw, learning the insatiable taste and scent of her. She tasted so erotic he felt light-headed. Her skin lacked the hair that most seniph females had. It was silky smooth, the texture of cream. "You have the softest skin," he murmured, his hands dipping into the curve of her back.

"Yours is opposite, rough and hard," she said, kissing a line down to his Adam's apple.

The sensation of her lips on his neck almost sent him over the edge. He moved to the base of her throat and ran his tongue along the pulse there. He felt her heartbeat, not only with his tongue but with his whole being. It was an erogenous zone for seniphs, the gate to pure sexual connection.

Kane nipped the delicate skin, careful not to use his teeth, only his lips. He slid his tongue and the edge of his teeth along the hollow above her collarbone, learning the taste and scent of her.

"Kane, this is torture."

"My kind, sweetheart." He kneaded her flesh, working his way along the base of her throat in a primitive pattern that was as old as his culture.

"I don't—" She gasped and said, "Oh, my gosh. This is awesome. I feel strange, and—"

His lips moved back across her neck as he slid a hand

down between her legs. He parted the soft wet flesh there and stroked her.

"Kane…"

"Shh," he said. "Relax and go with it, Nina." He continued to nip and stroke in an ancient rhythm.

She bucked against his hand and cried out as she reached a climax.

She grabbed his hair and forced his face to hers.

Her ardor inflamed him, and he plunged his tongue into her mouth while he felt the softness of her flat belly, her ribs. It took all of his control to slow it down and not make her his.

Her breathing sped up, and she gave a little sigh of pleasure as he cupped her breasts.

She arched against him and moaned softly.

He pulled her against his erection, his tongue mating with hers even as he teased her nipples into hard little nubs. "You feel and taste too good," he whispered, his breath hot and ragged against her lips.

"You, too. Your tongue feels—"

"Different."

"Yes, rough."

"I'm half cat, sweetheart. It's best you don't forget that." He braced himself against the side of the pool and lifted her until her hips rested on his stomach.

"I'm not complaining." She instantly wrapped her thighs around his waist and her arms around his neck, feeling the water's buoyancy supporting her.

He brushed aside her long hair and found her nipple. He flicked out his tongue and licked and suckled. He felt her quake in his arms.

She dove her fingers into his hair and forced his mouth closer to her.

He suckled the delicate flesh, aware of her racing heart pounding in his ears. The sensation of her rounded nipple hardening in his mouth, the feeling of her clinging to him, set him on fire.

She let out a little frustrated gasp. "Kane, I need you."

She settled against his erection.

A primitive yearning to make her his in every way burst inside every atom in his body. He'd never felt this drawn to a female, like she was a part of his essence.

"Kane, please."

He felt her hot plea against his lips, and he settled his hardness firmly against her bottom and moved his hips. She moaned at the friction.

A wave of desire swept through him, so powerful and so heady it caused him to shimmer.

"Whoa!" she said in a husky voice. "That feels interesting."

Kane marshaled his animal force and lust as he saw her gaze down at him. "It's just the energy when I shift."

"No, I mean this." She slid her hips up to his waist; then her hand closed around his erection. She explored the soft tip.

Kane sucked in a ragged breath, testing the last thread of his self-control. "Don't, Nina." He pulled her hand away. "You don't know what you do to me."

"I like this power over you," she whispered, moving her hips seductively against him. "What else can I make you do?" She licked and nipped his throat while her hands explored his chest, his nipples.

"You don't want to find out." Kane took her mouth as he parted her thighs with his fingers. He found the center of her desire and stroked her until she cried out.

When he knew she was on the verge of an orgasm, he slid his hard sheath into her soft magic. He felt her maidenhead only for a second; then she cried out and stiffened.

"Are you okay?" he asked; it took all of his willpower not to move inside her tight, moist heat.

"I am now," she gasped, as if she'd been carrying a burden and just set it down.

"Why didn't you tell me you were a virgin?"

"It isn't something I go around announcing— Hi, I'm a twenty-one-year-old virgin—"

"Thank you for letting me be the first." He heard the emotion thick in his voice before he cut off her words by kissing her. He'd never had a virgin before. It made that primal protective need come alive in him again.

"I've been waiting for this my whole life," she murmured against his mouth.

He couldn't hold back any longer, and he began to move ever so slowly inside her, widening her, letting his hardness fill her, allowing her to get used to the sensations.

Then she began moving with him. Kane felt her taking him deeper into her tight, hot sheath, touching her womb. They rode to a higher plane. He waited until she came with him and they both cried out in unison. Then he felt himself tumbling back to earth. In Nina's arms he'd forgotten Ethan and killing Daphne. He'd forgotten everything. Now realty came crashing down on him.

"I'll throw another log on."

Nina watched Kane sit up beside her. He'd pulled out the sleeping bags from the backpacks and made a comfortable bed for them by the hot spring. The top bag pooled around his hips as he bent and threw another piece of kindling on the campfire. She watched the firelight glowing along his broad shoulders, the muscles rippling beneath his skin.

She touched the scars that crisscrossed his back in thick slashing lines and asked, "How did you get these?"

"Long story." He seemed to grow self-conscious and turned to face her, hiding his back from her view. He nestled down beneath the sleeping bag and pulled Nina into his arms.

She cuddled up against his warmth and laid her head on his chest. A shifter's normal body temperature must be higher than that of a human. His skin felt like an electric blanket turned on high. She just wanted to wallow in his warmth. She couldn't believe how beautiful and hard his body was, and she'd never get enough of touching him. She burrowed closer, wrapping an arm around his waist and settling her ear over his heart. She eavesdropped in on the steady strum of his emotions, detecting reticence, grief and sadness. They were acute and stabbing. She knew the scars must have involved a life-altering tragedy in his life that he didn't want to talk about.

She encouraged him by saying, "We have all night."

He hesitated for a long moment, the only sound the pop and hiss of the fire and his deep, even breaths. Finally he said, "I should start with my father. He was a hard man, demanding, but he was a good provider. He cared about the pride and was well-liked."

Emptiness and unhappiness hovered around the borders of his mind while he spoke of his father.

"But Ethan and I never could live up to his expectations."

"I never knew my father. My grandmother told me he died when I was young."

"Do you miss having a father figure in your life?" he asked.

"Not really. You don't miss what you don't have."

They were quiet for a beat, absorbing that bit of wisdom. Then Nina said, "I'm sorry. I didn't mean to interrupt. Tell me what happened."

"I guess things began to fall apart when Ethan started showing symptoms of gleanerism. My mother noticed the mood changes and the flashes of red in Ethan's eyes before he actually turned."

"And you kept it from your father?"

"Yes, but with good reason. My father was the alpha male of our pride. I guess you know the rule."

"I do," Nina said, stroking his chest softly in hopes that he'd relax. "The alpha is responsible for killing gleaners."

"Yes." He grew quiet and seemed lost in a dark place.

After a moment, his Adam's apple moved in his throat as if it was hard for him to swallow as he continued. "My mother couldn't bear having my father destroy his own son."

"I've heard the ritual is brutal. The alpha shifts and fights the infected seniph—"

"To the death," Kane added.

She hated asking her next question. She'd heard vague stories of the ceremony, but she didn't know all of it. "What if the gleaner wins?"

"Then the whole pride takes part in the killing, and the alpha loses his status."

She wondered why seniphs still lived by such primitive rules. "The brutality alone would make me cringe," she remarked.

"It bothered my mother, too. She was fragile." He picked up a lock of Nina's damp hair and rubbed it absently between his fingers as he said, "She couldn't deal with losing Ethan that way, or any way, really, so she asked for my help and vowed me to secrecy. We arranged Ethan's escape together. I drove Ethan to the airport and put him on a plane to South Africa. I told my father the truth that night, along with a few lies."

He paused, deep in unpleasant memories, then said, "The punishment for letting a gleaner go is to fight the alpha. I knew my mother didn't have a chance against my father, so I told him it was all my doing." He paused, his green eyes darkening to almost black.

Nina could see Kane rushing to defend his mother. His bravery was boundless; she'd seen that in the way he wanted to protect his brother. What an ordeal it must have been, losing an only brother, knowing his mother would pay for the deception with her life. She hated to ask her next question, for she knew the outcome. "Did you have to fight your father?"

"No, I refused." He nodded, his expression marred by remembered anguish. "I went to the council and told them what I'd done. I asked them for the Right of Punishment."

"What's that?"

"A pride law that states the council can determine a fitting punishment."

"You were beaten?"

"You could say that." He nodded.

"I'm terribly sorry." She ran her hand along his back, feeling the deep ridges, hating that he must have suffered for a long time.

After a moment, he seemed lost in thought and said, "But it wasn't as bad as afterward."

"What happened?"

"The council stripped my father of his title and he was forced to fight a contender for alpha—part of my punishment. He killed my father." There was a solemn catch in his voice and in his breathing.

She felt him take a jagged breath, then another until he forced his breathing to normal again. She couldn't imagine the agony and helplessness of seeing his own father's cruel death. No wonder she sensed such darkness in Kane.

He added, "Then I fought the champion and became alpha."

The harsh, merciless tone in his voice sent a shiver

through her as she asked, "What happened to your mother?"

A sad gleam flickered in his eyes. "Her car ran off a mountain shortly after my father died."

"Suicide?"

"I'll never know. But I suspect she couldn't live with my father's death, or Ethan's disease. Wherever she is, I'm sure she's happier."

His loss and sorrow pulled Nina into the bleak dark hell that Kane had lived through. She didn't know how he could bear all that he had. Some people's lives seemed destined to ill fortune and misery, and he'd had his share of it. She also felt Kane's love for his brother. Kane had sacrificed everything for him, including his own life. She didn't want to give Kane another blot on his heart by destroying his brother. There must be another solution in dealing with Ethan.

"I'm so sorry, Kane." Tears stung her eyes as she laid her palm on the side of his cheek, feeling the thick stubble there.

He dropped the strand of hair, tipped up her chin and wiped the tears away with his thumb. He looked deep into her eyes and didn't seem to be speaking to her at all, but to himself. "Why is it that I can forget everything in your arms?" He rolled on top of her, settling his delicious weight down on her.

Nina clung to him. He needed her—that was all that mattered right now. She didn't want to think about what lay ahead. Live for the moment. The mantra echoed in her mind.

Chapter 12

Kane listened to the embers popping in the campfire. Shadows flicked along Nina's long black hair, shooting blue diamonds through it. She lay on her side, nestled in his arms, spent after Kane had made love to her for the third time.

Her head rested in the hollow of his shoulder, her sensuous breasts pressed against his side. Her long hair had dried and blanketed his chest and arm and felt like velvet next to his skin. In fact, everything about Nina felt smooth, delicate and perfect. He'd never felt such inner peace as when he held her in his arms. Her bewitching body, caresses and scent were a salve to his soul.

He listened to her soft breaths and the light sound of her snoring. He grinned, certain he'd never heard anything that gave him more pleasure. She'd definitely deny it if he told her later. He carefully moved her until her head rested over his heart.

She sighed, her hand tightening around his waist, one leg slipping up to rest on his upper thighs. He ran a finger along the downy skin at the small of her back. And he couldn't forget entering her for the first time. When he'd looked into her bright blue eyes and she had trustingly yielded her maidenhead to him. He'd experienced an overpowering need to keep her close to him forever. And it grew stronger with each passing moment he spent with her. He felt it now, and it bothered him, because eventually he'd have to give her up. They couldn't be together. What if he accidentally shifted and he woke to find that he'd done the same thing to Nina as he'd done to Daphne? He wouldn't be able to live with himself. No, he couldn't take that chance. They would both be better apart. The sooner he resigned himself to that fact, the better. Once they found Ethan and made sure he was safely away, he would have to find a way to let her go.

He exhaled deeply; then his eyes grew heavy. Nina's aura was so peaceful, calming and cozy, he found himself drowsy. Try as he might, he couldn't keep his eyes open.

Psssst!

Nina's eyes popped open as Koda's voice woke her. His form materialized in front of the cave's opening, hints of morning sunlight forming halos of bright pinks and orange around his swirling energy.

For a second he was a mass of white fluctuating

light. The intensity dulled, and his features drifted into place. His emotions controlled the color of his image. This morning he must have been angry, for his grizzly bear features were all surging flecks of red mist. He prowled toward her, his massive paws floating on air as he approached. He paused not two feet away and stared at them entwined in each other's arms. He shook his head, then looked down his nose at her.

What have you done, Nina?

A blush heated Nina's cheeks. She'd never had to face Koda in such a compromising situation. It wasn't pleasant having her private life open before him, and she couldn't keep the chagrin from slipping into her thoughts. *I don't need you spying on me, or giving me a lecture.*

Koda bent and sniffed Kane's face. His nose wrinkled as if he smelled something displeasing. *This two-skin is dangerous. He cannot accept his animal side and the urges that go with it. Until he does, he can never truly realize the extent of his own power, nor will he ever be happy or let himself truly care for anyone.*

Who said anything about caring?

I know you have feelings for him, because your powers of suggestion falter when used on him. Your fondness for the two-skin negates your abilities to control him.

So that's why her physical commands didn't work on Kane.

Okay, so I like him. So what? I'm not looking for any happily ever afters. She was practical enough to believe they didn't exist for her. They never had. *I don't* need you lecturing me on my love life. So, why are you here?

I'm here to warn you. You'll have no future with him.

You said get a life. So I got one—not much of one, either. Just a few hours of bliss. Am I not allowed a small smidgen of happiness without your insightful commentaries—that, I might add, are always after the fact? I knew what I was getting into. Angry tears stung her eyes. *Please, leave me alone.*

Beware. Trouble follows this two-skin, and it will follow you, too.

Stop talking in riddles, for goodness' sake! Just tell me what's coming.

You know the rules. Koda gave her a long-suffering look with his airy sparkling eyes; then he disappeared in a blink of bright scarlet dazzling light. His exit looked like a firecracker exploding. He must have been livid.

She glanced over at Kane nestled beside her. His five o'clock shadow darkened the sharply chiseled planes of his face. At the moment he looked peaceful in sleep. A ghost of a smile hovered about his lips and softened his expression. He was so large and intensely male and beautiful she still couldn't believe they had slept together. She wasn't gorgeous like Fala and Takala. Handsome guys weren't attracted to her. She blinked back a wash of tears.

For a few hours he'd been totally hers. She found herself resenting Koda for breaking into her precious few intimate moments of happiness. Spirit guides had no right to do that. No one had that right.

She lifted a tawny strand of hair sticking to Kane's strong, square chin and brushed it back. He moaned softly in his sleep but didn't awaken. She looked over at him and recalled their intimacy. He'd told her she was beautiful and whispered sweet encouraging words to her, but nothing beyond that. Koda's reading of Kane was most likely correct. Even if Koda was right, he didn't have to point it out—especially after she'd just had the most life-altering night of her life. Kane had warned her that he was too hardened to get close to anyone. He'd been honest all along. She had known what to expect, but her heart had a hard time coming to terms with the truth.

Abruptly panic, anxiety, annoyance and a sensation of being trapped snarled Nina's thoughts. The vibrations were close, chilling. Shivers gripped her. She felt her body temperature plummeting. Uncontrollable trembling shook her. Perhaps this was the trouble about which Koda had warned her.

She picked up Kane's arm so she could slip out of the death grip he had on her waist, but he startled awake. Confusion and terror clouded his eyes for a second; then he saw her. Relief flooded his expression as he tenderly stroked her lips with his thumb. "You're all right," he said.

"Of course I am. Why wouldn't I be?" Something had frightened him. She could feel the fear and relief and concern battling each other inside him. His perceptions fought with the shivers gripping her.

"I didn't want to hurt you in my sleep."

Nina realized what was behind his fear. She bent and

kissed him, then said, "You can't hurt me, Kane." You will in the future, but not at this moment. "As long as we're touching, I'll know when you shift and want to harm me."

"You won't be able to escape fast enough."

"I will."

He didn't look convinced, and his face darkened into a severe veneer of doubt and uncertainty.

Another wave of emotion bowled into Nina, and she shook from it.

"What's wrong?"

"I'm sensing a creature's distress. We have to hurry or we might be too late."

In minutes, they dressed and headed out of the cave. Nina led the way. Above her, the sun rose in the east, jutting shades of pink, orange and yellow across the sky. An eerie quiet filtered the air. She couldn't detect one bird's song, one animal scurrying away. The only sound was the crunching of their footsteps through the heavy snow. The same sensation that she'd felt when she'd last met the gleaner. The hairs on the back of her neck stood straight up. Was this the moment she'd dreaded, facing the gleaner and Kane? What would happen if she tried to destroy his brother? How far would Kane go to defend him? Nina knew she didn't have a chance of destroying the gleaner if Kane interfered. A cold sweat broke out on her body. It was hard to think of Ethan as just a monster any longer. He had a brother who loved him deeply. Still, Nina couldn't allow his killing to continue.

The creature's emotions led Nina to a ravine. Huge

rocks jutted out along the walls. At the base, the rocks had cracked and left a recessed nook, large enough for a man to slip inside and stay warm, a perfect hidey-hole.

"Look, tracks." She pointed to the cranny's entrance. The trail led away from it.

Kane passed her and reached the niche first. "Look at this. Two sets of human footprints and drag marks. Something heavy was pulled out of here."

Nina bent down and glanced into the opening. Someone had made a cozy campsite. The snow had been swept out of the hole. A backpack sat near the ashes of a campfire. "Someone was abducted. I must have sensed the emotions of the person being taken."

Kane bent down and sniffed the snow. "Ethan was here." He ran his hands back through his hair, jerking on the golden strands as if he meant to rip them out. "How could they capture him?"

"Good question. Whoever it was sneaked up on him. They couldn't have gotten near him if he knew they were close." Nina let her gaze roam over the area.

Kane scooped up the backpack and opened it. He pulled out a passport. Inside was Ethan's human photo, the red glare of his eyes illuminated by a flash. Kane's eyes glassed over with emotion.

Nina spotted something shining in the snow. She picked up a dart. "Looks like they drugged him."

"Who's responsible for this?" Kane turned, his expression sharpening into suspicion. "Have members of your family taken him?" He grabbed her arms. "Tell me the truth."

"No," Nina said adamantly. "I lied when I told you they knew where I was. They know nothing about Ethan."

"Then who has him?" Kane's fists tightened at his sides, his frustration and anguish gripping his whole body.

Swirling emotions flooded Nina's senses from all sides. She grabbed Kane's arm to warn him, but he must have sensed the danger, for he shoved her behind him.

Two-skins materialized out of the forest, prowling out from behind snow-covered trees, rocks and bushes. Nina stopped counting at thirty. They moved in perfect hunting formation, circling Kane and Nina, sleek lion muscles pumping, fangs bared. Six males, larger than the others, with darker manes, approached them. Scars pocked their furred bodies. One had a brown mane and only one eye. He led the others.

"No sudden moves," Kane whispered to her. "I'll handle this."

She was glad Kane's large, powerful form separated her and the seniphs, but she knew they wouldn't have a chance if the shifters attacked. Even an alpha male couldn't fend off thirty of his own kind. She knew exactly how Daniel must have felt in the lion's den.

One Eye and the five males stepped forward.

"Quinton," Kane addressed One Eye first, then the other five males. "Why is the council here?"

Quinton spoke first. "You've broken trust again, Kane. Betrayed us all. You knew Ethan was in the area, yet you kept it from us. Worse, you haven't destroyed him. You must face a tribunal." When Quinton spoke, his voice, commanding and rasping, came from another dark, cold dimension that lacked human emotion.

Nina's shivers made her whole body quake. The enmity and aggression coming from Quinton alone jackhammered her insides. This seniph was ready to kill Kane. Nina stepped over to Kane's side and slid her hand in his.

He didn't protest, only shot her a hard look. Then he spoke to Quinton. "You have Ethan?"

"You dare toy with us?" For the first time, Quinton's majestic brow wrinkled slightly with uncertainty, but not for long. His anger took over as he roared, "Do not play games with me. You have him."

"I don't."

A woman and two deputies appeared at the back of the group of seniphs. All three wore blue uniforms, parkas and boots. One of the men was squat, fleshy, sporting a bulldog face. The other was lanky and squinted nervously. Nina recognized Clive and Jake, the deputies who'd been burying the animals at the Baldoon farm.

The woman was taller than the two deputies by a few inches. A sheriff's badge gleamed over her left breast. A tight bun at the nape of her neck flattened her hair to her head. She was stunningly beautiful, most likely an alpha female. Was this the Arwan the deputies had been discussing?

The two deputies had their Glocks drawn and aimed at Nina and Kane. The sheriff gave them a command to wait; then she approached them. The measuring way in which the sheriff eyed Nina made her more uncomfortable than she already was.

"Where have you hidden him, Kane?" the sheriff asked.

"Arwan." Kane's lips tightened into a thin line. His razor-sharp eyes bored into Arwan as if he were trying to see that part of her that would betray him.

"I'm sorry, but this is my job."

"I know." Resignation forced a deadpan note into Kane's voice as he asked, "You led them here?"

"It wasn't hard following your tracks from the cabin. I figured you'd go to the cave."

Kane must have been close to this woman. Jealousy stung Nina. Could the presence she had felt and the tracks she'd seen at the cabin been Arwan's rather than Ethan's?

"Where is Ethan?" Arwan asked. "You can't protect him any longer. For your own sake, tell us."

"I have no idea."

"Don't lie, Kane." Arwan's upturned eyes softened when she looked at Kane.

It appeared Arwan cared for Kane in more than a friendly way. Nina felt her green-eyed monster resurfacing.

"I'm telling the truth," Kane said.

Quinton stepped forward. "We'll find out when you've spent some time with the doom demons. Now, go peaceably with us, or we'll force you."

Doom demons? Nina's brow wrinkled in thought. They were a new species she'd never heard of, but it didn't surprise her. Her grandmother had warned her of the many types of demons in the underworld. Even her grandmother, the previous Guardian, hadn't battled all of them. Whatever they were, doom demons didn't sound pleasant.

"Take me, but leave her." Kane motioned toward Nina.

"She knows too much, and she's as guilty as you of hiding the gleaner. She must stand before the tribunal."

"She's done nothing. This was all my fault. Let her go—run, Nina!" Kane shoved her. The air around him shimmered and pulsed; then he shifted. His clothes ripped away with his human skin as he leaped on Quinton.

The other two-skins dove in, driven to a frenzied attack by the sudden violence.

Nina lost sight of Kane, hidden within a huge mass of fur, whirling claws and fangs. She screamed and ran straight into the middle of the fray.

"Freeze!" Shots rang out.

A bullet whizzed past Nina's ear. The loud blast not only stopped Nina but all the other shifters as well. She searched for Kane, but the lion bodies on top of him were snarled together like fallen dominoes. Then she spotted Arwan, gun drawn and aimed at Nina's heart.

"Keep your hands up," Arwan ordered. She scowled at her fellow pride members. "Get off of him. Right now. All of you, *off.*" Arwan's gaze looked frantically for Kane, her expression exposing more than mere apprehension.

Nina prayed Kane was still alive as the animals

parted, some limping away with bites and torn flesh. When she saw Kane at the center, she let out the breath she'd been holding. Minor bites and scratches covered his furry snout and body. His lion eyes were still vicious and wary from the heat of the battle. He snarled dangerously, flashing fangs, crouched and ready to strike again if his enemies came too close. The old shoulder and arm bites hadn't reopened, thank goodness. Nina wanted to get to him, and it took all of her willpower to stay rooted to her spot.

Several seniphs lay on the ground near his feet, their bloody bodies not moving. Quinton was one of them. The other five council lions gave Kane a wide berth, eyes guarded, their spines taut and riddled with wounds. All the two-skins seemed accepting of the violence, as if it were routine. Three female seniphs had cautiously approached Quinton and licked the wounds on his face and body. Nina saw him coming around. She guessed all two-skins thought nothing of their primitive animal natures. But as an outside observer, it was brutal to watch. Her heart still hammered in her chest, and it had left a sick feeling in the pit of her stomach. Almost as bad as having a gun pointed at her, but not quite.

"Kane, you go peaceably, or she dies." Arwan looked down the barrel of her gun at Nina.

Kane seemed to see Nina for the first time since the battle. Impotent rage darkened his green eyes almost to black.

"What's it gonna be, Kane?" Arwan asked.

"You win," Kane said in a frustrated growl that sent shivers along Nina's spine. It sounded so foreign, hearing his voice coming from his seniph body. The huge lion mouth made it deeper, more guttural and fearsome.

"Chain him, and cuff her." Arwan motioned to the two deputies, calling them by name, Clive and Jake. Nina's suspicions had been correct. Clive resembled the bulldog. Jake was the lanky one.

Kane allowed them to shackle his neck and feet. They were the kind of iron chains she had seen used on large boat anchors, a good two inches thick. The padlocks were the size used on treasure chests. They weren't taking any chances of Kane escaping.

Then Jake came over to Nina, pulled off her gloves and cuffed her wrists. Nina could see Kane struggling to control his temper. She knew he'd fight to the death for her. His willingness to save her from harm awed her and caused an oppressive weight to settle on top of her chest. At least he cared for her a little, or was it just his overprotective alpha nature stepping to the fore? Either way, she didn't want him harmed for her sake.

"Hurry it up," Nina whispered to Jake.

At her human orders, he grunted with contempt. In seconds the cold metal clamped around her wrists. He threw her gloves on the ground then trudged through the snow to rejoin Clive.

Arwan crept up beside her. "You go with me, human."

The deputies dragged Kane off, the other seniphs flanking them.

Kane glanced over his shoulder at Nina and said, "You should have run." Remorse and sorrow filled his eyes. His expression was one of total acceptance of his

fate, human in every way and at odds coming from
the face of such a majestic, powerful being. It was the
first time since meeting Kane that Nina sensed any
defenselessness in him. Even when he'd been looking
for Ethan, he hadn't given up hope of finding him. Nina
felt Kane's sadness at having failed Ethan and herself.
In that instant she knew she loved Kane, both sides of
him.

Arwan grabbed Nina's handcuffs, jerking her in
the opposite direction. "Stop gawking and get moving,
human," she ordered.

The jealousy in Arwan's voice came through loud and
clear. Nina glowered at her and wondered what Arwan
had in store for her.

Chapter 13

The loud vibrations of the tire chains on the police cruiser thundered in Nina's ears. She glanced through the wire bars at Arwan driving. The sheriff hadn't said one word to Nina the whole long walk back to the cruiser. Nina could feel the uncomfortable tension rolling off Arwan like water off a roof. She didn't like or trust humans.

Nina decided to wait for Arwan to speak first, for she knew the alpha female in Arwan liked complete control over every situation and if Nina initiated the conversation Arwan would rebel and clam up. So Nina shoved her cold manacled hands down between her legs and stared out the window. The morning sun sat higher in the sky, and Nina had to squint as she looked at the grape orchards and white cleared fields. They were getting close to Brayville.

"You're not just human." Arwan had to speak over the sound of the chains, and her voice sounded shrill inside the closed space. "What else are you?"

"Clairvoyant."

"You reek of witch."

"My sisters call me that all the time." She heard Arwan hold back a snort of laughter and finished with, "But you're just smelling the white magic that makes my clairvoyance possible."

"What's your name?" Some of the brittleness melted from Arwan's voice.

Nina decided it was time to lie. If the seniphs knew her sister was the Guardian, they would surely kill her right away. At least hiding her identity might give her time to plot an escape. "Nina Gray."

"That so?" Arwan didn't sound convinced.

"I'd prove it to you, but Kane burned all my ID when he abducted me."

"You're not willingly with him?" Arwan turned her beautiful hazel eyes toward the rearview mirror and gazed at Nina.

"Well, at first I was his prisoner…." Nina hesitated, unwilling to discuss the twists and turns of their short-lived relationship.

Arwan shot Nina a perceptive gaze, reading the subtext behind Nina's reluctance. "He can be very persuasive."

Had Kane slept with her? Sure he had. He'd probably bedded all the women in the pride at one time or another. "How well do you know Kane?" Nina asked.

"Been best friends since I can remember. Why did Kane take you prisoner?"

"He guessed that I knew he was a seniph." Something stopped Nina from telling Arwan about her ability to sense living creatures' emotions and how Kane had used that power to help track Ethan. Arwan's sudden false sense of chattiness put Nina on guard. She reminded Nina of the popular girl in high school who talked to you only to get information, then dropped you off her radar.

"So, what drew you to the area?"

"I had a job near here. I was on my way home and stopped at the café in Brayville. Unfortunately, we bumped into each other at the door. His aura freaked me out, and I knew he was a seniph then. I didn't hide it very well, because he followed me."

"Oh, I must have been in the restroom, or I'd have seen that." She contemplated the turn of bad luck, then said, "If you know about us, then you must be well aware of all shifters."

"I know more than I need to," Nina said in a deadpan voice.

"Well, that explains a lot." Her eyes turned hard and gleaming as she said, "Then you know that gleaners can't be allowed to live."

"I know. I'm just sorry he's Kane's brother."

"Me, too. I know it looked like I didn't care back there, but I was just covering my butt. Somehow the council got wind of the gleaner killings at the Baldoon place and assumed it was Ethan. They demanded I find the gleaner, and if I didn't I'd suffer the same punishment as Kane." She heaved a frustrated sigh. "I would have protected him if I could. I didn't know you'd both arrived at Ethan's den when we did."

"How did you know where to find Ethan's den?"

"I knew Ethan would stay on the Van Cleave property, and Kane would head for the cabin or the cave looking for Ethan. I figured Ethan would hide near those two areas and seek shelter and warmth there, so I went to both places."

Nina felt another tinge of jealousy. Arwan had probably played with Kane and Ethan in that cave, been a big part of their lives, of Kane's life. Nina had had only a few days with Kane.

At Nina's silence, Arwan continued. "I went to the cabin first. I saw Ethan's tracks, but they disappeared, as I'm sure you found out. Then I backtracked and followed your and Kane's footprints. They led to the cave and then to Ethan's den. I wanted to go alone so Kane wouldn't be implicated, but Quinton insisted the council attend the hunt. My hands were tied. It was damn bad luck that you two found the den at the same time."

"Quinton dislikes Kane? Why?"

"Long story, but the short of it is Quinton is Daphne's cousin, and he's been out for Kane's blood ever since Kane took her life, even though Kane was exonerated for it—hah, looks like Kane got a little of Quinton's blood today." Arwan's lips stretched in a savage grin. "Quinton's lucky he's still alive."

"I'm sure he knows that." This seemed like a natural segue into her next question, and she asked, "What was Daphne like?"

"Her clothes look better on you."

Nina frowned down at Daphne's jacket and at the edge of the long sweater peeking out below it. She'd forgotten she was wearing Daphne's clothes. "How did you know these were hers?"

"Her smell is all over them." Arwan wrinkled her nose, repulsed.

"So, you two got along?"

"She resented me because I was Kane's best friend."

"Jealous type, huh?"

"Not so much at first, but when she couldn't give him kids, she grew insecure and took to drinking. A mean drunk, too. Didn't care who she ran with, either. She was called before the council for drinking with human men and putting the pride in danger several times. Personally, I don't know how Kane stood her. She made his life hell. Honestly, I was glad when Kane ended her life, and so was the council, all except Quinton."

Nina wasn't surprised by the coldness in Arwan's voice. Seniphs appeared to take death in stride, unless they were related and felt a need for revenge like Quinton. Poor Kane. He hadn't confided in Nina about Daphne's darker side. Despite his trying to convince Nina that he didn't believe in love, Kane had cared enough to stick by his barren wife. It gave Nina a tiny hope that they could have a future together—if, and that was a big if—they survived this present danger.

Silence settled between them while they both mulled over Daphne in Kane's life. Then Arwan said, "If you know where Ethan is, it would be better if you told me. I can help him escape."

"You'd do that?"

"Sure. I'd do anything for Kane. He's my friend."

Nina sensed a frosty possessiveness in Arwan's voice, and it prompted her to ask, "How long have you loved Kane?"

Arwan laughed derisively, sobered and narrowed her eyes at Nina in the rearview mirror. "You're good. No one else has ever asked me that."

"It's pretty obvious to me." Nina spoke past the growing ball of emotion threatening to choke her. "Were you two lovers at one time?"

Arwan laughed again, this time with full-blown bitterness. "That's a joke. He's never given me the time of day."

"I'm sorry." Nina felt some of the tension leave her chest.

"Don't be, human, it's none of your concern anyway." Arwan made a face in the mirror at Nina, then said, "Let's get back to Ethan. You didn't answer my question. Do you know where he is?"

"I don't. Honestly, we'd just found the den when you arrived."

"Who has Ethan, then?"

"I wonder if he's still alive."

A Teflon smile stretched across Arwan's lips. "You seem okay for a human. A shame you have to stand before a tribunal."

Nina didn't see one bit of compassion in Arwan's expression as she asked, "Will it be bad?"

"You'll probably suffer the same fate as Kane. Death."

The word tumbled down between them with the force of a dump-truck load of bricks. Nina's fear rose up and clenched her chest until she could hardly breathe.

Kane glanced around at his small cell, a ten-by-ten area with a toilet and solid walls. A set of iron bars spanned the wall that held the door. The air smelled of pine cleaner, stale urine and seniph musk. They'd stashed him in solitary confinement. Beyond the door was a vestibule and another wall of steel six inches thick. Only way in was a solid-steel electronic door. Hannibal Lecter had had it better than Kane. At least Hannibal had had glass.

Kane tugged at the manacles holding his wrists and ankles to the wall. They wouldn't budge. They'd been forged to hold seniphs, and he knew it would take an elephant to pull those chains from the wall. He was wearing only a loincloth that the deputies had given him. The minor wounds he'd gotten from attacking Quinton were still bleeding, but it had been well worth getting them, if only to finally put Quinton down. He knew it would bode ill for him, because Quinton was First Councilman and usually the deciding factor in death sentences. It would have all been worth it if Nina had run when he'd told her. She should have obeyed him. Damn her! All he could think about was how he could get her out of the mess he'd dragged her into.

The buzzer of the security door shrilled inside the cell. The steel-plated outer door slammed shut. An iron key rattled in the lock, and the inner door hissed open. Arwan approached him and said, "I hate seeing you in here, chained like a common criminal."

"What have you done with Nina?"

"Sorry about putting you in solitary, but the council ordered it. And don't worry about your human concubine—she's in a regular cell up front. It's a shame she'll die. I'm starting to like her."

"Don't let them hurt her." Kane pulled on the shackles until his knuckles showed white and the tendons popped on his hands.

"Tell them where Ethan is, and they won't use the doom demons on her." Arwan crossed her arms over her chest, her eyes roving slowly over his body in an appraising way.

Kane noticed she had removed her Glock for security purposes. Overkill, because he couldn't reach her anyway, chained to the wall as he was. "I don't know where he is," he said. "I think someone's setting me up. Telling the council about Ethan, abducting him and then forcing you to find me just when we reached Ethan's campsite."

"I'm really sorry, Kane. I couldn't cover for you and lie to the council about a gleaner being in the area."

"I know. I didn't want you involved. You did the right thing."

"The only person who has a grudge is Quinton."

"I wouldn't put it past him."

"Let me arrange for your escape." Arwan gripped his shoulders. "Together we can find Ethan and free him, too. You don't have to stand before the council. We can leave here and never come back."

"Can you get Nina out?"

"No." Arwan frowned, shaking her head. "Too much security on her, and too much risk. It's you or no one."

"Then I can't go."

"You don't have to die because she will. Why do you care about that human anyway?"

"I feel responsible for her being here. I'm not leaving her. That's final. You can still help Ethan, though. I know he's a gleaner, but he was your friend, too."

"We were close a long time ago." She ruminated for a moment, then seemed to come to a conclusion. "I'll do it for you, not for him. I'll snoop around Quinton and see what I can find out. Please, Kane, consider my offer. There's no need for you to die like this." Arwan's features screwed up in a worried frown, her face not so pretty at that moment. "I can't bear to lose you."

Before Kane knew it, Arwan stepped over to him and kissed him. Her lips were urgent and demanding, the purring in her throat loud and welcoming.

Kane turned his head away, giving her his cheek. "Arwan, don't."

She grabbed his face and forced him to look into her wounded hazel eyes. "I love you, Kane. Please, let me arrange for your freedom. We can leave together. Never come back. Charles can run the vineyard for you and send the money—"

"You've got this all figured out, don't you?"

"Just trying to save your life," she said. "I never dreamed you'd be so ungrateful."

Kane had thought he knew Arwan as well as he knew himself, but this female standing before him was a stranger. "Don't get me wrong, I'm appreciative. I just need you to realize I can never think of you in that way. I only care for Nina." He froze. The declaration that had slipped out surprised him.

"You'd love a human before me," she spat out, bearing all her emotional claws. "First it was Daphne, that alpha bitch. Now this mousy little human." Her expression filled with scorn. "I've stood by you for years waiting for you to love me, Kane. Well, I'm done waiting. You've just lost the best thing that ever came into your life." Her eyes glistened with unshed tears as she turned in a huff and left.

When she buzzed open the outer door, two doom demons blocked her way. They were huge fiends with gray hairless wrinkled skin, purple glowing eyes and horns on the front of their snouted faces. They walked upright and resembled giant anteaters with six human-looking tactile fingers. Long black robes covered the nasty spikes of bone that protruded from their spines. They were demon inquisitors for hire.

One of the demons held a tray of clamps, knives, beakers of acid and various shapes of curved blades used for torture.

"Well, well. Kane Van Cleave. We meet again. It's been some time. Nice to see you again."

Kane recognized the demon right away. He had worked on Kane the first time he'd faced a tribunal on charges of letting Ethan go. In fact, every scar on his back had come from this monster. "Great to see you, too, Grimel," Kane said with hatred in every word.

"You remembered my name. I'm so pleased." Grimel smiled, his big yellow fangs showing. He turned, and Kane saw that Grimel held the same whip he'd used to torture Kane the first time they had met. It was a nasty flaying device straight out of the Tower of London's medieval dungeon. Eight flexible metal lashes were attached to a single clublike handle. The metal strips could be heated to sear the skin during a beating.

"You made certain I couldn't forget." Kane glared at Grimel.

"Yes, I like my clients to remember who marks them—if they live."

Kane saw the tears in Arwan's eyes as she slipped past them. Then the key rattled in the lock as Grimel opened the inner cell door. Grimel's companion smiled at the prospect of the long hours of torture ahead of them.

Kane thought only of how to save Nina and Ethan as he watched the doom demons approach him.

Two hours later, Nina held her throbbing temples and paced the length of a cell the size of a small bathroom. She was sequestered in the middle cell. The two on either side were empty. The sound of her footsteps echoed off the white concrete walls and floor and braided with the country music playing inside the office. From her vantage point, she could see the main part of the sheriff's office. Clive had his feet propped on a desk, looking at internet porn and drooling over two large-breasted naked women.

A German shepherd lay at the foot of his desk, eyes on her, watching her pace.

She reached the wall, turned and rubbed her arms, caught in another wave of the shivers. The buzz in her mind split in two directions, pain and agony coming from two sources. Both were close, originating from somewhere inside the jail. Was one of them Kane? Nina had seen Arwan give the order to Jake to go get the doom demons, but they hadn't come through the main office. Nina had no idea what they looked like, but she had sensed the pall of evil their arrival had brought in the form of the shivers that now plagued her. It bothered her that she had no idea if the emotions were coming from alive or dead victims. Thoughts of Kane's death caused tears to blur her vision. She had to find him and know for sure if he was alive. Dear God! Please let him be alive.

Nina blinked back the tears, turned and paced in the opposite direction. She stopped, rested her forehead on the bars and gazed out at the German shepherd. Then an idea struck her. "Here, doggy," she whispered.

The shepherd stood up and obeyed her command.

Clive had a one-track mind and didn't notice she'd called the dog.

When the shepherd came to her, Nina was glad they'd removed her handcuffs when they had secured her in the cell. It made it possible to stick her fingers through the bars and touch the dog's neck.

What is your name?

Gabriel.

Do you know who is being hurt, Gabriel?

Two lion men.

Where?

One in solitary confinement with torturers. A mental tremble went through Gabriel.

Is this man's name Kane?

I've heard the lion men call him that.

Nina prayed Kane still lived and breathed. *Where is the other person being tortured?*

In the old tunnels under the jail.

Who's hurting him?

Don't know. I'm not allowed to go down there. I smelled his blood down there, though.

Please, help me get out of here.

I'll try.

Who was the second seniph? Nina felt one of the shivers stop completely. A tight belt of fear clenched her chest and heart. Please, please let Kane be okay.

Chapter 14

Three hours later, Nina had all but given up hope on her escape. She could detect one creature still in trouble, but that signal was slowly fading as the other one had.

She heard someone whistling an unintelligible tune. Then Clive walked toward the cell with a tray of food in his arms. Gabriel padded behind him.

The scent of fried chicken wafted through the air, and Gabriel had his nose tipped up, scenting it with a doggy smile on his face.

"Here's your dinner, missy. Don't know why we're spending money to feed you. Gonna kill you anyway, but Carrie makes the best fried chicken this side of the Mississippi. It's a fitting last meal." He leered at Nina's body.

"Thanks." She centered her gaze on the dog and kept the deputy talking. "How is Kane?"

"Can't tell you that. Orders are not to speak to you."

"Can't you even tell me if he's alive?"

"Nope. Most can't survive a second session with doom demons."

"Kane's faced them before?"

"Sure enough, the first time he let his brother go. He lived to tell about it, too, though he ain't a bragger. Keeps to himself since Daphne's death. It's a shame. Poor guy's had a bad run of luck most of his life. Seems to follow him." Clive shook his bean-shaped head. "Good man, though. All the Van Cleaves were good people, save for Ethan. Tragic that one, yes, sir. Real shame for Kane that Ethan has lived as long as he has. Brought a lot of trouble on Kane, I can tell you. Kane's rich as Croesus, but it ain't helped him none. He takes good care of the pride, though. No one can fault him there. I'm thinking that's why the council spared his life the first time. Don't know what will happen this time. Suspect he'll have to die."

Nina's brow wrinkled at the lack of emotion in Clive's voice as he spoke of Kane's death. He could have been discussing the newest brand of toothpaste. "What are these doom demons?" she asked.

"Nasty devils. Gotta knack for torturing the truth out of anybody and anything. You'll find out soon enough."

Worry snarled inside Nina. "I just want to know if Kane's okay."

"If he ain't dead, he'll die soon enough after the

tribunal." He seemed to realize he'd spoken too much and shoved the tray at her. "Here you go."

Nina and Gabriel shared a knowing look; then they both moved in unison.

Nina tossed the tray up into Clive's face.

The dog attacked from behind.

While Clive fought off the dog and flying food, he cursed the animal for being disloyal, then cursed Nina.

She dodged the food and tray clattering to the floor as she wrestled his gun out of the holster. One quick blow, and she clonked him on the head with the butt end.

He fell hard to the ground. Nina grabbed him now and gave him an order to sleep for a week. Then she pulled Clive back against her bunk.

Gabriel gulped down the chicken leg and breast in three bites, then backed off.

She shoved the deputy and the remnants of the tray and the plastic fork and spoon and paper plate under her bunk and covered it with the blanket.

She touched Gabriel's head. *Nice job. Now let's go find the two lion men.*

At the thought of Kane's fate, her stomach clenched in fear.

Nina skulked through the sheriff's office, following Gabriel. The area was small, barely room for two desks and Arwan's office, which was enclosed in glass walls. The shades were open. Arwan wasn't at her desk. Clive's screen saver flashed a rainbow of dots across his monitor. A police scanner squawked somewhere in the room. Her gaze shifted to the front door. Any second, someone might walk in.

Nina touched Gabriel's back. *Where is everyone?*

Don't know.

Which way to solitary confinement?

I'll show you.

Gabriel padded over to a door near Arwan's office. Nina opened it and heard Arwan's loud bawl. "You left them alone with Kane?"

"Grimel told me to stay out," Jake said.

"Now we'll have to pay a fine. The procurator will be angry he's lost two of his best doom demons. And who will torture the human now? The procurator won't be as accommodating since we killed the best inquisitors he has. I'm surrounded by incompetence! Get the bodies out of here. And don't take them through the front door. That's all I need, for the council to see this. Take them out the back and incinerate the bodies. I've already called Elmer and Chris for backup. They'll be here any minute. Don't leave this cell until they get here. Nobody gets in or out. No more screwups, do you hear me?" Arwan's voice warmed to match her anger. "And make sure you put the crystals in the right place. We pay wizard engineers a hundred thousand dollars for an impenetrable magic cell that can hold Hercules, and what the hell happens? We let two demons get killed in it." She was screaming now. "Can't anyone do their job around here? I'm living in freakin' Mayberry. Where the hell is Clive?"

"Feeding the prisoner. What do you wanna do about Kane?"

"I'll get the healer."

Nina heaved a sigh of relief. At least Kane was still alive. He must have passed out, and that's why she couldn't make a mental connection. Footsteps thumped toward her. She told Gabriel to stay, then ran back through the office and quickly slipped back into her cell.

Arwan poked her head into the cell-block area and eyed Nina. "You been fed?"

"No."

Arwan's perfect face, still livid with ire, scrunched up in a frown; then she rolled her eyes and threw up her hands.

"Trouble?" Nina asked, innocently.

"Yeah, and its name is Clive." Arwan turned and stomped away, ordering Gabriel to find Clive.

"He was looking at porn on the internet before he left," Nina called out, hoping Gabriel took her on a wild-goose chase.

"If he's over at the drug store looking at dirty magazines on duty again, I'll fire his butt, then I'll kill him," Arwan said more to herself, though she was furious enough that her voice carried back to Nina's cell.

Nina heard voices; then two men ran past the office, toward solitary confinement. Elmer and Chris? Nina wanted to help Kane escape, but he was passed out, and, with the added guards and special cell they held him in, she thought it impossible.

One lone sensation still pulsed inside Nina, the chill of the pain putting ice in her veins. This must be the second lion man Gabriel had told her about. It seemed the sensations were stronger here in the cell block. Maybe coming from below her. She made sure Jake wasn't around; then she unlocked her cell and slipped out, locking it back. The severity of the shivers led her to several large bookcases standing against a wall. This was crazy. The shivers were stronger on the other side of this wall.

Nina ran her hand along the bookcase, pulling out books. She tapped on the back. It rang hollow. She shoved forward on both bookcases.

Nothing.

She then pushed on the sides. One rolled aside, hiding a bricked entrance. The smell of dry, stale air, mold and mildew wafted through the entrance. She went through and pulled the bookcase back over the opening. Flames burned in sconces on the wall, throwing eerie shadows along the cobwebs floating from the staircase's ceiling.

Halfway down, faint moaning, deep and throaty, drifted toward her. She'd heard that hollow bass-drum voice before. The gleaner? Here? The hairs on the back of her neck stood straight up, but she forced herself to continue down the stairs.

She reached a bricked tunnel that split into two paths. The moaning came from the left side. Her entire body trembled now as she turned that way. She gulped past the lump in her throat and walked the length of the tunnel.

A room opened up before her, and she paused. Shackles dangled along the walls. She spotted Ethan.

Six crystals surrounded him, their red magical rays shooting up to the ceiling. Gleaner containment, thought Nina ruefully. He was in human form, his head and body slumped forward. The iron chains around his feet and hands held him up. He'd been stripped down to a loincloth, his body covered in welts and cuts. A nasty-looking bullwhip lay coiled on the floor near his feet. She had to look away from his battered body. No one should be treated that way. She could only imagine what Kane must look like. A sick feeling coiled in her gut.

"Hey," Nina said, carefully standing behind the crystals.

He started awake, fear of more torture in his flaming eyes. They seemed not as bright as when he'd first eaten. When he saw it was her, he almost looked relieved. "You. Come to kill me, too? Take a number."

"A gleaner with a sense of humor." Seeing him in human form and hideously violated, she couldn't help but pity him. "I'm glad you still have one."

"I try." He shot her a look that was similar to one of Kane's arrogant proud expressions, except for the scary red eyes. His hair was cut shorter than Kane's but the same color. And he was a little smaller than Kane, but he had the same well-developed musculature as his brother. His resemblance to Kane was obvious.

"Why didn't you come to Kane for help?" she asked.

"I didn't want to get him in trouble. That's why I stayed away."

"Why did you come home at all?"

"I had business here."

"What, killing Emma Baldoon?"

"No." He bit the word out and actually looked contrite for a second. "That was pure survival. I came here for another reason."

"To plague Kane?"

"You think I wanted to hurt him? He's my brother."

"You didn't give it much thought when you left the first time and he had to take the blame for letting you go." She suspected there was a selfish streak in Ethan.

He was silent for a moment, his expression battling old ghosts. "I admit, I used to resent him."

"Why?"

"Kane could do no wrong in my father's eyes—'Can't you do it like Kane? You'll never be as good as Kane.' At first I was glad Kane was getting punished for my escape."

"How did you learn of it after you'd left?"

"Through Daphne."

His shame was transmitting to her loud and clear, and she said, "You loved her?"

"I don't know. I think I wanted her because Kane married her. I just wanted one thing he didn't have. I flat-out seduced her, even before she married him."

"Weren't you younger than she?"

"I was seventeen. She was twenty-two. An older alpha. I thought I was hot stuff seducing her over the internet."

"How'd you meet?"

"We had a couple of weekends in New York when I could get away. My mother had a sister in that pride, so I used that as an excuse to fly to New York. I tried to convince her to run away with me, but she married Kane anyway. Then I turned and had to leave. For a long time I hated Kane for not being the one who got sick. He had the vineyard and Daphne. He had everything. I was on the run in Africa. I was so young and dumb," he said with self-loathing.

"Did you stay in contact with her?"

"She wrote to me in Botswana. Before my sickness got too bad, I came back to see her, right before she died." He hung his head and shook it back and forth.

"Did she care for Kane at all?"

"More for his money. And the whole kid thing killed what feelings she had for him. She felt ashamed she couldn't breed. I didn't care or want kids. It was stupid of me to covet her. I'd like to blame my actions on the disease, but it was just plain envy. I know that now." Ethan's eyes glazed over and turned ruby red, the flames there visible for only a second.

"Did he ever know about you and Daphne?"

"No."

"He's never stopped caring for you." When she thought of the misfortune of both brothers, she felt a tug in her heart.

"I know. The things I've done to him, I can never make reparations for."

"I think just knowing you're okay will be enough."

"I hate my existence, the stalking, killing, hiding. I know exactly why my people kill monsters like me. In truth, I'm tired. I can't live like this anymore, killing everything near me just to survive. I hate to think about the lives I've taken just to eat. My life was over the day this disease turned on inside me. I've got nothing to live for."

"You could help Kane."

"Gladly. I want to help him. He's done so much for me I can never repay him." Ethan hung his head.

Nina could feel his remorse and shame and wanted to believe him. But it would destroy Kane if Ethan was put to death. Somehow she would have to find a solution to help them both. "Who did this to you?" she asked.

"Our fine and upstanding sheriff." A snarl pulled at one side of Ethan's mouth.

"She said she didn't know where you were." Nina felt her face grow hot with indignation. "She let Kane take the blame for hiding you. He was tortured to find out where you were. Oh my God! Is she that despicable?"

"You don't know the half of it."

Nina made a decision. She found the iron keys to the shackles hanging on a hook. She grabbed them, then picked up the crystals and moved them aside. "Come on, you can tell me more while I get you out of here."

Later that night, Nina was back in her cell, reclining on her bunk. She tried not to worry too much about Kane, but she couldn't help it. Every time she closed her eyes, all she saw was his gorgeous face.

A piercing shriek split the air.

Nina smiled. That must be Arwan throwing a tantrum at finding out her dungeon prisoner had vamoosed. After speaking with Ethan and learning all about Arwan, they formed a plan that would free Kane and take down Arwan. She needed to be stopped. The things that Ethan had imparted about Arwan gave new meaning to the words *artfulness* and *cunning*. Nina was willing to bet no one in the pride knew what their sheriff was capable of.

Nina had helped Ethan drag Clive's body down to the tunnels, and he promised to leave him tied up somewhere and not to harm him. Nina would have escaped, too, but she had to remain in order to carry out their plan. She wished she could get to Kane and warn him about Arwan, but he'd find out at the tribunal. Everyone would.

Nina hoped she'd done the right thing in trusting Ethan. He had seemed sincere about helping to free Kane. She didn't want Ethan to die, and they had avoided the uncomfortable subject, but she knew Ethan was sacrificing himself by carrying through their plan. He had agreed to come to the tribunal. There was no other way.

Yes, there is. He doesn't have to die, you know. Koda shimmered into her cell, his airy form yellow gold this time. He took up most of her squatty little cell.

What? Nina frowned at him.

Die. Koda repeated.

After learning of Ethan's contriteness and his willingness to help Kane, Nina had shared an unbreakable connection with him. She didn't want Kane's brother harmed, just his killing stopped. Koda in his infinite wisdom knew that.

How can we save him?

I can take him to Sehsola.

Why didn't I think of that?

Because you're not a spirit guide, and you've had your mind centered on getting yourself in trouble.

I don't need a lecture right now, thank you very much.

Always a pleasure to help you. Koda's tone was on the snide side.

Nina rolled her eyes heavenward. *Tell me, is it allowed? Can you take Ethan there?*

If he agrees to go.

I'll have to convince him.

Tell him he won't be alone. There'll be other outcasts there.

Yes, you're right.

Sehsola was a magical dimension created to hold truculent supernatural beings who were a threat to earth's inhabitants. Maiden Bear had created it long ago. All past Guardians had used it, if they took pity on a defiant enemy. Nina felt certain Fala would be using it, too.

Thank you, Koda, you've been helpful.

Aren't I always? Koda rocked back on his hind legs and sniffed haughtily.

Honestly, not really.

He dissolved in a huffy poof.

Come back. Tell me how Kane's doing.

Nothing.

She hated when he disappeared like that. She curled into a ball on her cot and imagined Kane's strong arms around her. That may never happen again. She chewed on her lower lip and felt a spasm of pain in her belly.

Chapter 15

The next morning, Nina walked beside Jake as he led her into the courthouse to the tribunal. She strode up the front steps, the links of her handcuffs rattling and blending with their footsteps. Snow had been removed from the portico, exposing solid gray granite stones. She passed the massive Romanesque columns and felt intimidated by them. A seniph with a squirrel face and squat body, clad in a yellow robe, stood at attention near the door. He was already opening the heavy oak door for them to enter.

The hinges rasped out a solemn, haunting groan. The discordant sound went through Nina and made the lump in her throat tighten. Was Ethan already here? She prayed he'd been telling her the truth about wanting to help Kane. The snow-covered streets seemed deserted, all the businesses closed. Was the entire pride attending the tribunal?

Jake led the way down a hall and paused at a second set of doors. The doorkeeper's Beefeater expression never wavered as he avoided making eye contact. His yellow robe hissed softly as he opened one of the massive oak doors.

They walked through.

The door slammed and locked behind them.

Loud voices suddenly stilled.

A sea of faces stared at her, judging her. A collective wave of suspicion and repugnance thundered at her, almost doubling her over. It was like hearing a thousand cats purring directly into her head. She wanted to rub her throbbing temples, but the handcuffs stopped her.

The whole pride must have turned out for the tribunal, all in human form. She stiffened her spine and her courage. You can get through this for Kane.

The courthouse didn't adhere to the human's judiciary design. Shaped more like a miniature coliseum, it held four galleries and circled a lower arena, where she stood at the moment. Near her sprawled a large ring, cordoned off by iron railings. At the front, a curved dais held the six council members, all robed in black. Gold honor stoles draped their necks and fell down their chests. What looked like hieroglyphics was embroidered in black on the stoles, which harkened back to the seniphs' arcane beginnings. She wondered if they'd been doing this ceremony since Tutankhamen's time. Had he been a seniph, too?

Quinton sat front and center. Bruises and gashes

dotted his face and neck. His lower lip looked torn and twice the size it should be. His bad eye was all white and added an even more zombielike quality to his face. He didn't appear at all happy or at all impartial from the Pontius Pilate-glare she was getting.

Nina didn't realize she'd paused until Jake gave her a little nudge. The rotunda's acoustics were phenomenal, and her footsteps echoed like bass drumbeats in the ensuing silence.

"Bring in the other accused," Quinton barked and pointed to a robed bailiff who stood at the end of the dais.

The bailiff disappeared through a door behind the platform.

After a moment, he reappeared. Arwan followed him, looking very official and trustworthy in her sheriff's uniform. She looked bold and beautiful and all official business, her platinum hair braided in a chignon, her hazel eyes sparkling like hand-blown glass, her cheeks rosy red. She captured the attention of every male in the room. And she walked with the confident air of a woman aware of her own feminine power and her ability to manipulate any one of them.

Where was Ethan?

Kane walked in behind her, his chains rattling like Jacob Marley's ghost.

A collective gasp erupted from the assemblage.

Nina sucked in her breath. Kane's head had been shorn; only stubble remained on it. He wore a loincloth, and she could see the deep lacerations over his muscular legs, stomach, chest and arms. They matched the scars on his back. There wasn't one place on his beautiful body that didn't look ravaged. Dear God! She wanted to go to him, but when she took a step toward him, Jake stayed her with a hand on her shoulder.

He said, "Stay where you are."

Kane saw the exchange, and his eyes shot green fire at Jake. Then his gaze met Nina's. The remoteness and detachment in his expression frightened her. He had reverted back behind that wall he had built around his heart. He didn't let his gaze linger long, and it shifted to Quinton.

"Lay out your claims against me and the human," Kane said, motioning toward Nina while avoiding eye contact with her.

She felt her emotional connection to Kane slipping away by the second.

Quinton pulled out a scroll that looked made of papyrus and unrolled it. His fat lip snarled as he began to read, "Kane Van Cleave, you are accused of bringing a gleaner into our midst, harboring said gleaner, lying to this council, the sheriff and your pride. You also jeopardized the pride by abducting a human, mating with her without approval—" all the females present gave a loud gasp at this "—and eliciting her help in your subterfuge."

Nina pursed her lips and frowned. Kane had told her they brought humans into the pride to eliminate inbreeding, but he hadn't told her they needed approval first. So Kane had been breaking another law by sleeping with her. It didn't seem fair.

"What say you to these charges?"

"Guilty."

"No!" Nina yelled.

"Quiet." Quinton looked down his nose at her from his high seat. "Humans are not allowed to speak in a tribunal."

"Even when I know the accused is lying?"

Another gasp from the gallery.

Kane shot her a "butt-out" glare. "I am guilty and take full responsibility," he said. "The human had nothing to do with it. Let her go."

One of the council members with a gray goatee and a gouge over his right eye spoke. "Kane, you know we cannot do what you ask. She is a risk to us all."

"I kidnapped her and forced her to help me."

"He's lying," Nina said, impassioned to save Kane from his own sense of honor. Where was Ethan, damn it!

Quinton pounded the dais with his fist. "Quiet, all of you!"

Silence grew so heavy in the air it throbbed against Nina's eardrums. From years of hunting, seniphs had a way of stilling their breathing and bodies. She heard only her own heartbeat and breaths booming in her ears.

Another council member broke the hush. "Let the woman speak. I wish to hear what she has to say." He addressed Nina. "Do you have proof of these accusations?"

"I do." Though he's not here yet.

Several other councilmen nodded and voiced their agreement on listening to her.

Quinton relented. "Very well. Speak then, witch."

She wanted to say, "First of all, I'm not a witch," but she kept to the subject. "The real guilty party here is Arwan."

Another sharp inhale from the onlookers. Arwan stiffened and looked at Nina as if she wanted to rip her eyes out and eat them.

"How so?" Goatee asked.

"Ask her why she imprisoned Ethan in the dungeon of the old jail."

Kane's eyes widened in surprise.

"She's lying," Arwan ground out. "Kane has hidden Ethan away. Not even the doom demons could get the truth out of him."

Quinton looked at Kane. "If you have any loyalty to this pride, tell us where he is."

"I don't know."

"He doesn't," Nina spoke up. "I escaped my cell and found Ethan in the basement. He told me himself that Arwan put him there and tortured him. She has made fools of you all. I let him go."

Another twitter of disbelief at Nina's bravado.

"Liar!" Arwan bawled. "I had no reason to imprison Ethan. I would have destroyed him if I had found him. And she expects us to believe that Ethan didn't kill her with his burning powers?"

"Magical crystals were draining his strength and keeping him under control," Nina said.

Arwan laughed out loud, mockingly. "Another lie." She walked along the dais, meeting the eyes of each council member. "Are you going to believe this slutty witch over me?"

"No," came a loud cry from the bystanders.

"It's the truth!" Nina cried.

"Silence!" Quinton bellowed, his voice carrying with a foghorn's intensity. The room quieted; then he said, "If anyone else speaks, I'll clear this court."

A hush blanketed the air, but Nina felt the animosity for her rise a hundred points. If looks could fry, she'd be well done by now. What if Ethan didn't show up? Had she misjudged him? She might have signed Kane's death warrant by trusting his brother to do the right thing.

Kane stepped forward, his chains rattling. "The witch is lying. I'm guilty. Sentence me, but let her go."

Nina looked askance at Kane, but he wouldn't look at her and missed it.

Quinton said, "She's wasted enough of the court's time. Kane, face your peers for sentencing."

Nina wanted to scream that Ethan could confirm the truth of her words, but she knew it would be futile to argue with Quinton.

Kane turned to the seniphs in the gallery. He didn't bow his head but looked straight into the eyes of each shifter there.

"You can no longer hold the alpha. You will be stoned to death in accordance with our laws, at sunrise tomorrow morning."

Some of the females wailed aloud. Nina felt as if her insides were being pulled from her body.

"Do you accept your fate?"

"I do." Kane's baritone carried loudly through the court. "What about the human?" Kane asked.

"She will be bound and stoned with you."

"No," he ground out. After a moment his eyes gleamed as if he remembered something, and he blurted, "I invoke the Law of Champion in her behalf."

"What is that?" Nina whispered to Jake.

"Instead of being stoned, a champion will fight for your life," Jake said.

"What if I don't want that?" Nina glowered at the side of Kane's head, because he refused to make eye contact.

"Then you die with Kane."

Louder, Nina said, "Thank you all the same, but I turn down your law. I'd rather be stoned."

"Then I accept for her." Kane cut his eyes at her, one brow arching cynically.

Nina didn't see one hint of the man who had held her and made love to her. This Kane was aloof, cold, hiding behind the emotional barrier he'd erected. Pain squeezed the region over her heart. She turned away from Kane and asked Quinton, "He can't do that, can he?"

"Yes, for he's admitted he's the reason you are involved in these charges."

"Well, just peachy," Nina said. "I don't have a choice, it appears. What kind of kangaroo court is this? Other people can choose what affects you, no one listens when you're telling the God's honest truth—"

"Quiet." Quinton peered down his scabbed and swollen nose.

"It has been done. A champion will be chosen."

Nina tried to cross her arms over her chest in a huff, but the handcuffs pulled at her wrists and she grimaced and lowered her hands.

Quinton spoke to the gallery. "Anyone willing to champion this human step forth."

Nina thought Kane would be the first to stand up for her, but he didn't move. She watched as ten males stood up and walked down the gallery isles. All were young, muscular, cocky and eager. One towered over all of them. He must have been seven feet tall, barrel-chested, with linebacker-size shoulders and arms. A shock full of curly black hair stuck out all over his head. He was the most frightening of them all.

Nina bent near Jake again. "I didn't think anyone would stand up for me because I'm human."

"Don't get a big head. We only tolerate humans. They are competing for title of alpha."

"Oh—wait! Does that mean they'll fight Kane?"

"Yes."

"But he's wounded. It won't be a fair fight."

"He'll die in battle and save face. A true warrior's death. It's better than being stoned."

No, no, no! Kane was going on a suicide mission to save her. "If my champion is defeated, what happens?" Nina asked.

"Kane will continue to fight until he's defeated."

"Oh, no!"

Jake's gaze roamed up and down her body. "The winner also wins you and keeps you as a concubine. You will never be able to leave the pride."

"Nice." Nina watched as the ten men lined up before

the dais, facing the crowd. One of them, who had a beaver face, winked at her. She averted her gaze as quickly as she could.

Quinton waved a hand toward the group. "Choose your champion."

Nina stepped forward, but Jake grabbed her shoulder and pulled her back. "Not you," he whispered in her ear.

"Wait a minute, this is my champion."

"The person who invoked the law chooses."

"What kind of archaic rules are these?" She shot him a look of mute appeal and dread as she wondered which shifter Kane would choose.

Kane looked each man in the eye then pointed to the Jolly Dark Giant. "I choose Tibor."

Nina felt the pit of her stomach drop. No, no, no! Tears filled her eyes and spilled down her cheeks. Ethan, where are you?

Ten minutes later, Kane listened to the catcalls and whoops from the gallery as he circled Tibor inside a metal arena that had been set up in the courtroom's center. Some seniphs were in favor of Kane. Most wanted Tibor to be vindicated. Two years ago, Tibor had challenged Kane for title of alpha. Kane had won and spared Tibor's life. Because of that act of mercy, Tibor had been the brunt of jokes for two years. Tibor had an ax to grind, and Kane knew this fight would be to the death and no mercy would be involved. And Nina would at least have a life.

He had a hard time keeping his gaze away from Nina.

Her vivid blue eyes gleamed with worry, disappointment and a tenderness that tugged at his insides. And the tears. He couldn't stand to think he'd made her cry. He hated that he'd dragged her into this, and he hoped she forgave him. The moments he'd shared with her had been the happiest he'd had in a long time. But he knew reality would come back to forge a path between them. He should never have let himself grow close to her. Never.

And where had she come up with that lie about Ethan? He didn't believe she'd spoken to Ethan and that Arwan had imprisoned him in the dungeon jail. Arwan may have had a crush on Kane, but she would never stoop to such lies. She wouldn't betray him like that. Yes, she had brought the council to Ethan's den, but she had just been protecting her own life. Maybe Nina was just trying to protect Kane and delay the inevitable. But who had taken Ethan? And was Ethan dead already?

He was glad he'd remembered a way to save Nina at the last moment. At least she wouldn't have to die. Thoughts of Tibor with his big beefy hands all over delicate little Nina made jealousy pour through his veins like hot lava, his beast's anger rising like a high tide within him.

They had shifted to fight, and Tibor in lion skin was an impressive sight, even to Kane. He outweighed Kane by seventy pounds and was half a foot taller. The muscles beneath his fur rippled as he crept slowly around Kane. Kane could smell the fear pheromone coming through Tibor's sweat glands, and it was a heady smell for the beast in him. He felt the need to spring building in him, the need to sink his teeth into flesh, the need to dominate. *Don't be in a hurry. Concentrate on the eyes and wait.* The attacker never had the advantage. It was the second blow of a careful defender that did the most damage. He'd learned that from his father.

Tibor attacked, jaws and claws thrashing.

Kane leaped over his opponent and aimed for his neck. He felt Tibor's jaws sink into his haunch.

Kane bit Tibor's throat, but his aim was off. He had a mouthful of fur and skin. Not the windpipe.

Tibor recovered and slammed his body into Kane. All Kane could see was the killing gleam in his opponent's eyes.

Chapter 16

Nina couldn't stand it any longer. She might lose her life, but she couldn't watch Kane die right before her eyes. She grabbed Jake's arm and commanded him to sleep.

He fell at her feet.

She hopped over him and ran for the makeshift arena.

"Get her!" Quinton yelled.

Nina was already over the iron rail and inside the ring. Tibor's and Kane's massive jaws were going at each other as they rolled on the ground. After three tries, she managed to latch her handcuffed hands onto Tibor's tail. She gave him an order to sleep. He tumbled over and thumped against the floor, eyes tightly closed, lips blood-covered and still snarling.

The spectators screamed obscenities at her for

interfering, and she wondered if this was what it had been like for the gladiators of Rome. Some were leaping down from the gallery, shifting. They bumped into each other and began to fight among themselves. Utter chaos.

Someone pulled the emergency fire alarm, and the sprinkler systems rained down. Nina could hardly catch her breath for the water hitting her face. This captured the attention of the seniphs, too. True to their feline nature, they didn't look happy about getting wet.

Nina saw them sputtering and shaking off water as she ran to Kane. He rose, shifting into human form. He was naked, blood leaking from the bites on his body.

He said, "You shouldn't have interfered. It will just make it worse." The water hitting his wounds caused him to flinch in pain.

Nina felt someone grab her from behind. Arwan called out, "Watch her hands."

A small contention of chaos still continued at the main door. Through the huddled fray, Nina caught quick glimpses of Ethan's face. He'd made it. She wanted to leap with joy, but all she could manage was a long, ragged exhale of relief.

One of the contenders, Beaver, jerked Nina to her feet from behind and locked her arms against her chest. At the same time, six men leaped on Kane and stopped him from rushing to Nina's rescue.

She struggled to touch her captor to give him an order, but she couldn't break her hands free. Beaver had a death grip on her arms. She stopped struggling, her attention drawn back to the door.

Ethan tossed three seniphs up against a wall like they were tennis balls. He warned them he didn't want to hurt them, but he'd kill them if they attacked again. His eyes had such a killing flame in them that the seniphs backed off out of fear. The pride members who'd formed a closed ring around him also parted.

The sprinklers had stopped, and Nina had a clear view of Ethan. Their eyes met and connected for a second. His expression said, "Hey, I made it. Don't be angry."

Ethan turned to the dais where the councilmen looked stunned. "I wish to be heard. Then you can do what you will with me."

"No," Kane blurted as two men dragged him to his feet and clamped the chains back on his arms and legs. One of the men was licking the blood off Kane's hands.

Ick. Nina had forgotten how much seniphs (no matter what skin they were in) liked the taste of blood. She shifted her gaze back to Kane. He knew Ethan was making the ultimate sacrifice. He seemed to be oozing torment from every pore. She could feel it like a rainstorm inside her mind.

Ethan shook the water from his face and said, "Don't worry. I wish to clear your name, brother, and set the record straight. It's time." Even though Ethan's eyes flashed flames, Nina saw flickers of compassion for his brother there.

Nina felt her heart softening toward Ethan.

Arwan stood in front of the dais. She reached for her gun. Quinton had been watching her, and for an old seniph he moved with light-speed reflexes. He leaped over the dais and knocked the gun from her hand. They stood snarling at each other, Quinton with his blind eye looking monstrously ominous and Arwan looking deadly in her stunning beauty.

Quinton said, "Yes, we will hear what the gleaner has to say." He growled at several of the robed porters to cuff her.

Arwan's gaze bored holes in Nina.

Quinton walked around and resumed his seat, his authoritative voice ordering seniphs back to their soggy seats.

Reluctantly, they sat and waited.

Ethan strode past the arena and stood before the council. "My brother did not know I came home. He had nothing to do with it. But she did." He pointed to Arwan.

A collective disbelieving gasp whispered through the galleries.

Nina shot Quinton a self-satisfied glance; then she looked at Kane. He appeared shocked and rapt as he avoided her gaze.

Beaver finally turned Nina loose, and she smiled a prim "thank you" at him, but he looked so absorbed by Ethan's testimony, he didn't notice. Everyone ignored her, including Kane.

Goatee asked, "Now we will have the truth. Why did you come here?"

"This is not something I like to admit, but I have been blackmailing Arwan for years."

"For what?"

"She killed Daphne."

The spectators gasped.

Quinton looked confused and leery. Shock turned Kane's expression into solid unreadable rock.

"He's lying," Arwan gritted out, then snarled at the two guards holding her. "You're going to believe a gleaner?"

Quinton's face bulged with irritation. "Explain." He picked up a towel one of the robed guards had brought each councilman and angrily scrubbed his face.

"I thought I wanted Daphne." Ethan cast an apologetic glance at Kane.

Every muscle in Kane's body tensed, veins throbbing dangerously in his neck.

Ethan seemed unable to look at his brother any longer, and he turned back to the council and continued. "I came home to persuade her to run away with me, but like today, I was late. I walked in on Arwan as she was staging the crime scene to make it look like Kane had killed Daphne."

"Prove it!" Arwan yelled.

"I have pictures. That's why she chained me in the basement and tortured me. She wanted to know where I'd hidden the evidence. But Nina found me and let me go." Ethan smiled at Nina, his expression almost kind.

"Just cheap words," Arwan insisted.

Jake, who had awakened when the sprinklers let loose, now stepped forward. "She stole knock-out drugs from the department. Clive and me saw her do it. She acted real weird and said she needed them for a bear hanging around her house. I didn't connect that to the death of Daphne, until just now." Jake turned to Kane. "I'm sorry."

Kane nodded, but looked too betrayed and stunned to acknowledge him.

Quinton said, "Why did you blackmail her?"

"Because I needed money to live on. I couldn't contact Kane for it. I knew you'd be reading his mail."

The brothers shared a surreptitious glance. Nina remembered Kane admitting to secretly helping Ethan when he could. By remaining silent on that score, Ethan was protecting Kane and rising in Nina's esteem.

"So why did you come here? You could have blackmailed her from Africa."

"She refused to pay. I came back to force her...and—" he paused and hung his head in shame "—to tell Kane the truth. I wanted to square things with him. And, too, I'm tired of living."

"Then you've come to the right place," Goatee said.

Ethan looked at Kane. "I just need to know that you forgive me."

Kane nodded, his eyes glazing over.

Quinton said, "Enough." He turned to Arwan. "You have lied to the pride and abused your rank. You have lost all privileges granted you by this pride. Your name shall never be spoken again. You will fight all challengers for alpha female. And if you survive, you will be stoned by the pride." About fifteen young females looked wild-eyed and eager at the prospect of fighting Arwan. "You—" Quinton pointed at Ethan "—will face your brother in battle, and if you live you will be bound and stoned."

Nina couldn't remain silent any longer. "Please, may I speak?"

Quinton's swollen mouth stretched with impatience. "Very well."

"I beg you—" she swept her wet arms toward the gallery "—all of you, to have compassion for these brothers. Haven't they suffered enough? You would have them fight and kill each other. Where is your sympathy, your sensitivity? I know there is a human side to each one of you. Seek it out. Have mercy on Kane and Ethan."

"There is no other way for a gleaner," a balding seniph in the gallery shouted.

"Ethan doesn't have to die. I know of a way to save his life, and he'll never harm this pride or anyone else again."

"You do?" Ethan's brows snapped together.

"My white magic has access to many dimensions. One is a place called Sehsola, where creatures like Ethan can live without harming others."

Quinton asked, "Who are you, witch?"

Now might be a good time to tell the truth, so she said, "Nina Rainwater."

The galleries quieted. Tension gelled in the air.

Arwan said, "I knew you were lying about who you were."

"That makes two of us," Nina said with a small smile.

Quinton cleared his throat, clearly looking for the

best political approach he could find. "Do you share the blood of the new Guardian?"

"She's my sister."

"That's why we must let her go." Kane finally spoke, but he refused to look her way.

"She knows about us." A woman spoke from the gallery.

"And you know my sister is the Guardian. What is keeping you from exposing her to the humans? We can keep each other's secrets."

"We certainly don't want the wrath of the Guardian upon our heads," Goatee said, the other members nodding their agreement.

Quinton mulled this over in his mind. Then he said, "We'll put it to a vote." He gazed at the seniphs. "All in favor of this witch's plan, stand and be counted."

Almost the whole body stood in unison.

"Very well, the pride has spoken." He shook a finger at her. "But you must prove that the gleaner is gone from our world."

"I can. My spirit guide will witness it before you." Nina hoped that she could talk Koda into it. He tended to be shy when appearing before others.

Nina happened to catch Kane's eyes. His expression never softened, but he mouthed the words, *Thank you.*

She wanted to say something back like, "It's nothing. I'd do it again for you. A hundred times if I could hear you say you want me."

In that instant, Kane turned away from her and faced Quinton. "I'm prepared to face my punishment."

"What punishment?" Nina interrupted. "He's innocent."

"He knew his brother was here and did not attempt to destroy him, nor did he let anyone know. It's an inexcusable offense," Quinton said.

"He let Arwan know," Nina said, since Kane wouldn't speak up in his own defense. He seemed perfectly resigned to his own death, and it made Nina want to smack him hard and say, "Fight for your life, for me, for us." What she did was stand there, heart aching, and she shoved an angry, accusatory finger at Arwan. "She's the one who kept it from you."

Arwan rolled her eyes.

After a one-eyed glower in Arwan's direction, Quinton addressed the whole pride. "That is not his only offense. Kane took a human and put the pride in danger."

Nina wished he'd stop emphasizing the term "human" as if it were the name of a new strain of Ebola. Warming to her cause, she said, "These offenses might be great to you, indeed, but they are not unforgivable. Surely, caring for a brother does not warrant a death sentence." Nina walked down the dais, meeting the face of each member. She had always been a shy, unassuming person, but now she felt a burst of boldness that surprised even her. She would speak before millions if that's what it took to free Kane. The quieter and more aloof he grew, the more determined she was to save him.

"Don't any of you love someone or something so much you'll sacrifice everything you possess, including your principles, to protect it?" She paused and waited.

The silence was so dense, Nina could hear her own heartbeat racing in her chest.

After a moment of the members looking at each other as if waiting for someone to speak, one of the white-haired council members finally said, "I understand what she is saying. Kane's loyalty to his brother is admirable. Twice he risked death to save his brother. He has proven his allegiance to us time and again. What would we do without the Van Cleave wealth? His family has always supported and protected us. And let's not forget he's our alpha. We should spare him."

"Spare him, spare him." A group of young females sitting on the right side of the room began the chant. It swept over the crowd, getting louder, feet and hands joining in.

Quinton bellowed, "Quiet!"

The chanting stopped with a few loud shouts.

"He should be spared," Goatee said. "The pride has spoken."

Quinton narrowed his eye at the gallery, clearly not happy with the turn of events. Then his gaze shifted to Kane. With Quinton's battered face, it was the ugliest look Nina had ever seen. After his face contorted in vacillation, dislike, resentment, he bent and with an impatient wave of his hand caused the council to huddle together.

They argued quietly for what seemed like years, but was only a few moments. Then they separated.

Quinton addressed Kane. "Alpha, your life will be spared, as long as you have no further contact with this *human*. She has caused enough trouble here."

That's nice. Somehow she was being punished for this whole mess. She guessed humans made easy scapegoats.

"Do you accept these terms?" Quinton asked.

Kane hesitated, finally glancing at Nina. His green eyes turned to obdurate jade, his usual proud warrior demeanor washing over his expression as he raised his square jaw an inch, the lights shining off his shaved head. His hair had been strikingly beautiful, and she remembered running her hands through it as they made love, but he looked equally gorgeous and all rugged male with no hair at all.

"I do not," Kane said. "I won't be dictated to when it comes to seeing the human."

Was this Kane's way of saying he cared about her? Or was it his pride talking? He looked at her with such harsh intensity that it frightened her down to her core. It was a quelling look, a goodbye look. Now would be a really good time for Kane to show some kind of feeling for her. That she mattered to him, that the short time they had shared together had registered on his emotional meter. But he only stared straight through her like she didn't exist. Was he still so hardened that he couldn't admit he cared for her? She couldn't see a hint of feeling or softness in his eyes. There were too many minds bombarding her to sense what he was feeling. Her impressions were all gnarled and cluttered. If she could just touch him, but she had a feeling he'd pull away.

"But—" she said, making a final protest.

Kane interrupted her with a low growl. "Enough, Nina. Take Ethan to safety now."

Kane's handsome features blurred behind her tears.

Quinton addressed Nina. "Go, take the gleaner with you and never darken our borders again. Send your—" he faltered over his next words "—spirit emissary to us when the gleaner is secure."

Jake walked over to Nina and took off her handcuffs. "By the way," Nina said, "Clive is tied in the tunnel somewhere."

Jake's expression brightened as he released her wrists. "Thank you."

Nina rubbed her chaffed skin as Ethan strode up to her and said, "Let's go."

Quinton was pointing to Kane and saying, "As for you, you've chosen your own fate in the ring."

"No!" Arwan shrieked, enraged with Kane. "He should die now! Stone him! You're all yellow-bellied and weak as humans. I spit on you." She spat at Quinton.

He bellowed to the bailiff, "Take her out, and don't let me see her face again until the sunrise."

She fought the bailiff. Even handcuffed as she was, the bailiff had a hard time controlling her. He drew back and bit her on the back of the neck. She went limp, and he merely slung her over his shoulder like a sack of potatoes. Nina had never seen or heard of such a move, but she guessed it was some kind of love bite that calmed alpha females. It worked like a charm.

During the commotion, Ethan grabbed Nina's hand and wouldn't let go. "Come on."

He hurried her through the courtroom so fast she

struggled to keep up with him. "What will they do with Kane?"

"He'll fight opponents until he can't anymore."

"No." She glanced back and saw the men holding Kane release him into the ring.

"You don't understand. In the seniph world he's been allowed to keep his honor by fighting for his life. Do not disgrace him again."

"We can't just leave him here."

"If we go back, the council will lose their patience, and you'll lose your life. Kane will blame me for not keeping you safe. Then he'll have to fight anyway. No, I've let him down too many times. We have to leave. Love him for who he is, Nina. He may look like a man, but he's a seniph. We live by different principles. We are not afraid of the Land of the Dead."

Nina glanced behind her and saw Kane's bones writhing beneath his skin; then the tawny fur erupted as he shimmered into full lion form. Another opponent had entered the ring and was already in his other skin. She knew Ethan was right. They couldn't fight the whole pride. Kane was lost to her. She had to accept it, even though she felt her heart being ripped in half. She had to lean on Ethan's arm to walk.

Kane watched Nina until she left and he was certain Ethan and Nina would be okay. He closed his eyes for a second, burning her image into the back of his eyelids. This would be the last time he saw his brother or Nina. He would gladly give his life to assure her and Ethan's safety. and that's exactly what he'd done. He couldn't risk escape, in the process putting their lives in danger. Nothing really mattered to him other than knowing they were safely away.

Watching Nina leave and knowing he'd never see her again caused numbness to spread through his whole body, all the way to his soul. He'd never felt such desolate emptiness. Was it love? He'd cared for his family and Ethan, but it wasn't like this feeling. This felt like he was bleeding inwardly, as if he'd lost a part of himself. He still couldn't quite believe he was capable of loving so deeply, not with the dangerous wild creature inside him. But he was feeling it, and it hurt like hell, like someone was pulling his ribs out one by one.

Kane was jarred from his ruminations by his opponent's attack. He bit back viciously and savagely, taking out all his frustration.

Chapter 17

Two and a half hours later, Nina drove slowly down the main road of the Patomani Indian Reservation. For the tenth time, she glanced around her, half expecting to pass someone in the tribe. It was mid-afternoon, a busy time. She hoped not to encounter anyone. Her eyes were puffy from crying, her heart still ached and she wasn't in the mood to share her experiences with anyone. What she really wanted to do was go to her quiet place.

"What's wrong?" Ethan asked.

"Other than having a gleaner with me?" she said, trying to tease but only sounding sad. She couldn't help it. All she could think about was Kane. That hard expression on his face the last time she'd seen him would be burned into her memory for the rest of her life. Losing him was hard enough, but wondering if he cared about her was even worse.

"Put that way, I see what you mean."

Ethan's reply dragged her back from her misery. "It's just that I didn't get approval from the Guardian to take you to Sehsola."

Nina sighed loudly as she pulled into a snow-covered farming road. It bordered a huge field. The snow wasn't half as deep here in the southeastern part of Virginia as it had been in the mountains. It looked as if they'd only received three inches at best. The sun had gone behind a cloud, and the field was a gray wasteland, cold and frozen and barren.

She drove to the end of the field and parked near the woods. Ethan had driven Kane's Jeep to the courthouse, and they had just hopped into it and taken off. His scent still lingered in it, and she gulped past the lump in her throat that just wouldn't go away.

"If we're doing something wrong—"

"No, my sister would have agreed once I explained everything, but I just don't feel like dredging it all back up. I'll tell her later, when she's back from her honeymoon." Every time Nina breathed, she felt the bottomless empty fissure Kane had left in her chest. It wouldn't ever go away. "Come on, I'll show you the prayer cave. We'll walk from here." Nina closed the door softly and Ethan followed her lead.

She found a path she knew by heart. She could see tracks in the snow where her people had gone in to fast and pray. It was their holy place.

She thought of something and said, "You know, I didn't ask you, but my vow to save you can only work if you're willing to go to our dimension. Are you?"

"This world holds nothing but painful memories for me. What is your dimension like?"

"Sehsola's a peaceful dimension. You won't have to kill to survive there. In fact, violence is not allowed."

"You mean it's like heaven."

"That's right. You'll want for nothing."

"Nothing?"

Nina, with her usual acumen, sensed what he was too reticent to ask her. "You won't be lonely there."

"Even with this beautiful face." He teasingly pointed to his red eyes. He blinked and gave her a quick glimpse of the flames behind them. Blink, and they were just red and bloodshot again in his human form. Their sharpness was a tad disconcerting, though.

The look quickly reminded her not to forget he was first and foremost a gleaner, a charming one when he tried, but one none the less. And in a few days he'd have to kill again to stay alive if he wasn't going to Sehsola. "I wouldn't worry. The females there will be all over you," she said, hoping to lighten the uncomfortable moment.

He smiled and said, "This sounds more promising by the moment." The jocularity left his voice. "So, they must be hard up like me to be in this dimension."

"To be honest, they were a threat here on earth, like you, and the Guardians sent them there."

"Hmmm, desperate women in paradise. What more could a guy want?"

"Sunscreen, mouthwash, a locked door," she said.

Ethan chuckled. Nina only smiled sadly.

They reached the cave entrance, and she paused long

enough to listen. She didn't hear or feel anyone inside, so she pulled aside the branches that hid the opening.

The smell of incense and burning herbs met her. Damp cold air wafted from the dark abyss of the cave's inner recesses. Outside light could not penetrate it. Takala had explored those depths as a child, but no matter how much she tried to convince Nina to go with her, the primordial magic she sensed in the bedrock frightened her. She felt it teeming now, strumming against her mind. She had learned to tune it out, and she did so now, but she couldn't stop the shivers. One shook her body as she paused before a magical circle of stones and said, "We need to build a fire, and then I'll call Koda."

"Who's Koda?"

"My temperamental spirit guide."

"I heard that." Koda's voice projected through the air, rather than in her mind. Energy whirled into a writhing mass as his bear body materialized. Today he sparkled with the brightest aqua she'd ever seen. He really was beautiful. An attempt to impress Ethan, no doubt.

"Well, it's the truth," she said as she went over to a corner of the cave and scooped up an armful of kindling.

"I always do as I am commanded." Koda looked upward toward heaven.

"I hope this transfer has been okayed."

"Yes."

"And after we're done here, please appear before Quinton and tell him I kept my word." She wanted to add "And if you see Kane still alive, let me know." But it would have been like losing him all over again, and that was too painful.

"I shall."

"Good. Then let's get to it." Nina arranged the wood inside the stone circle. She reached for a lighter that was left in the cave, but Ethan said, "Allow me."

He narrowed his eyes at the kindling and concentrated. Suddenly it burst into flames.

Nina turned to Ethan. "Are you ready?"

He nodded.

She might have hugged him, but a touchy-feely goodbye didn't seem wise. Instead, she nodded and walked around the circle of stones, chanting an exchange prayer in the Maiden Bear's primitive language. Koda joined her. The acrid smell of magic coursed through the cave, pulsing against her body. Spirals of smoke curled up and formed huge hands with long undulating fingers.

"It's time. Jump." Nina pointed to the inner circle.

Ethan hesitated at the flames and the filmy fingers for only a moment. Then he said, "Thank you, Nina Rainwater. I'll never forget this kindness."

"I'll always remember you." *And your brother.* Tears swam in her eyes, blurring the flames and the smoky images.

Ethan leaped into the fire. The fingers closed around him and for a moment held him aloft.

Koda jumped into the circle, encompassing Ethan and the fingers within his large mass. They disappeared in a whoosh.

The fire went out, and Nina stood there, alone,

rubbing her arms. For a moment she had forgotten about Kane, but the emptiness of never seeing him again fell on her like blocks of iron. She dropped to her knees, covered her face and cried.

An hour later, Nina walked into her grandmother's kitchen.

Empty.

"Grandmother!" Nina called out.

She wasn't used to entering Meikoda's house and finding it empty. She was the old Guardian and high priestess. Meikoda's wisdom and indomitable strength drew the Patomani people to her in droves, especially the women of the high council. They were all powerful shamans and related. It wasn't unusual to find her aunts, great aunts and cousins, all twelve of them, crowded into the kitchen in the throes of studying ancient spellcasting or levitating, or just plain playing toothpick poker. Today it was still as death.

At least she could slip in without anyone hitting her with a hundred questions.

The front door opened with a loud thump. It crashed against the door stop and bounced a few times. A signal that her sister, Takala, had just entered. She had superhuman strength and had never really mastered it. Her grandmother had replaced the front door countless times. Takala barreled over, around and through anything in her way.

"There you are, Buddha." Takala bounded into the kitchen like a cyclone, yet managed to maintain an air of pride and arrogance in her stiff back and shoulders. "How was the job?"

Nina was still stinging from the moniker. She hated it, but if she asked Takala to stop calling her Buddha, her stubborn sister would just do it more. "Uneventful," Nina said, not wanting to discuss Kane.

Nina took in Takala's garb. She was in her Kate Beckinsale *Underworld* regalia. Her long legs were encased in tight black leather pants and knee-length boots with three-inch heels. Nina didn't know how she walked in those things. She'd fall flat on her face if she wore them. But they served a purpose. Takala kept a switchblade in the right one. A black leather greatcoat fell down below her calves. A tie-dyed T-shirt was knotted at the waist. A spiked black belt slanted across her hips. Silver hoop earrings flopped near her cheeks and matched the layers of silver necklaces falling down her chest and the many bracelets on her wrists. She wore dark plum nail polish and matching lipstick that would have looked horrible on anyone else. On Takala, it only enhanced her plump lips. Takala was a private investigator, and she said she dressed to impress her clients with her toughness, but Nina knew she just liked the attention of flashy clothes. Takala was much fairer than Nina, and her chestnut hair, highlighted by dirty-blond streaks, was wild and all over her head and shoulders. She had the tousled look down pat.

"You won't believe what I just heard." Takala headed for the refrigerator, her boots clicking on the linoleum. Because of her strength, her metabolism was always in overdrive and she ate constantly.

"Where's Grandmother?"

"Grocery shopping—aren't you interested in my news? You've been gone almost a week—I thought you might want to know what's happening around here."

"I do."

Takala pulled out a chunk of cheddar cheese, grabbed a paring knife from a drawer and began cutting off chunks and stuffing them in her mouth. She had a mouthful when she actually looked at Nina, actually seeing for the first time. Takala had one green eye and one blue. Meikoda had nicknamed her Lioness with Two Colored Eyes. Other people, who were brave enough, just called her Two Colors. Both her eyes were trained on Nina now. "Good grief, Buddha, what's wrong with you?"

"Nothing."

"Yeah, right. You always go around with mole eyes." She laid down the cheese and grabbed Nina's wrists. "You've been crying. These are cuff marks." Takala pulled down Nina's turtleneck, and Nina jerked back, but not soon enough. "No way, girlfriend! Hickies! I didn't think you were into bondage. I didn't think you were into anything—wait a minute. You're not a virgin anymore."

Nina blushed.

Takala laughed out loud. "Hallelujah! Welcome to the world of lust. Now spill everything and don't leave out one juicy morsel."

Takala had always been too nosy and observant and annoying, but Nina loved her for being all those things. "Tell me your news first." Nina pulled out a kitchen chair and sat down, dreading what she would be forced to tell Takala just so she could have some peace and quiet.

Takala picked up the cheese again and cut off a chunk. "Oh, Akando just told me Aden's getting hitched to a time jumper named Hannah Gray." She stuck it in her mouth, rolling her eyes in bliss at having something so tasty to chew.

"Really. A time jumper?" Nina couldn't help but sound incredulous. She'd never met one, only heard the legend of them. They were human vessels created for the Guardian to use to jump between dimensions in the pursuit of evil.

"Yeah. I heard she's pretty, too. And guess what else? She's a first cousin we never knew about. Tansy's daughter."

"Wow! I never knew she'd gotten pregnant, or even had a boyfriend."

"Grandmother told me that when Aunt Lena found out Tansy was pregnant, Lena forced her to go to a Catholic home for unwed mothers. Lena made sure no one found out and swore Grandmother to secrecy." Takala hacked off another chunk.

"It's too bad Lena cared more about appearances than she cared about Tansy and her grandchild. No wonder Tansy looked so sad before she died," Nina said, remembering she'd never seen a woman look so forlorn in her life.

"And Lena, too. Now we know why."

Lena had died right after Tansy. Nina had always thought Lena died of a broken heart from losing her daughter, but there was a lot more suffering involved. "Poor Tansy. Have you met Hannah?"

"Not yet. Grandmother has. She suggested we have them over for dinner tonight." Takala popped another wad of cheese in her mouth and ate it in two gulps, then said, "I had thought you and Aden might hook up, but now—"

"Why did you think that?"

"I don't know. He seemed to single you out."

"He's just a friend." Nina had always liked Aden and his wife. Two years ago he lost her in a car accident. Nina had babysat for Aden's two children when he needed help, and she might have thought herself attracted to him, but he hadn't seemed interested in any woman, including Nina. She suspected he was still in love with his wife. Long ago she had pigeonholed him into the "just friends" category. She was happy that he'd found someone to love again. When she thought of love, Kane appeared in her mind and she felt that sharp knife in her gut.

Takala cut another slice of cheese. "Now spill your news. Who's the dude? Was he a good lover? Must have been, if he seduced you."

"Anyone ever tell you you don't have a subtle bone in your body?"

"Thank goodness." Takala, not at all offended, grinned with cheese between her teeth. She was well aware of all her shortcomings and avidly accepted them. "And you don't have to be such a prude about it. I'm just trying to find out what's been happening with you."

"I know." Nina wished some of Takala's audacity

would rub off on her. "It's just I really don't want to talk about it."

"No problem." Takala waved the knife and cheese through the air in a dismissive gesture while trying to read Nina's expression with little success. Something in her steadfast gaze hinted that Takala wasn't about to give up and she'd broach the subject later. "Want to hear what I've been doing?"

"Working on a case?" Nina asked. Takala's last case caused two hit men to abduct her, and they had come very close to killing her.

"Not at the moment." Takala hesitated and set down the knife and tiny hunk of cheese that was left. She played with the bracelets on her wrists and looked uncomfortable about something.

Takala rarely held back anything, and Nina knew she was hiding something major, even catastrophic. "So?" Nina prodded her.

"I've been looking for Mom."

Nina's eyes widened and her jaw fell open. When she could speak again, she said, "Why, Takala? She's been out of our lives for years. I don't even know what she looks like. If she wanted to be with us, she would have contacted us. This is a terrible idea."

"Don't you ever wonder about her?" Takala asked with an empty hollowness in her voice.

"I used to, when I was little and I'd see other kids with their mothers bringing birthday cupcakes to school. Now, I don't want her in my life. We have each other and Meikoda. That's all we need." Nina hadn't thought of her mother since talking to Kane about it. She'd been ambivalent about it most of her life, but knowing Takala might actually find their mother put an entirely different perspective on it, one she didn't want to meet head-on. Even thinking about it made her stomach churn. "Have you told Fala about this?"

"No." Takala played with the bracelets on her wrist.

"Because you know she won't go for it. And I won't, either. If you find her, I don't want to know about it. And don't tell Grandmother—you know it will hurt her. Our mother was abjured. We can't even speak her name." Their mother was supposed to have taken over the powers of the Guardian, but she'd left the tribe and all her responsibilities on Meikoda's shoulders— including raising her three children, and that's why she was disowned by her people.

"I know. I wouldn't do that to Grandmother."

"I wish you wouldn't go stirring all this up now."

"You don't remember her—you were too little. But I do. I guess I need closure. I need to know if she's still alive." There was a catch in Takala's voice. She gulped back the emotion glistening in her eyes and said, "I just want to see her, tell her about us and Fala's wedding and mine."

"*Your* wedding?" Nina's jaw dropped even farther than it had with the last boom Takala had lowered on her. It took a moment of frowning at Takala before Nina asked, "You're marrying someone?"

"Akando, silly." Takala rolled her eyes at Nina.

"Fala just dumped him for Stephen. I thought he was still in love with Fala. Has he asked you?"

"No, but he will. I feel certain of it."

Takala was a great private investigator, observant when she was on the trail of a suspect or danger, but when it came to relationships, she was clueless. "I wouldn't go getting your hopes up." Nina tried to bring Takala back to reality. "He's rebounding."

"But I love him," Takala blurted as if that should sway Akando's opinion.

"How many guys have you thought you loved before Akando?"

Nina began ticking them off on her fingers. "There was Jason, Doug, Ernie—"

"Okay." Takala grew defensive. "They were wrong for me. But I'm sure about Akando. Just because you have a boyfriend now doesn't make you an expert. When am I going to meet Mr. Right, anyway?"

Nina had been holding back a dam of emotions, but it broke. "Never!" She leaped up out of her chair too fast, and it fell backward. She ran out of the room, bawling.

Takala yelled, "You want me to find this guy and beat the crap out of him, I will! Tell me who he is!"

The only response Takala received was Nina slamming her bedroom door.

Takala shrugged and said to the room, "What did I say?"

Chapter 18

The next day Nina sat in the prayer cave, wrapped in a coat and several blankets, shivering near a fire and avoiding everyone. Takala had badgered Nina until she had to reveal everything about Kane. Immediately, Takala told their grandmother what had happened—but thankfully not about searching for their mother—and now Meikoda was tiptoeing around Nina, shooting her expectant glances and waiting for her to talk about Kane. Meikoda had even made all the special foods Nina liked. But she had no appetite. Meikoda must have had a talk with Takala, because she thankfully hadn't approached Nina again on the subject. Nina just wanted to be left alone to grieve with her broken heart. She wanted the Quiet Place.

She felt the ancient magic deep within the cave strumming against her nerves as she called for Koda.

With surprising promptness, the spirit guide appeared before her. His diaphanous form shimmered a bright ginger. He hovered three feet off the ground and walked on air toward her. *I know you are hurting. I could feel your terrible sadness in the heavens. Even the Maiden Bear can sense it.*

I'm sorry to bother anyone. She stared at the fire, watching the flames flicker.

She sent me to help you.

Nina wondered why he'd appeared so soon after she summoned him.

What can I do to lift your spirits? Koda asked, sounding much more obliging than he ever had.

Maiden Bear must have had something to do with his new obsequiousness. Couldn't hurt having connections in high places.

Nothing—I don't know. I just hate feeling like this.... Nina paused, looking for the right words.

Koda filled them in for her. *Like you've lost all interest in life, like you feel suffocated, like you'll never be happy again?*

Yes, like that.

I warned you. He wiggled his bear brows in a superior way.

I don't need to hear "I told you so."

It might make you feel better to know that Ethan is safely sequestered in Sehsola.

Yes, it does. What were his first impressions there?

Happy ones. Three she-demons welcomed him with open arms.

She demons were unruly succubi. Nina felt an urge

to smile but couldn't bring herself to give way to it. *It's good to know he'll be happy.*

He sent you his warmest wishes and salutations and appreciation.

Did you let Quinton know Ethan's fate?

I did, and he thanked you, which caused him great grief and a lot of pride swallowing.

Nina was tempted to ask about Kane, but she couldn't and not cry again. *Koda, I need to go to the Quiet Place. I'm sure after some time there I'll feel better.*

I can't take you there.

But it's my place.

I'm forbidden.

Find a way. I know you can. Plead with the Maiden Bear if you must.

Koda wrinkled his long snout and stared at Nina for a long time. Was that sympathy in his eyes? Finally he said, *There is one way.*

I knew it.

Don't sound so happy. It's permanent, Nina. If I take you without permission, you will have to stay in the Quiet Place forever. You'll be trapped there, and your gift of tongues will pass on to someone else.

You mean I'll be totally free. Nina had enjoyed helping others, but that was before she'd fallen for Kane. She had been content with her drab life. Yes, she knew she had just been existing. She hadn't been living. But now, after tasting Kane's passion, she knew she couldn't go back to that kind of life again.

Take me, Koda. Take me out of here.

It's a big step. Stop and reflect. Don't make a hasty

decision. I promise you there will be other men in your life.

But I don't want other men. Nina stood, crossed her arms over her chest and splayed her legs. *The man I want is lost to me forever. I beg you to take me to the Quiet Place.*

Koda sighed loudly. *You should consult the High Council. Talk to the Guardian.*

Nina knew her grandmother and Fala would forbid her to do it. They didn't know how she was hurting. Only she knew that. *No, it's my life. I'll make my own decision.*

Their eyes warred for a long while. When he didn't see her waver, he finally spoke. *Very well.*

Nina began walking around the fire, singing the ancient prayer that always took her to the Quiet Place.

Hear me O Maiden of the Light
Guide me through heaven's heights
To alight in silent flight
in the place of quiet sights

Koda joined the litany. She could feel his supernatural energy building behind her, his guttural voice rising in her mind. The flames swept higher, almost touching the cave's ceiling. The heat of the fire chaffed her cheeks and dried her lips. The air swelled around her and pulsed, keeping time with her heartbeat.

"Granddaughter, stop it this instant!"

At the sound of her grandmother's stentorian command, the fire instantly went out.

Koda dissolved in a glimmer of light, taking his magic with him.

Coward!

Just like Koda to desert her when trouble arrived. Nina really couldn't blame him for this one. Most spirits avoided Meikoda if they could. She had been the Guardian for decades, and the high priestess of all white magic. All she had to do was inhale wrong and she could suck the life force out a spirit into her own body and absorb it. And as every spirit guide knew, Meikoda didn't have a lot of patience with them.

At the moment, Meikoda didn't look all that tolerant of Nina, either. Her face was drawn back in a narrow-eyed frown. Blue fire spit from her bright eyes, and they glowed like two shooting stars.

Her grandmother was the prime example of why looks could be deceiving. She was small, hardly five feet tall. Wrinkles were embedded in every sharp plane of her face and neck. She wore an unassuming jean skirt and white blouse and a thick blue wool sweater she had knitted herself. Her long white hair was braided and hanging down her back. She looked like a diminutive elderly lady, but she was a vessel of power. Nina felt her body humming with it.

Nina lowered her eyes, offering the elder the deference she and her sisters had learned to bestow as young children. Nina knew Meikoda loved her, but she wasn't the demonstrative grandmotherly type. She had to teach Nina and her sisters to live with their gifts and the huge responsibilities that went with them. It was not for the weak-hearted or the disrespectful. Meikoda demanded obedience. And up until this moment, Nina had had no trouble showing her deference. But she was already wondering if she could call Koda back when she was alone again.

"I always knew you were the most sensitive of your sisters, but I never took you for a quitter." For a tiny woman, Meikoda's voice was strong and clear and electrified the air.

It went through Nina like a blade. She stiffened, and her fingers drew up into fists at her sides as she said, "I'm not."

"Then what were you doing, child? You mope and weep, and now I find you breaking your connections to me and your sisters, to those who love you, for one of loneliness and solitude."

Tears spilled down Nina's cheeks. She realized now there were others to consider, others she loved. She'd been selfish. "I'm sorry," she choked out.

"First Fala. Now, you, Nina. You were the most level-headed of my grandchildren. I thought you would never have your head turned by a man."

"He's special, Grandmother."

"You love this man so much?" Meikoda approached her and took out a tissue and blotted at Nina's tears.

"I do. I know it was wrong to go to the Quiet Place. I just didn't want to feel like this anymore."

"A broken heart will follow you wherever you go." The angry brightness in Meikoda's eyes had dimmed, and Nina could look into them. It was the most compassion Nina had ever seen on her grandmother's face. "The Quiet Place will not mend it or silence it. As long as you have memories of this man, you will feel the pain. Only time will heal it."

"Nothing will heal it."

"Not if you keep it all inside. Tell me about him, particularly how he won your heart, for I am certain no man can deserve you." Nina began to protest, but Meikoda stopped her with a raised finger. "You may persuade me on the way back to the house and unburden your spirit at the same time."

"Yes, ma'am."

Nina watched Meikoda stuff the tissue in her sweater pocket, then turn and leave with a swish of her skirt. Nina dragged her feet as she followed her. She really didn't want to discuss Kane, but she had no choice now. Maybe her grandmother was right. Maybe it would help to close her emotional wounds if she spoke about her seniph.

The sight of Takala standing on the porch, looking for them, alerted Nina that something was wrong. Takala wasn't hard to miss in her outfit. She wore a tight suede miniskirt and matching brown vest, long beige-and-white-striped tights, mid-calf boots and a green bomber jacket. And, of course, the pounds of silver, which sparkled like a solar flare in the sun.

Takala leaped over the porch railing like a gazelle clearing a six-foot bush and ran across the yard. "Have you told her, yet?" she asked, looking at Meikoda, her eyes gleaming with mischief.

"Told me what?" Nina asked.

At that moment, the storm door on her grandmother's little rancher opened and Kane stepped out.

Nina had been walking by Meikoda and she stumbled.

With surprising reflexes for her age, Meikoda caught Nina's elbow before she fell.

"Whoa, guess you haven't told her," Takala said.

Meikoda said, "I was waiting for her to convince me he was worthy enough to speak to her. I believe she has."

The sight of Kane tunneled her vision, and she saw only him. His presence blocked out everything else, and she breathed in the sight of him. He wore a green and yellow rugby shirt and chinos. Cuts and bruises marred his face and neck. A fine sheen of blond hair had begun to grow on his shaved head. Two days' worth of stubble darkened his chin. And his eyes gleamed with deep green fire. He looked gorgeous, and alive!

Nina could only stand there, stunned, taking in the sight of him.

Takala pushed Nina forward, saying, "Come on, Buddha, you're ruining this Kodak moment for me. I had hoped for at least a Scarlet and Rhett reunion."

Nina suddenly felt afraid as she saw Kane walk down the steps toward them. When she thought he was lost to her forever, she could accept not knowing how he felt about her. Now she would find out, and she dreaded the outcome.

As if Meikoda read her mind, she whispered to Nina, "Your first love is not always the one you end up with. The point is that he opened you up enough to make you see your own beauty and that you are every bit as desirable as Fala and Takala ever were. He made you see you are worthy of loving. Embrace it. Stop doubting yourself, and you may be surprised."

Easier said than done, Nina thought.

Kane approached them, his body growing larger and larger by the moment, seeming to fill up the whole outdoors. His gaze lazily combed her body from head to toe as if he couldn't believe she was standing before him.

Her heart sped up, and she felt a sudden flush wash over her. She could sense his desire, and she wondered if he was remembering their lovemaking as she was.

"We will have a long chat inside, after you have a moment with my granddaughter." Meikoda gave him a long, hard warning look that could burn the flesh off his body.

"I'd like that." Kane didn't flinch, only met her gaze squarely, unblinking, looking at her with guarded respect. Most supernatural beings could not stare into Meikoda's powerful eyes for long. It didn't seem to bother Kane.

Nina closed her eyes and let his rich baritone wash over her. She thought she'd only hear it again in her memories, but he was really here, standing four feet away. It felt like miles for some reason.

When Meikoda was satisfied that she wasn't going to budge Kane from his purpose, she said to Takala, "Come along. We'll fix some tea for our guest. We'll read Mr. Van Cleave's future in the leaves."

Takala didn't look happy about leaving Nina alone,

and she punched Kane on the arm and said, "Hurt my little sister, Bruce Willis, and you won't have a head to shave." She hurried to catch up to Meikoda. When Takala was behind Kane's back, she mouthed the words *He's cute,* then gave Nina a thumbs-up.

Nina could see the thoughts swirling behind Kane's eyes. She could feel his uncertainty now. An uncomfortable silence rose up between them; then he broke it. "So that's your sister Takala."

Here we go. Men attracted to her sisters. Never to her. She could write this script. He'd ask if Takala was dating anyone; then he'd start calling her. Nina would have to watch him pick Takala up for dates, watch her not come home at night, wonder what they were doing. Wait! That's what the old Nina would think. He had been attracted to her. He had come here to see her. And she had felt his lust for her. She was doubting herself. Stop it!

"Yes," Nina said. "She's one of a kind."

"She doesn't look at all like you."

"I know." Nina wanted to wring her hands, but she crossed her arms over her chest.

"What about your other sister, the one who's the Guardian?"

"She's a taller version of me."

"I had hoped to meet them both."

"Sorry, all you get is Takala. Fala's on her honeymoon and won't be back for another few days."

"I look forward to meeting her."

That was a good sign. She didn't want to talk about

her sisters like it was the weather and she said, "So, you survived."

"Yes. Has Ethan gone to your dimension?"

Had he come here only to check on his brother? "I'm afraid so," she said, hearing coldness slipping into her own voice.

Disappointment pulled at his expression. "I had hoped to say goodbye."

"You're too late." She remembered how he hadn't told her goodbye in the courthouse. She'd never forget the cold determination in his eyes when he'd ordered her to leave. "He's very happy."

"I'm glad."

Nina changed the subject. "So, how did you get away?"

"After five challengers, the council let me have my freedom."

"I guess they didn't want you wiping out all the males in the pride."

"Not with our birthrates so low."

Talk about uncomfortable. She was standing here discussing birthrates like it was a headline in the daily paper. She felt them becoming more and more self-conscious as the seconds ticked by. It appeared he hadn't come to terms with his beast, and he was still overly cautious. She summoned her courage and said, "So, you know about Ethan now. I guess we should go get that tea."

"Not yet." He grabbed her arm.

Immediately Nina felt Kane's desire and uncertainty and something she couldn't name. But it was compelling and intense and poured through her mind like waves of hot chocolate. She hadn't felt this feeling coming from him ever before. Not ever.

"Nina, I have to tell you something."

"What?" Nina folded her arms over her chest and assumed a calm pose, while her stomach coiled in tense knots. She held her breath and waited, her whole world seeming to rest on his next words.

"I treated you horribly the last time I saw you. I should never have let you go like that without telling you how I feel. Will you let me tell you now?"

"I don't know. You really hurt me." She looked him square in the eyes.

"I know." He slid his hand down her arm and grasped her fingers. The warmth of his skin penetrated all the way to her bones. "I couldn't admit to myself that I needed you. And I was afraid I might hurt you if we were together, but I'll die without you, Nina. My life is nothing if you're not in it. If you don't want me, I understand. I don't deserve you." Raw, open tenderness glazed his eyes.

It was the first heartfelt weakness she'd ever glimpsed in Kane, and it gripped the core of her soul and wouldn't let go. "I know you don't," she said in a choked whisper, "but I still love you anyway."

He gazed at her as if he couldn't believe her words. "I love you, Nina Rainwater."

He crushed her against him and held her tight. It felt so wonderful to smell him, to feel his hard, muscular body next to her own, to know he wanted her, to sense the power of his beast. She sighed against him and laid her ear over his heart and listened to it pounding.

"I promise you, I'll never hurt you. I'd die first."

"I know that," she said, loving the sound of his voice rumbling in his chest. "Now shut up and kiss me."

Kane did just that, and when Nina felt his hot, urgent lips on hers, she sensed the beast's passion for her as well as the man's. They merged into one, and she knew Kane had finally accepted his beast, and both halves of him loved her. The power of it took her breath away.

* * * * *

nocturne™

COMING NEXT MONTH

Available May 31, 2011

#113 THE VAMPIRE WHO LOVED ME
Sons of Midnight
Theresa Meyers

#114 DÉJÀ VU
Lisa Childs

You can find more information on upcoming Harlequin® titles, free excerpts and more at
www.HarlequinInsideRomance.com.

HNCNM0511

REQUEST YOUR FREE BOOKS!

2 FREE NOVELS PLUS 2 FREE GIFTS!

 Harlequin®

n o c t u r n e™
Dramatic and Sensual Tales of Paranormal Romance.

HN11

Harlequin® Blaze™ brings you
New York Times *and* USA TODAY *bestselling author*
Vicki Lewis Thompson with three new steamy titles
from the bestselling miniseries SONS OF CHANCE

Chance isn't just the last name of these rugged
Wyoming cowboys—it's their motto, too!

Read on for a sneak peek at the first title,
SHOULD'VE BEEN A COWBOY

Available June 2011 only from Harlequin® Blaze™.

"Thanks for not turning on the lights," Tyler said. "I'm a mess."

"Not in my book." Even in low light, Alex had a good view of her yellow shirt plastered to her body. It was all he could do not to reach for her, mud and all. But the next move needed to be hers, not his.

She slicked her wet hair back and squeezed some water out of the ends as she glanced upward. "I like the sound of the rain on a tin roof."

"Me, too."

She met his gaze briefly and looked away. "Where's the sink?"

"At the far end, beyond the last stall."

Tyler's running shoes squished as she walked down the aisle between the rows of stalls. She glanced sideways at Alex. "So how much of a cowboy are you these days? Do you ride the range and stuff?"

"I ride." He liked being able to say that. "Why?"

"Just wondered. Last summer, you were still a city boy. You even told me you weren't the cowboy type, but you're…different now."

He wasn't sure if that was a good thing or a bad thing. Maybe she preferred city boys to cowboys. "How am I different?"

"Well, you dress differently, and your hair's a little longer. Your face seems a little more chiseled, but maybe that's because of your hair. Also, there's something else, something harder to define, an attitude…"

"Are you saying I have an attitude?"

"Not in a bad way. It's more like a quiet confidence."

He was flattered, but still he had to laugh. "I just admitted a while ago that I have all kinds of doubts about this event tomorrow. That doesn't seem like quiet confidence to me."

"This isn't about your job, it's about…your…" She took a deep breath. "It's about your sex appeal, okay? I have no business talking about it, because it will only make me want to do things I shouldn't do." She started toward the end of the barn. "Now, where's that sink? We need to get cleaned up and go back to the house. Dinner is probably ready, and I—"

He spun her around and pulled her into his arms, mud and all. "Let's do those things." Then he kissed her, knowing that she would kiss him back, knowing that this time he would take that kiss where he wanted it to go. And she would let him.

Follow Tyler and Alex's wild adventures in
SHOULD'VE BEEN A COWBOY
Available June 2011 only from Harlequin® Blaze™
wherever books are sold.